I0817837

Sweet LIKE A PSYCHO

A SECRETS OF SUBURBIA NOVEL

IVY SMOAK

This book is a work of fiction. Names, characters, places, and incidents are fictitious. Any resemblance to actual persons, living or dead, events, or locales is purely coincidental.

ISBN: 9781942381181

2020 Hardcover Edition

To all the words that hurt.
Look who's laughing now.

CHAPTER 1
Violet

Everyone has secrets. It was a phrase my mother used to say. The words echoed in the wind around me, a ghost from my past whispering in my ear. I tightened my scarf to help block the cold. Again. And again. Until the fringe hung evenly on the front of my coat. I breathed a sigh of relief even though the wind still rushed past my ears.

The rain from earlier tonight should have left the ground slippery, but the dense canopy of trees in the woods had preserved the freshly fallen leaves' texture. And I was thankful that it had. My feet crunching through the brown leaves helped to drown out the sound of the wind.

It was growing colder every night. Soon the woods would be covered in a blanket of peaceful snow. And with the snow would come silence. There was nothing better than silence.

I wound through the trees, ducking beneath broken limbs as I descended the hill from my house. It had been a long time since I walked to the lake. My usual trail was hard to make out. The path my feet had made over the years was nearly covered in fresh foliage and buried under a layer of autumn leaves. I preferred staying in my house. Indoors, to be more specific. There was too much noise out here. And too much uncertainty. There was really no reason to come out when I had such a beautiful view of the lake from the comfort of my own home. But I had been itching to see it in person again.

Before the woods could block my view at the base of the hill, I glanced to the right to see the row of cookie-cutter houses in the distance. My family had lived in one of those houses. A perfect house. In the perfect neighborhood. A perfect little life. At least, that's how it looked from the outside. You could never truly be sure. After all, everyone has secrets.

I grimaced at the phrase and adjusted my scarf higher this time in order to cover my ears. Once. Twice. Three times, until it lay perfectly even again.

It was only another minute until I reached the edge of the lake. It was beautiful. And deserted. And freezing. I resisted the urge to adjust my scarf again. Instead, I pictured my mother kneeling beside the water. Sometimes I wondered if it was really a memory or just a figment of my imagination. Because in all honesty, it was one of the only vivid memories I had of my mother from when I was a child. She had knelt down to look me in the eyes, holding my face and wiping away the tear stains.

"One white lie never hurt anyone," my mother had said. "Everyone has secrets. But a big lie?" She lifted her ruined silk blouse that I had butchered to make a dress for my Barbie. "You do not lie about big things. Big lies have big consequences."

The gentle touch of her hand on my face had become sharper, her fingertips biting into my skin.

I had wanted to confess. I had wanted to tell her I was sorry. But for some reason, the words hadn't wanted to escape.

And I couldn't nod my head because she was holding my chin so tightly in her hand.

"Consequences, Violet. There are consequences to big lies."

I remembered her pushing my head under the cold water for so long that I breathed in a lungful of it. I could still hear my stepfather's laughter in my head. He had watched it all unfolding and didn't care one bit that my mother was trying to drown me.

I blinked and the image of her disappeared. One of my only living, breathing memories of my mother. It was bittersweet. There had been such a tender moment there. But I wasn't sure it outweighed the feeling of fire in my lungs when I couldn't breathe. I still missed her desperately, even though I shouldn't have. I stared out at the still water of the lake. I most certainly shouldn't have.

But it was better to hold on to the sweetness of a moment. It was better to remember the good things instead of the bad. I knew that better than anyone. I had lost my mother when she was far too young. A short life was one of the hardest things to cope with. It made you forgive any wrongs. Or maybe it just made you crave even the bad memories because you just missed the person so damn much.

I felt a tear run down my cheek. And I was very aware of the fact that there was no one to wipe it away now. I drew closer to the lake and stared down at my reflection. I wasn't a little girl anymore. I was well into my mid-twenties, yet I still cried at the lake like a child. I still escaped here when I needed a moment to myself. Everything had changed, yet nothing at all.

The silence suddenly felt overwhelming. Maybe a part of me still craved being in one of those stupid perfect houses in that stupid perfect neighborhood. I wanted the façade even if it wasn't real. I didn't want to hurt this much.

A loud boom echoed through the trees, sending birds fleeing to the sky. Through the layers of my scarf it sounded like a gunshot. Every now and then a crazy person would hunt in these woods even though it was against the law. Another shot went off and I flung myself to the ground. Only I was on the edge of the lake...so instead of solid ground, I plunged into the water with a splash that sounded almost as loud as the gunshot in my ears.

For a moment it felt like my head was being held underneath the surface. Like my mother's hand was gripping my hair so tightly it hurt. But then it felt a lot more like I was being pulled into the cold depths from below. Something heavy and sinister clutched to my ankle. Pulling me lower and lower. I reached for the surface as I continued to sink.

It was the layers pulling me deeper. I knew how to swim, it was just impossible with these heavy clothes. I wrestled with my scarf that was much too tight after all my adjustments. And I unzipped and pushed my coat off my shoulders.

This time when I kicked my legs, I easily rose to the surface. I gasped for air as I hauled myself up onto solid ground. On my hands and knees, I choked and sputtered up water.

I finally breathed out only air and saw my exhale in a puff of smoke. It was cold, but it wasn't that cold. I lifted my head and squinted my eyes. A soft orange glow was on the horizon in the distance. *Fire.* I was still trying to catch my breath, but the enormity of the situation made it harder to fill my lungs. *Shit.* It felt like my heart was beating out of my chest.

I pushed myself up onto my feet and ran back toward my house, to the hill that overlooked the perfect little neighborhood below. It didn't look so perfect anymore. One of the houses was completely engulfed in flames. Or what was left of it. There was barely any house there. It was just rubble ablaze. The boom hadn't been from a gun. That house must have exploded.

I could already hear sirens in the distance. They'd take care of the flames. They'd make sure they didn't spread into the trees. They wouldn't let them reach me.

But nothing I thought eased my rapid heartbeat. My mother's words still echoed in my head. Everyone has secrets. The problem was, I had three of them. And I lived out here for a reason. I shook my head. One white lie never hurt anyone. And as far as I was concerned, neither did three. I reached for my scarf to adjust it, but my hand came up short.

I looked back at the lake. I had a dozen other scarves, but that was my only winter jacket. For a moment I was frozen. It wasn't just because I was freezing cold. It was because I didn't know what to do. Run back down the hill to help? That house would be swarming with people in just a minute. Jump back into the water and find my jacket? It was too cold. But it wasn't the temperature of the water that was preventing that option. I didn't want to feel like I was drowning again.

A chill ran down my spine. And it wasn't from the cool wind against my wet clothes. Or even from the horrific scene in front of me.

I started walking farther up the hill. My mind was having trouble calming down, but it was like my body knew what to do. I had to get home. Houses didn't just explode out of nowhere. Well, maybe sometimes they did. A gas leak or some other easy explanation. But sometimes a person caused the leak. Human error. Or worse. There'd be an investigation. Cops would swarm the woods searching for the culprit. I was the only person that lived out here. And I did not want them invading my privacy. I had too much to lose.

My whole body was shaking by the time I reached my house. I wanted to believe it was because of my soaked clothes and the cold wind. But I knew it wasn't. I felt like I was running out of precious time.

The chipped white paint on my wrap-around porch was already illuminated with the red and blue of distant sirens. The cops would be here soon. I opened and closed the front door as quietly as possible, but the creak of the rusty hinges marred the silence.

I tried to take a slow, steadying breath so I could concentrate on everything I needed to do. *Wet clothes.* I touched my soaked sweater. Changing wasn't an important task, but I couldn't stop shaking. Maybe it would help. I pulled the thick layers off, jumping on one foot then the next as I removed my jeans. I tiptoed upstairs to my bedroom with the pile of wet clothes in my hands. Each creaky stair made me cringe. No matter how much work I put into this house, it still seemed to be falling apart.

I discarded my wet clothes on the bathroom floor and grabbed my robe. After I took care of everything, I could take a nice hot shower and try to rid the image of the cool lake from my mind. And hang up the clothes. But my feet wouldn't move. I just stared down at the pile of clothes on my spotless tiled floor. *Ignore the wet clothes!* I backed out of the bathroom. And then went back in. Backed out. Then in. Then out. Then in. Three times. *Damn it!* I ran out of the bathroom and grabbed some hangers from my closet. *Stupid wet clothes.* I carefully hung up the soaked garments on the shower curtain bar above the tub. And then evenly spaced them out. It was absolute perfection. It was also an absolute waste of valuable time.

My mind was racing. How long had I spent doing that? Five minutes tops? They'd still be taking care of the fire. I grabbed my binoculars from the vanity, pulled one of the horizontal blinds down, and peered out the window. There was no sign of the fire spreading into the woods. Just its glow in the distance and the red and blue lights in the sky.

And...and a person. I blinked. There was a woman running through the woods. More specifically, running up my hill in the middle of the woods. The woman glanced over her shoulder at the fire and then picked up her pace. She ran right past my pickup truck and into the cover of the trees again.

I didn't have a doubt in my mind that the lunatic running through the woods was the culprit of the explosion. Which made my deepest fears a reality. The cops would follow her. They'd follow her all the way up here, directly toward me. I glared daggers at the spot where the woman had disappeared through the trees. She'd just led the cops straight to my doorstep.

I put the binoculars down next to the other identical two and tried to focus again. It had taken me a few minutes to run back home. A few minutes to hang up my wet clothes. I pulled my hair into a bun on the top of my head as I paced around the bathroom. There was still time. The cops wouldn't necessarily know that she had run into the woods. It was dark now. It would be hard for them to find her trail even in the light since the ground was covered in fall leaves. They wouldn't know she had basically run up to my house. I'd be fine.

My pep talk didn't calm me down. At all. Especially since it ignored the fact that someone may have seen the woman run into the woods. Nosy neighbors could probably point the cops in the right direction. My direction. And I knew for a fact that the Windy Park community was full of nosy neighbors. I heard their whispers. I knew what they said about me.

I ran out of the bathroom and crouched down at the foot of my bed. My fingers dug into the side of the loose board as I pried it up. Just like it had been a long time since I had been to the lake, it had been a long time since I had lifted up this loose board as well. Things were good. I was good. I hadn't let my memories bother me in a long time. But here I was. Staring down at every incriminating thing I owned. Well, not necessarily incriminating. Just…suspicious. Suspicious to stupid cops who heard stupid gossip from stupid neighbors.

The ironic thing was that I had planned to go through all of this tonight anyway. I let myself remember once a year. I used to always do it on the anniversary of when my heart was shattered into a million tiny pieces. But it had gotten pushed back every year, had changed seasons a few times even. Sometimes it was just a little too hard to remember. Maybe six years was the amount of time that would finally allow me to find peace.

I picked up the shoebox and tossed the lid off. Inside were just a bunch of short letters from my boyfriend. *Ex*-boyfriend. How unusual was it to keep notes from an ex? I didn't really know. I had no one to ask. But it felt unusual that I hadn't dated anyone since he had skipped town. Six years. Six years I had waited for him to come back. That wasn't exactly bad, just pathetic. I looked down at the letters. In a lot of ways, this box held my most valuable possessions. It was like I had packaged up my heart in this box and closed the lid on it. I could practically feel my heartbeat in my fingertips as I held the box in my hands.

Why was I hung up on him anyway? He was a complete asshole. He had just left in the middle of the night. He left me. He was the reason I was at the lake tonight. It was our meeting spot. We had both grown up in Windy Park and it was an easy place to sneak off to. We were young and in love. And then...we suddenly weren't.

He was the reason I was stuck in this godforsaken rundown house. Some of my best memories of him were here in the woods. Throwing rocks at the window of this house. Telling ghost stories of its previous inhabitants who had left it abandoned. I shook my head. There was nothing haunted about this house. It just held all the memories of him. And I couldn't leave. I don't know why I couldn't leave. But I felt most at home tucked away in the woods. Stuck in the past.

I lifted up the letter from the bottom of the box. The last note I had ever gotten from him. We used to sneak them to each other between classes. A slight brush of skin as our palms touched to exchange them. A tingle that made me feel more alive than I ever had. My eyes scanned the creased page.

Vi,

Only three weeks until we're out of here. Us against the world, babe. Us against the world.

Forever and always,

Joel

Six years ago we had planned to run away together. He was going to take me to LA. We had big dreams, the two of us. Until he decided he didn't want to be a *we*. He was probably a screenwriter in Hollywood by now. I wouldn't know. I didn't own a TV. And I never went to the movies. I barely left the freaking house. He had never needed me to accomplish his dreams. All I'd ever done was hold him back.

I stared down at the page, still confused about what possibly could have changed in the several hours between him writing this note and the time that evening that he skipped town early without me. But in my heart I knew. He had figured out my secret. And abandoned me. I needed him more than ever and he had abandoned me. *Big lies have big consequences.* My mom's words rattled around in my head again. She was certainly right about that. The problem was, I never meant to lie. I was always going to tell him. I was just waiting until he whisked me away from this town like the knight in shining armor I thought he was. Yup, he was most definitely a hotshot in Hollywood by now. I wasn't much of a dreamer, yet I had believed every word out of his mouth. Surely the box-office numbers would reflect his master storytelling.

I tossed the letters back in the box. They weren't the reason I had opened up the floorboard. A few harmless notes from an ex weren't incriminating. All they meant was that I was a creepy broken-hearted loner in the woods. No, the letters weren't the incriminating thing hidden beneath my floorboards. It was the handgun that I was worried about.

CHAPTER 2

Tucker

Cops and firefighters were already swarming the scene, ruining any chance we had at gathering untainted evidence. Not that I was expecting any evidence. It was probably a gas leak. Tragic, but just an accident. Case closed.

I pulled up to a house on the opposite side of the street and put my unmarked Dodge Charger in park. There wasn't anything to be done except wait until the fire was under control. I was drawing close to the end of a twelve-hour shift, and this mess would be better handed off to someone who wasn't dead on his feet. Or the cops could just handle it. There was no point in sitting here counting down the minutes.

"Think the captain will care if we leave it to the night shift?" I asked and turned to my partner.

"She was the one that requested we get our asses over here," Damien said. "So I'm guessing yes."

Fair enough. I drummed my thumbs on the wheel. It took me a minute to realize that the song stuck in my head had played the first night I had met Julie. I remembered dipping her in my arms and her smile making it impossible to stare at anyone but her. I used to be able to look forward to going home to a warm bed after a long shift. Until I realized that I wasn't the only one she'd been sharing our bed with. My hands tightened on the wheel.

"You have to stop thinking about Julie," Damien said.

"I wasn't."

"You were." He put his feet up on the dash. "She sure as hell isn't thinking about you, though, so why are you wasting your time?"

I ignored him.

"When was the last time you got laid?"

"Recently enough." It was a lie. It had been four months since I broke it off with Julie. And I hadn't found anyone else I was interested in. I didn't have time to date anyway.

"You've been hard to work with ever since the two of you split."

"You've been hard to work with ever since we got paired up."

Damien put his hands over his heart. "That hurts, man." But then he immediately smiled. "Not that I believe it for a second. I'm the best thing that ever happened to you."

I shook my head. "It's questionable that you think another man in your life is the best thing that ever happened to you."

"You're switching my words around. I said that *I* was the best thing that ever happened to *you*."

"Yeah right."

"Let's hit the bar after this. Get you out of your slump."

"I'm not in a slump."

"So you *have* gotten laid since your split?"

It wasn't worth the time lying to him. We could both sense a liar a mile away. It was part of the training.

"Tucker." He drew out my name in a weird seductive way. And I was worried that he was right. If I thought him saying my name was seductive, I was most definitely in a slump.

"Four months isn't that long," I said instead of giving in. I was too tired to have this conversation with him right now.

"Um…yes. Yes, it is. As soon as we get the all clear from the goddess, we're going out."

I wasn't sure whether to focus on the fact that he had just called our captain the goddess or the fact that I was 100 percent not going to a bar with him tonight. If I was in denial about my lack of a sex life, he was certainly in denial of his chances with the boss. But before I could respond, his phone bleeped in this hand.

"Speak of the sexy devil. I'll put on my charm and plead our case to get out early. Don't see any reason for us to be here when the officers clearly have it covered. You know she can't resist me. Torres speaking," he said as he opened the door and stepped out into the cool night. He slammed the door, leaving me alone in the car.

I let go of the wheel and sighed. Damien was right. I needed to move on. But this town didn't exactly have a high population of bachelorettes. It was filled with suburban housewives like the women who resided in this neighborhood. I stared out the window at the fire. Two covered gurneys were being ushered away from the flames. *Shit.*

I was hoping for an easy case. That was impossible now. It would be elevated to a homicide investigation. I was about to open up the door to get filled in by the local cops when the printer beside me whirred to life.

I lifted up the first page. It was a file about Benjamin Harlow. I scanned the page. Not a civilian. He was a detective like me. There were only three reasons his file would be coming out of the printer. Either he was a suspect, he was dead, or he was injured. Detectives didn't tend to do much arson, and based on those gurneys and half of the house literally being blown to bits, I was worried that he wasn't just injured.

Suddenly I wasn't tired anymore. Not only had this arsonist blown up a house, but they'd possibly killed a detective. That meant this case was a top priority. Which meant solving it would help get the captain off my back about my recent uh...less than stellar job performance.

I grabbed the paper and stepped out into the cool night.

Damien was still talking on the phone. I ducked under the caution tape and flashed my badge at the nearest cop. "Any idea what happened here?"

"Arsonist. Took out two of our own." He shook his head.

Two? Damn. I'd go from narrowly avoiding suspension to being the hero of the department if I solved this one. "You sure it was arson?" I thought he might have a few guesses, but he seemed pretty sure.

"Don't you smell that, detective?"

I took a deep breath. Despite the smell of smoke, there was one more pungent scent in the air. "Kerosene?"

"The house was doused in it. A trip-wire was attached to the front door. We didn't stand a chance."

I wasn't expecting him to say that. I thought they had arrived on the scene after the explosion. "Cops were here before the explosion?"

"Yeah, we were called in as backup to an ongoing investigation."

"What ongoing investigation?"

The cop laughed. "It's above my pay grade. Guess it's above yours too." He turned his head. "Ma'am, you have to stay on the other side of the tape."

There was an older woman in a housecoat wrestling with the yellow caution tape. She ignored his request. He put his hand on his gun and started to walk towards her, but I put my arm out to stop him.

"I got this," I said.

He laughed again. "You don't have the case file and now you're helping with crowd control? No wonder more cases don't get solved around here."

I ignored him. Damien would fill me in on all the details when he was done flirting with the captain, but for now, I figured I might get some valuable intel from the neighborhood gossip. Or I'd end up driving an Alzheimer's patient back to their house. It could go either way.

"Ma'am, you really can't come any closer. This is an active crime scene. And that house could blow again any second."

The woman proceeded to stomp on the tape dividing us. "But I know who did it. I knew that woman wasn't quite right in the head. I knew it. I told everyone so. I have a great eye for this sorta thing."

"I want to hear all about her, but first we need to move to a safer location." I guided her over to my car.

"I think her husband was beating her. She must have finally snapped and blown the place up."

"What woman blew the place up?" I asked.

"The one who lived here."

Lived. In the past tense. It would be fitting if the woman responsible was killed in her own death trap. "What did you say your name was?" I asked.

"Sally. Sally Bennett. I know everything that goes on in this neighborhood. And she was having an affair with her gardener. Who just so happens to live right down the street."

"And how is it that you know all this, Ms. Bennett?"

"Mrs. Bennett." She held her head up a little higher. "People like to tell me things."

"The woman who lived here told you she was having an affair?"

"No, but it was so obvious. She and Ben were always together. It was as clear as day. Don't know how her husband didn't know. Or maybe he did. Oh! Maybe he was the one who set off the explosion!" She seemed so excited by the prospect of such juicy gossip.

"What did you say this woman's name was?"

"Aren't you supposed to know that? By the way, I'd be happy to identify the body...bodies?"

I bet you would. She was totally fishing for information. "Yeah…I…" I looked down at the papers.

"Adeline Bell is her name. Oh and that right there is her gardener." She pointed to the paper in my hand.

"Benjamin Harlow?" I lifted up the picture of the detective.

She shook her head. "You have the last name wrong. His name is Ben Jones. Such a gentleman. But yes, that's definitely him. My God. Did he have a secret family? He did, didn't he? It's always the ones you least suspect." She shook her head.

I rubbed my eyes. It would have been hard to pick out the truth from this woman's gossip when I was fresh. It was nearly impossible after a twelve-hour shift. By the morning she would probably have everyone in the neighborhood believing that Mr. Bell had blown up his cheating wife and that Ben Jones was a polygamist. "What did Adeline look like?"

"Long blonde hair. She was quite beautiful. If you ask me, she could have been a model in her prime."

"And you think she died in the explosion? You said that she *lived* here. Not *lives*."

"Oh, no. I just meant I doubt she'll be coming back anytime soon. I wouldn't come back if I was her. And there isn't much to come back to." She gestured towards the still-burning shell of a house. "Her house is basically dust. And she took off so fast…"

"Wait, you saw her?"

"I've been trying to tell the cops, but they haven't been listening. She took off in the woods a few minutes ago. Saw her with my own eyes." She pointed towards the woods.

I glanced over at Damien still flirting on the phone. And all the cops were just standing around. I could easily catch up to the culprit if she only had a few minutes head start. This was my big chance. "Thanks for the tip, Sally."

"Any time, officer."

I didn't have time to correct her. I was a detective. Not a beat cop. And I was about to prove it to her and Officer Prick. I folded up the picture of Ben Harlow or Ben Jones or whoever he was and shoved it into my pocket. The guilty woman would crack over a picture of her dead lover. Not that there were going to be many beautiful blondes who smelled like kerosene out in the woods on a cold night like tonight. I shoved the rest of the printouts into Damien's hand as I ran past him.

"Where are you going?!" he yelled from behind me.

I ignored him as I ran toward where Sally had pointed. It didn't take long to find the trail. It had rained earlier, and there were clear shoeprints in the muddy, crunchy leaves. I turned my phone's flashlight on and ran into the woods.

***

Gotcha. The house was clearly abandoned. Paint was chipping off every visible service. There were dozens of cracked boards on the porch. It was practically as dilapidated as the house that was on fire. Yet, the lights were on in one of the rooms upstairs. And I could see the silhouette of someone walking around inside.

The trail from the crime scene had led straight here. It was like she was begging to get caught. In a lot of ways that aligned with what Sally had said. This woman could be lovesick. Dying to be caught after her regrettable decisions killed the man she was having an affair with. I looked over my shoulder and noticed how good the vantage point of this house was. It was located on top of a hill that looked down on the woods surrounding it. But it also gave a damn good view of the neighborhood where the fire was still being fought.

I paused by the rundown pickup truck and pulled out my gun. Maybe this situation wasn't so black and white. It felt sinister up here. A chill ran down my spine and I tried to ignore the feeling. I was tired. I needed to wrap this up so that I could go home. To my cold bed. *Get a grip.*

I lifted my gun and tried to quietly walk up the decrepit porch steps. Each creak echoed in the quiet night. I should have told Damien to have my back. As far as I knew, he was still on the phone with the captain, though. I was out here all alone. All my backup down the hill was at least ten minutes away. I should have called in a bomb squad. But then they'd get all the credit. If I got blown up...well, the odds of that were pretty small. She wouldn't have trip-wired two houses. Right?

Before I could lose my nerve, I banged on the door. "Police! Open up!"

No answer.

Of course. The arsonist wasn't just going to invite me into her lair. I lowered my gun and was about to kick down the door when it squeaked open.

A woman stood there with her gaze trained on the ground as she pulled the silk sash closed around her robe.

"I'm Detective Reed," I said, keeping both hands on my gun instead of offering a handshake.

She didn't respond. Instead, the silence stretched between us as she tied the sash three times. Not that the sash being tight hid a damn thing. Her thin, silk robe didn't leave much to the imagination. My eyes snapped back up to her face.

She was staring at me staring at her. And even though the accusing expression on her face should have made me look away, I just couldn't. She was indeed beautiful. High cheekbones, full kissable lips, a perfect pale complexion with rosy cheeks. But her hair was brown, not blonde. And I felt myself breathe a sigh of relief.

"Can I help you?" she asked. I thought her voice would be filled with indignation based on how she was staring at me. But it wasn't at all. She sounded timid. Scared.

I realized I was probably terrifying her. I slid my gun back in its holster. "What are you doing out here?" *In the middle of the woods? In a robe?*

"I live here."

I wanted to laugh. But it didn't look like she was joking. And she was...wet. Her damp hair was piled on top of her head in a messy bun. And there were splotches on her robe like she had thrown it on instead of taking the time to dry off properly after a shower. A very recent shower. Here in this house. She really lived here? "You live out here in the middle of the woods?"

"In a house. Why is that so strange?" She stared at me.

"It's literally falling apart." I tapped one of the broken floorboards with my heel. "This must violate all sorts of codes."

She stood up a little straighter. "I've been fixing it up. I'm not breaking any codes." But she didn't sound very sure of herself.

If this was fixed up I didn't want to think about what it had looked like before she got her hands on it. Or maybe she was just the worst house flipper on the planet.

"Is there something I can help you with, Detective Reed?" She put her hand on the doorknob. "If you don't mind, it's getting rather late and I..."

It was pretty clear she was trying to get rid of me. "I have a few questions for you."

"For me?" She didn't look surprised. She looked like she was expecting it. Only a guilty person expected questioning.

I cleared my throat as I pulled the paper out of my pocket. "Do you know this man?" I unfolded it and held it up for her.

She leaned forward slightly to get a better look. "No, I've never seen him."

"Are you sure?" She didn't look back at the page. Instead, her gaze met mine.

"Positive. I've never seen him in my life."

"Maybe you know him as Ben *Jones*?"

"I don't know him at all."

"What about the name Adeline Bell?"

"Doesn't ring any *bells*." She laughed awkwardly at her own joke for just a second and then pressed her lips back together. "I don't know anyone by that name."

I folded the paper back up and slipped it into my pocket. Either she wasn't sorry at all about his death or she really didn't know him. But I couldn't read her at all. And usually I could read strangers like the back of my hand. "Have you seen any suspicious activity outside tonight?"

"There was an explosion in the neighborhood down the hill. Windy Park. You should look into that instead of tramping around my property."

"That is what I'm looking into."

She stared at me. "And you're here because..."

"A trail from the house on fire led me right to you."

"Do you go following every path you see? There's a sidewalk out front of that house that blew up. Why not follow that around the neighborhood?"

"So you didn't see anyone outside your house? A blonde woman perhaps?"

"Nope."

It was a lie. There was only one reason to lie. She was somehow involved in all this. I looked back up at her wet hair. Was it wet with water, or wet with dye? It was the only thing that didn't fit Sally's description.

"You're sure?" I asked. "No one? Nothing unusual at all?"

"Nope. Absolutely nothing."

Absolutely a lie. "Would you mind letting me take a look around…"

Her hand shot to the doorjamb, blocking any view I had inside of her home. "Yes, I mind. This is private property."

Damn. I really wished cop shows didn't make it so clear that people can refuse to let law enforcement in. "Fair enough," I said. For just a moment my eyes traveled down her body again. I silently cursed. Maybe Damien was right. I needed to get laid so that I'd stop ogling murder suspects.

She cleared her throat.

I snapped my attention back to her face. "You really shouldn't live out here all alone." I couldn't help it. No one that looked the way she did should be alone period. And now a murder suspect was loose in these words. Or maybe she was the suspect.

"I never said that I was alone," she said. It should have sounded harsh, but her voice was timid again. Like there was something more hidden in her words.

But it didn't matter what she meant. It was clear she wasn't going to give me any more information. "I'm sorry to have bothered you. If you hear or see anything, though, let me know." I handed her one of my business cards.

She took it from me, grabbing it with the tip of her index finger and thumb like she was worried our hands might touch.

"And be careful out here, Mrs..." I waited for her to give me her last name but she didn't. Instead she slammed the door in my face.

CHAPTER 3

Violet

I locked the door and then just stared at it. *God, I just lied to a detective. Why the hell did I just lie to a detective?* It had felt right in the moment. But as soon as the words left my mouth I regretted them. I could have told him about the woman running through the woods. I could have pointed him in the direction that she had fled. I could have given him every detail he wanted and gotten him out of my hair.

But instead I *lied.* I shook my head. He hadn't left me with much of a choice. I couldn't have the cops poking around in the woods. I couldn't have them running all around my property with police dogs and metal detectors and whatever else cops used in the search for a criminal. What if they found something? I couldn't risk it.

I bit the inside of my cheek. Had the detective known I was lying? It looked like he did. Like he could easily see right through me. *Shit shit shit.*

"It wasn't a big lie," I said into the empty room. "It was a little white lie. A nothing lie. There are no consequences for a nothing lie." *Right?*

I should have run back upstairs to finish what I had started just in case he came back, but instead I found myself pushing my ear against the door. There was no squeak of floorboards or crunch of leaves. I closed my eyes and tried to listen. The silence was incredibly loud as I pressed the side of my face harder against the wooden door.

Detective Reed's gaze had been so intense. It felt like he had locked me in place when he was staring at me. Like I could barely even breathe. *Does he feel as frozen as me right now?*

I moved away from the door. Of course he didn't. There was no way that he was as affected by our meeting as I was. It was his job to make me feel frozen. For his eyes to bore into my soul, see my darkest sins, and to travel down my body...I shook my head. *No.* That was most certainly not his job. But he had done that, right? I hadn't imagined it?

I swallowed down the lump in my throat. All my nerves were on hyperdrive. The only man I had interacted with recently was mailman Joe. And he was like seventy. This was a normal response to a man my own age. Especially one who looked like Detective Reed. I glanced down at the business card in my hand. Detective Tucker Reed.

I tiptoed to the window in the living room and peered through a gap in the curtains. I expected to see him retreating through the woods, but he was just standing there. Staring at the door. Frozen. I could feel my pulse beating in my head. I hadn't imagined it. He had been looking at me. Really looking. And it didn't seem like it was purely for detective reasons.

I let myself stare unabashedly at him from behind the safety of the curtain. He didn't look how I expected a detective to look. Beer bellies and mustaches were the dominant features of the detectives in my mind. But he was most certainly not like the detectives I pictured in my head. He was wearing a formfitting wool jacket that was undoubtedly not hiding a huge stomach. If anything it was probably covering perfect six pack abs. I glanced down at his left hand. There was no ring on his finger. Hot and single. I was good at smelling trouble a mile away. And Detective Reed was most certainly trouble. After all, he was clearly the reason I had lied. I couldn't think straight when a man with a chiseled jaw, five-o'clock shadow, piercing brown eyes, and a deep sexy voice was staring right at me.

Yes, he was the reason I had lied. He had made me act poorly. It was all his fault. *Jerk.*

He turned his head and I threw myself down onto the floor. *Ow.* I cradled my elbow that had just whacked the hardwood floors. Or what was left of them.

When I peered back out the window, the detective was gone. And a part of me wondered if I had imagined him.

***

I placed the handgun and old letters back in their box. There was no reason to move the gun. It'd been sitting there for six years without causing me any harm. No one would find it here. My original plan was to grab the gun and chuck it into the lake. But the red and blue lights hadn't ceased lighting up the sky. The cops wouldn't be going away anytime soon, despite me denying the fact that a very guilty looking woman had been running through the woods. The gun was safer with me than out there where they could find it. Like I had told the detective…he needed a warrant. And I couldn't see why anyone would give him one to search my house. I was a law-abiding citizen. I paid my taxes. I was most definitely not going to be a suspect in their investigation of a house fire. I lived all the way out here for a reason. They'd leave me alone.

I put the floorboard back in place and stood up. Yup, it was most definitely safe there. Just like it always had been. But I still wondered if police dogs could sniff out guns. I wanted to Google it on my phone, but I knew searching that question would inevitably lead me down a terrible, inescapable rabbit hole of useless facts. It was the same reason I had to ban myself from looking up anything on WebMD. No matter my symptoms, it always made me think I had a brain tumor. Or maybe there was a reason for that. My fingers itched to look up whether I did or did not in fact have a brain tumor. I took a deep, calming breath. *You are banned from that site. You are banned from searching police dogs.*

And honestly, who cared if police dogs could smell guns? The gun wasn't loaded, and it was mine. Well, technically it wasn't mine. It had been my stepfather's. But I didn't steal it or anything. No, it wasn't registered in my name, but I was pretty sure I had a right to it since he was dead.

Did that look bad? God, it probably did. I looked back down at the floorboard. Honestly, I was terrified of the thing. I didn't know how to properly use it. And I didn't know how to discard of it or I would have done it years ago. The gun had been lying in my floorboards untouched ever since I moved in. And now I had an unregistered gun in my house. With my fingerprints all over it. It did look bad.

I took another deep breath. No one was going to find it. Because no one was coming into my house without an invitation. I walked over to my nightstand and stared down at the detective's business card. It was easy for me to suddenly focus on him instead. He had been in the back of my head all night. All I had wanted to do since he left my front porch was send him a text. Google and WebMD searches wouldn't have appeased me long anyway when my true desire was to talk to him. I stared at the card. A little harmless flirting would either help get him off my back or make me seem suspicious. *Probably the latter.*

I lifted up the card. The temptation was too strong. I needed to get rid of it before I did something I regretted. I walked into the bathroom, opened one of the drawers in my vanity, and pulled out one of my three lighters. I lit the corner of the business card and watched his information slowly disappear forever. Not that it mattered. I had remembered his number. And once something was seared into my brain it was pretty hard for me to forget it. Regardless, I watched it burn closer to my fingers. At the last second I tossed it into the toilet. It sizzled and went out with the most satisfying sound. *Huh.* I watched the remainder of the card grow damp. Maybe they should have suspected me for setting a house on fire. I had always liked the sound of fire. But more so the sound of a fire being extinguished. I was a lot of things, but I was most definitely not a pyromaniac. I flushed the toilet and placed the lighter back where it belonged.

Tonight was always going to be hard. I was surprised at how little the memory of Joel stung me now, though. Maybe six years truly was the magical amount of time to heal. I doubted it had anything to do with Detective Reed. A handsome face didn't just erase years of painful memories. One chance meeting wasn't enough for me to forget the fact that the love of my life had abandoned me here.

Despite the fact that I wasn't sad, I still walked out of my bedroom and down the hall, trying hard not to let the floorboards creak. If I was being honest, I found myself wandering into Zeke's room most nights. Sad, happy, grateful…all of my emotions were always heightened by him. Seeing him sleeping peacefully reminded me how little all the Joels and Detective Reeds in the world really mattered. Zeke was the only man that I needed in my life. And since he was five, he didn't seem to mind his mother snuggling with him when she needed a little comfort.

I climbed into his twin sized bed and wrapped my arm around him.

"I don't feel good," he said and nuzzled his face into his pillow.

I hadn't expected him to still be awake. I kissed the top of his head. "I know, sweetie." I had put him to bed right after dinner. He had been complaining about his throat hurting. Although...he didn't have a temperature. And a liar was always good at spotting another liar. Maybe he had learned it from me. But I hadn't pressed it tonight because I had a date with the lake and memories that I should have buried long ago. "So you're not feeling any better?"

"No. I think I have to stay home from school tomorrow."

"You do, huh?"

He turned to face me. "Probably. I wouldn't want to get the other kids sick."

"Zeke." I placed my hand on the side of his face. "Are the other children still teasing you?"

"No." He said it too defensively, and his tone broke my heart.

I had been called into the principal's office a week after he first started kindergarten. A very uncaring principal who just wanted to inform me that my child was being teased. He didn't offer any way to help the situation. Just thought it was important for me to know that my boy was being called Zeke the Freak.

I hoped the last few months had been getting better. But they hadn't. Fake stomach bugs. Headaches. He even claimed he had AIDS. I doubt he really knew what that entailed. The honest truth was that my sweet boy had the dreaded faker's disease. Zeke was spending more time on WebMD than me to look up fake illnesses.

"Little dude, you have to go to school. It's important."

"Why? You don't leave. I don't want to either."

I pressed my lips together. I knew that part of his name calling was my fault. I was the crazy lady who lived at the top of the hill. I could handle housewives' wrath. But my son? None of my idiosyncrasies were his fault. Why did bored suburban moms teach their kids to behave so poorly? Just because I liked to live out here alone didn't mean my son was strange.

Sure, he didn't exactly look like normal kids. I let him dress how he liked because I believed it was important for children to express themselves. His blonde hair was in short dreadlocks, he always wore bright yellow rain boots, and he preferred cargo shorts to any other kind of pants or shorts, even if it was frightfully cold. But that made logical sense. He held all sorts of things in his pockets. Whenever I needed a pen he could hand me one in under two seconds. It was impressive. The kind of thing that kids should have admired. But no. I looked down at my beautiful little son. Zeke the Freak. Children could be so idiotic. He was the light of my life. He was wonderful, and smart, and kind. He was perfect.

"Maybe you can have tomorrow off," I said as I tucked a dreadlock behind his ear. "How does a three day weekend sound?"

"Yeah?" He looked up at me with his adorable little face.

"Yeah. You've earned a holiday." He hadn't. He was a few absences away from having to repeat kindergarten. But that was bullshit. He was smarter than all those little assholes making fun of him. And if his principal wanted to try to cross me, I'd pull the crazy card and scare him into agreeing with me.

"Thanks, Mom." He snuggled back into my arms.

I wished that I could turn back time and name him something different. Something that didn't rhyme with a hateful word. But children would find a way to be mean no matter what. That was what kids did. Hurt each other with words.

Zeke's chest started to rise and fall slower. Knowing that he didn't have to face his enemies tomorrow had put him fast asleep. I blinked away the tears in my eyes. All the thoughts of my ex, handsome detectives, and unregistered handguns disappeared. What was I going to do about Zeke? I needed to figure out something soon before he repeated my mistakes.

CHAPTER 4

Tucker

"Where the hell have you been?" Damien jogged over to me when I reached the bottom of the hill. "I've been running around the woods aimlessly for half an hour looking for you."

"Sorry, I was…" I glanced back up the hill at the rundown house. I was what? Flirting with an innocent civilian? Not exactly. I hadn't been flirting. I was simply questioning her. And she definitely wasn't innocent. That woman was hiding something. I'd bet my badge on it. Not that such a bet would mean much...I was about to lose my badge anyway.

"You were what?" His breath was ragged from running.

I didn't want to talk to him about the woman I had just met. He'd ask me too many prying questions and joke around about why it took me so long to question her. Besides, she was clearly married. And my number one suspect. I just wasn't sure why neither fact made her less appealing to me. "Aw, Torres, were you worried about me?" I patted his shoulder and kept walking through the woods.

He caught back up to me. "No. These woods just give me the creeps. And it doesn't help that there's an escaped psychopath somewhere in the vicinity. Seriously, don't take off like that."

I could have kept teasing him about being worried. But I was glad someone had my back. Because no one else in this town did. "I'll tell you next time I'm about to follow a lead." I ducked under a branch.

"A lead? What lead? You weren't even briefed yet."

"A neighbor saw the woman who lived in the house run into the woods. I thought I might be able to catch her."

He tugged the zipper on his coat higher. "No wonder I got the creeps walking out here by myself. One crazy woman on the loose is bad enough. But two? Let's get the hell out of here." He picked up his pace.

"What do you mean two? Are there two suspects?"

"Nah, I was just referring to Violet. I'd stay out of these woods due to her alone."

"Who's Violet?"

"Sometimes I forget you're not a local. The crazy woman on the hill." He gestured behind us.

The crazy woman on the hill? I glanced over my shoulder at the hill, but I could barely see it in the darkness. "You mean the one who lives in that dilapidated house?"

"Don't tell me you met her?"

"I thought she might be the arsonist. There were footprints leading from the crime scene practically to her doorstep."

Damien laughed. "She rarely leaves her house. Pretty sure she's scared of germs or something. She's a total nut-bag but not an arsonist."

"Are you sure it's not the same person? Her hair was wet. Maybe she had just dyed it. She fit Sally's description otherwise and…"

"Who the hell is Sally?"

"That nosy neighbor at the crime scene."

He shook his head. "And you believed the observations of a bored housewife?"

"Sally was a very credible source." She wasn't. She was exactly how Damien described her, only more of the gossipy variety. She had been fishing for information more than offering anything valuable. I was pretty sure she was already spreading rumors of Benjamin Harlow being a polygamist.

"Well I'm a more credible source than your new friend. And you're barking up the wrong tree with Violet."

"But she lied about seeing something. I think if we go back and question her again she'll…"

"No need. We're off the case."

I stopped on the edge of the woods. "What do you mean we're off the case? I already have a lead."

Damien kept walking back toward my car. "There are no leads. Not for us anyway. I did what you wanted, we get to go have that drink now."

"Well undo it. I really think we should go question…"

"Fine. I didn't technically get us off the case. The captain said we no longer have proper clearance. It turned into some next level shit. The FBI will be here soon."

Jesus. The FBI? Solving this case wouldn't just save my career. It would set it on a much better trajectory. We passed the crime scene where the fire was finally being contained. I didn't want to let this go. I had more questions to ask the cops and neighbors. I scanned the marred yellow caution tape that Sally had been fighting earlier, but she was nowhere in sight. The case had been so easily abandoned by everyone but me.

"Open the damn door, Tucker." He knocked on the passengers' side window of my car.

I pulled the keys out of my pocket and unlocked it. Damien had more information than he was letting on. He had been chatting with the captain for as long as I was running around in the woods. He had to have found out a lot about the case before we were called off it. I didn't have much of a choice but to take him up on his offer of drinks now. I had already cracked this case wide open, I just needed a few more details. The more Damien drank, the more he'd talk.

***

"So you're scared of Violet because she has obsessive-compulsive disorder?" I asked. Damien was three beers in while I was still nursing my first. It was the perfect time to pry more information out of him.

"I never said that I was scared of her. And I have no idea what her freaking diagnosis is. I said the woods give me the creeps because they're filled with crazy women."

I should have been getting details about the case. But for some reason my mind had decided to focus on Violet. It had nothing to do with her beauty and everything to do with the fact that she was guilty. At least, that's what I was telling myself. I needed to know more about her to figure out the perfect plan before showing up on her property again tomorrow morning. "OCD isn't exactly creepy."

"It's not about the OCD. It's everything else. It's about the fact that she used to be so normal and then lost her mind and decided to isolate herself from the world."

I took a sip of my beer and waited for him to continue. I knew that he would. Once he got going on a story it was hard to stop him, even if the story was terribly boring and I desperately wanted it to end. But I was dying to hear more of this one.

He leaned forward slightly and dropped his voice. "She was a few years younger than me in school. I saw her around and she wasn't crazy then. She was normal. Popular even. I was away in college when it happened, but apparently her whole family abandoned her. Just went poof in the night. Her boyfriend too. They left her all alone, flew to the opposite ends of the country just to get away from her. And that's when the crazy came out. At least when it started to show to everyone else apparently. Her family probably ditched her because they already knew she was a loon."

"So you just heard about this? You weren't there when any of it happened?" He was as bad as nosy Sally. Rumors weren't facts. He knew that.

"Sure, rumors spread like hotcakes. But these ones are true, I'm telling you. I mean, if the woman is sane, why does she live out in the middle of the woods in that rundown shack?"

It wasn't a shack. The house would have been beautiful in its prime. I couldn't exactly argue with the rundown part though. It had been the first thing I'd noticed about the place. "Well if she was alone it would be crazy. But she's not." I remembered how defensive she got when I implied that she shouldn't be out in the woods alone. "She's married, right?"

He rose both eyebrows and laughed. "Married? Are you kidding? Who would marry that whack-job?"

I took another sip of my beer. So it had been another lie. She was alone in that house. Why had she been so quick to lie to me? The question had been turning around in my head for the past hour, always leading toward one conclusion. She was hiding something. "Maybe she's out there because she's trying to run from something she did."

"Not this again. We're off the case, man."

"Just hear me out. What if we solved the case instead of the FBI? We could do no wrong after something like that."

He just stared at me.

"All we have to do is go question Violet again and…"

"You have the hots for her."

I laughed. "No, definitely not."

He slowly shook his head. "You're smitten."

"Who uses the word smitten? I'm not smitten."

A huge smile spread over his face. "She was hot. I haven't seen her in years, but I remember her being at least an eight."

She was a ten, hands down. If Damien didn't see that, he was blind. But the captain and Violet certainly didn't look anything alike. Damien tended to go after curvy, powerful women who he pretended he knew how to handle. Violet wasn't like that. She seemed…delicate. Like a violet actually. A lying, timid yet audacious, sexy as sin violet. I shrugged away the thought. "I'm not attracted to her. But speaking of women…how did your chat with the captain go?"

"Great. Pretty sure she's going to say yes to a date any day now."

Keep dreaming. "So what did she say about the case?"

"That two cops were killed in the explosion, which is why we had to rush over there. Everyone thought there was also a civilian in critical condition. He left in an ambulance before we arrived on the scene, but they IDed him at the hospital while I was on the phone. He's actually some hotshot agent from out of town that's part of an ongoing investigation."

"Benjamin Harlow?"

"Yup, that's the one."

"Is he going to be okay?"

Damien shrugged. "It didn't sound good. He's in critical condition. I doubt he'll make it through the night."

Damn. I was really hoping to question him about everything. He'd even be able to ID Violet if she was the one that had been living in the house. But that theory was pretty much out the window. If everyone knew about the crazy lady on the hill, surely Sally would have known. She would have just said Violet had done it and then gone home. That wasn't it. I was missing something.

What I needed was a good night's sleep so I could sort through the details with a fresh perspective. All I could focus on right now was that there were two cops down. And that Benjamin guy would be a third soon enough. This case was big, just like I had suspected. Any more information Damien could give me would be helpful. "So...what's the ongoing investigation?"

"That's all I know. The case was ours for less than ten minutes."

"Did you hear anything else about Benjamin? It was strange...Sally knew him. But she said his last name was Jones instead of Harlow."

"Maybe I was wrong about you having the hots for Violet. Clearly you have a thing for Sally. What's she look like?"

Frumpy and twice my age. "I'm not interested in Sally or Violet. I'm interested in solving the case."

"How about the two dimes at 10 o'clock?"

I didn't even turn to look. "Aren't you trying to score with the captain?"

"Yeah but big fish take time. I'm just looking for tonight, not the long haul."

"I'm going to pass."

"Suit yourself. I'll see you in the morning." He grabbed his beer and headed over to the table behind me.

I sighed and pulled out my wallet. Damien had barely given me any information. I was going to have to solve this thing on my own. And on my own time because I was already on thin ice at work.

CHAPTER 5

Violet

I sneezed and pulled the comforter up to my chin. Everything hurt. My whole body was betraying me, begging to stay in bed. But I had promised Zeke a fun day off. He needed to get his mind off the snarky five-year-olds in his class, and I had the perfect day planned. A little cold wasn't going to get in my way of putting a smile on Zeke's face. Even thinking about him coming home in the afternoon with a frown on his face killed me.

I tickled his side, waking him up in a fit of giggles. "It's a three day weekend." I tried to yell it and sound excited, but it came out as more of a hoarse whisper.

He squirmed out of my tickle attack. As soon as he could breathe, he sat up in bed and looked down at my face. "You're sick."

"I'm not sick." I was most certainly sick. I sneezed again, crushing any doubt in either of our minds. My plunge in the lake had done me in.

He put his tiny little hand on my forehead. "I must have given you what I had. I'm sorry, Mommy."

"We both know you weren't sick last night."

"I *was*. I feel better today though." He climbed off the bed. "I'll make you pancakes."

I tried to hide my smile. For a moment I thought he'd go to school after all and abandon me in my dire state. He had just admitted that he felt fine. But he was going to stay and take care of me. It wasn't the fun day I had planned, but it sounded pretty perfect to me. Minus the pancakes. My little dude could not cook. Last time he made me buttermilk pancakes he didn't dilute the powdered buttermilk. They tasted like chalk mixed with acid, but I didn't have the heart to tell him that. I had eaten three of them. *Three.* I could have died. That's how much I loved him.

"How about cereal instead?" I asked.

"But you love pancakes and whenever I don't feel good you make me my favorite foods."

"I do love your pancakes, but…"

"I'll be back." His bare feet padded along his bedroom floor and into the hallway.

Crap. I could add a tummy ache to my ailments in a few minutes if I didn't figure out a way to distract him. But my body wouldn't move. If I could just get up, I'd at least be able to help him cook. I could sneak in the right ingredients when he wasn't looking.

The slam of a cabinet door downstairs hinted that I was running out of time.

Ignoring my achy body, I pushed myself out of bed. It was freezing. I folded my arms across my pajama top and ran my hands up and down my arms to try to warm myself. I had turned the heat up last night. It shouldn't have been this cold. *Please don't let there be something wrong with the heater.*

A lot of the work around the house I could handle on my own. But I wasn't great with anything electrical. I remembered when I was young, my mother could make a call and a repairman would come out right away. For me? I'm pretty sure they just pawned my job off to employees lower down the totem pole until some newbie who didn't know the difference between copper and aluminum wiring finally got stuck with it. It was no wonder that my heater had crapped out. The last person to fix it was clearly only an apprentice. He shouldn't have been out here alone. Plus he kept glancing over his shoulder the whole time like I was going to murder him when he wasn't looking. The rumors about me were probably growing if he thought that.

I grabbed a pair of socks for Zeke before leaving his bedroom. There was no point in us both being sick. "Put these on before you catch a cold too, little dude," I said and shoved them into his flour covered hands. "Want some help with the pancakes?"

"No, I got it." He hopped from one foot to the next, pulling on his socks.

I scanned the counter while he jumped around the kitchen. What the hell was tomato paste doing out? He had to know that wasn't the right ingredient. Maybe I shouldn't have let him stay home from school. He still had a lot to learn. "You know...all the best chefs have sous chefs."

"A lady named Sue helps all chefs? There must be a lot of Sues in the world."

"No, sous as in s-o-u-s. They're basically cooking assistants. I'll be your sous this morning. So...what should I do with the tomato paste?" *Besides throw it out.*

"We're out of eggs and I think it's about the same consistency. We're just going to mix it in."

So he knew the word consistency yet didn't have any taste buds? I needed to work on refining his pallet. But it was hard when he basically refused to eat anything that wasn't dinosaur shaped. Or filled with sugar. *I'm a terrible mother.* But something with sugar was certainly better than tomato paste in pancakes. "You know, we might have some apple sauce or something a little sweeter that…"

"You're the *assistant.*" He handed me the can opener and hopped back onto the chair by the island. It was adorable to watch him stand on the chair while he...bare-handed some flour. Without measuring. These pancakes were going to be worse than I thought, if that was even possible.

"Aye, aye, Captain," I said. But instead of following his instructions, I picked up the can and can opener and looked for a good hiding spot. "Oh, no…the can opener isn't working," I said as I tossed it behind some pots and pans. "It must be broken, so anything canned is out. But if it's okay with you, I can still find that applesauce," I said as I closed the cabinet door.

He didn't respond.

"Is that okay, Zeke?"

He was just staring out the window, his hand paused on the spoon he had been stirring with. His momentary distraction had been great timing because it had given me time to save our breakfast. But now he was alarming me.

"Zeke?" I abandoned my sous chef post and walked over to him.

He tilted his head to the side. "There's a stranger out there." He pointed out the window toward our driveway.

It felt like my heart was beating out of my chest. Sure enough, there was a man snooping around my truck. Strange, yes. A stranger? Not exactly. Detective Reed had made it pretty clear that he was going to be a pain in my ass last night. I had just foolishly thought that I had gotten rid of him.

"Mommy, who is that?" Zeke looked up at me.

"No one important. Stay here, okay?" I quickly walked out of the kitchen, grabbed a light jacket from the closet, wishing that I hadn't left my winter one at the bottom of the lake, and shoved my feet into some boots.

"Mom?"

"Stay in here, Zeke." I closed the front door behind me as I ran down the porch steps. "Hey!" My weak sick voice was gone. I was livid. He had no right to be here and I had made that perfectly clear last night.

Detective Reed looked up at me and had the audacity to smile. *Smile! While he was trespassing!*

"What are you doing on..." I sneezed. "On my property?"

His dark eyebrows pulled together in the most sympathetic way. And for some reason it made me even angrier. I didn't need his sympathy. He shouldn't be here judging me. He wasn't allowed to be here at all.

I sneezed again.

"Are you feeling okay?"

"Do you have a search warrant?" I asked, ignoring him.

He shook his head. "No, but I brought coffee. And doughnuts." He lifted up the Dunkin bag like a peace offering.

I stared at the bag of doughnuts. It was my only way out of the poison pancakes my son was about to make. Zeke loved doughnuts. He'd abandoned any thoughts of making me a home cooked meal if I could snag those. But I had a feeling the price was going to be pretty high. "Well, thank you for bringing breakfast." I put my hands out, hoping that somehow there wouldn't be a catch.

"If you agree to talk to me about what really happened last night."

No such luck. I dropped my hands to my side. "I told you everything I knew."

"Did you though?"

I sneezed again.

"You should be wearing a warmer jacket. It's freezing out. Here..." He unzipped his own coat and started to shrug his shoulders out of it while balancing two coffee cups and the bag of doughnuts.

"I'm not taking your jacket. And I don't have anything else to say to you. I made myself perfectly clear last night and..." I stopped talking when he draped his jacket over my shoulders. I immediately felt some of the achiness in my bones diminish. I couldn't even remember the last time a man had offered me his coat. *Joel. It was Joel.* I glared at Detective Reed. "Get off my property before I call the cops."

"I am law enforcement. And I came in peace." He lifted up the to-go bag again, like he could dangle cheap food over my head.

Suddenly I had a craving for disgusting pancakes. At least those were made with love and didn't come with any strings attached. "We both know that you're not supposed to be sneaking around here without the right documentation. So...get." I shooed him away.

He laughed.

I was pretty sure my knees felt weak because I was sick. Not because his laugh was disarmingly deep and sexy.

"Look, I think we got off on the wrong foot last night," he said.

You think? "I disagree. I think we both are on the exact right foot." I turned away from him and started walking back toward my front porch. *The right foot? Who says things like that?* The fever had reached my brain and was making my mind all mushy. I was in desperate need of a good WebMD search, but knew I wouldn't risk going down that inescapable rabbit hole of brain tumors.

"I'm just trying to talk to you, Violet."

I stopped. He knew my name? I waited for him to catch up to me and then looked up at him. Someone had either told him who I was or he had looked me up. Neither would have been great. And the way he was looking at me made sense now. He wasn't staring at me with pity. He was staring at me like he was trying to figure out if the rumors were true. I wasn't deaf. I heard the whispers. I was used to the stares. *The crazy lady on the hill.* That's what my neighbors called me. My petty, stupid, horrid neighbors.

But I wasn't a kid getting teased on the playground. And words didn't hurt me anymore. I stood up a little straighter and swallowed down a sneeze. The act made my eyes water and I hoped he didn't think I was about to burst into tears. "You have exactly one question. One. And then you have to leave." Maybe I imagined it, but I swore his gaze drifted to my lips for just a second before snapping back up to my eyes.

"Why did you lie to me last night?"

He had found me out. But I had lied a bunch of times to him last night and I wasn't sure which thing he was referring to. It was better if I kept with my story and kept him far away from me. "I didn't lie about anything. Now get off my property." I grabbed one of the cups of coffee and the bag of doughnuts and ran up the creaky steps.

As soon as I slammed my door with a kick of my boot, Zeke was upon me.

"Who was that?"

"A…friend. He brought us doughnuts!"

"Doughnuts!" He grabbed the bag from me and ran back into the kitchen, hopefully abandoning any more questions and any more ideas about cooking me breakfast.

I lifted off my coat and silently cursed. It wasn't my coat. I was still wearing Detective Reed's pity jacket. Now not only had I lied to a detective, but I had stolen his jacket too. *God, I'm going to end up in prison. Especially if he finds out my secrets.*

CHAPTER 6

Tucker

I couldn't get Violet out of my head. All day, my mind just kept going back to her. My current casework was piling up on my desk, but the only thing I could focus on was the case that got away. I needed to figure out if my hunch was right. Even if there was only a slim chance that I could solve this case, I needed to take it. I turned off my computer.

"Where are you heading?" Damien asked as I stood up from my desk.

It felt like he had been watching me all morning and afternoon, waiting for me to sneak off and work on the case we'd been dropped from. It had made the searches I needed to do on the database nearly impossible. The only information I was able to get was that the woman who had owned the house that exploded was a ghost. No pictures. No medical records. No previous addresses. No nothing. And I was only able to get that useless information because Damien had to go to the bathroom. The whole day was pointless. The only thing I wanted to do was continue to question my lead suspect. Which was what I was about to go do. "I'm going home," I lied.

Damien leaned back in his chair and propped his feet up on his desk. "Not heading out into the woods to harass a beautiful psychopath?"

"Violet is hardly a psychopath."

"That wasn't the answer I was looking for."

"I promise I'm not harassing any psychopaths." Damien didn't know that I had already stopped by Violet's place before my shift started. And he didn't need to know that or the fact that I was planning on stopping by again. All I needed was an in with Violet. If I could get her to trust me, she'd tell me what she saw last night. *Or she'll tell me what she's done.* And she had responded well to the food I had brought. She had a dinner coming her way and hopefully a little more conversation.

"That's still not the right answer. You're going to her house again, aren't you?"

"Of course not." Out of habit, I reached for my coat on the back of my chair, but my fingers came up empty. Another reason why going back to Violet's wasn't a bad idea. She had stolen my jacket. I kind of wanted it back. That combined with the fact that she was a suspect were definitely the only reasons I was going back. It had nothing to do with her rosy cheeks or the adorable way she sneezed and looked angry at the same time.

"Then give me a lift home, will you?" Damien asked, pulling my thoughts away from Violet. "My car's in the shop and Uber drivers always give me low ratings when I tell them I'm a detective. I think it freaks them out."

"We both know you can fix anything wrong with your car by yourself. Besides, I saw you drive up today. I have better things to do than chauffeur your lying ass around town."

"I'm only lying because you are. We're off the case, man."

"I know that."

"Do you?" He dropped his feet from his desk and leaned forward in his chair. "You're already on thin ice around here.

If you keep pressing this, it'll be the last straw they need to kick you to the curb."

I knew that. But I also had a feeling in my gut that I was about to solve the damned thing, which would do the exact opposite for my career. "I know what I'm doing."

"No one knows what they're doing when beautiful women are involved."

"Touché."

"Just don't believe anything Violet says. She's cra…"

"Crazy. I know." But she didn't seem crazy to me. She seemed…lonely. Whenever I talked to her she threatened me to get off her property. But I was pretty sure her eyes had been begging me to stay. Tonight I was going to up my flirting game. Besides, Damien's constant pestering reminded me that it had been quite a while since I had been on a date. This would be good practice. Not real flirting at all. Just practice for when I got back out there.

"Please just go home. And if you do decide to be an idiot and go to her house, call me so I can be your backup!" Damien called after me as I headed toward the door.

I didn't respond. I just waved my hand in the air to say goodbye. Having him with me was not part of the plan. How was I supposed to worm my way into Violet's good graces if Damien was scowling at me the whole night? Or worse…hitting on her. I wasn't sure why the thought made me angry. It wasn't like I was actually going to be hitting on her tonight. Just innocent, fake flirting.

***

I put the car in park, ignoring every part of my brain telling me to turn around. Fake flirting was going to be difficult when Violet was bent over her air-conditioning unit with her perfect ass jutting up into the air. I stared at the black leggings she was wearing. A very perfect ass. She might as well have had a neon sign on her saying, "Trouble."

I ran my hand down my face and over the scruff on my chin. I was a detective. Not a horny teenager. I could keep it in my pants for one night. This was going to make or break my career.

She bent over even more as she examined the air-conditioning unit.

I groaned. *She's crazy*, I tried to tell myself. But I didn't believe the words. *She blew up a house.* I wasn't sure I believed that either. *So what the hell am I doing here?* I grabbed the bags of take-out before I could change my mind.

My car door slammed and Violet jumped, hitting her head on the side of the unit.

"Ow," she mumbled. But then it was like she slowly registered what had caused her to hit her head. She quickly spun around and stared at me. There was a spot of grease right beside her nose. She was holding a hammer in her hand. A hammer that had no business being anywhere near her air conditioner.

"You again," she seethed and pointed the hammer at me. "How many times am I going to have to ask you to get off my property?" But before I could respond, she sneezed in the most adorable way, and then proceeded to wipe the grease spot across her cheek, smearing it everywhere.

I would have laughed, but for some reason it made her look even sexier. "You'll probably have to ask me a few more times," I said with a smile. "It just so happens that I like coming around to see you." This flirting thing was easy. I wasn't out of practice at all.

She squinted her eyes at me. "Okay. Then let me ask you a few more times. Get. Off. My. Property. Get off my property. Off. Now." She pointed to my car. "Go."

I ignored her and walked closer. "I noticed you weren't feeling well earlier. I brought dinner for us to share." I lifted up the take-out bags. "Together this time, though." I gave her my most charming smile.

For one second, her gaze dipped to my smile. But then she immediately snapped her attention back to my eyes. "Go to hell." She started to storm past me.

"Whoa." I caught her arm. "I'm not here on business. I'm here to have dinner with you. You know...like a date."

She looked down at her arm and then back up at me. Her left eyebrow rose. "Like a date?" She laughed. "Look, you're clearly from out of town, so let me help you out. I'm insane." She pulled out of my grip and then gestured her hands around her head in a comical way, although it was a little intimidating since she was still holding the hammer. "People stay away from me. Be one of those people, Detective Reed."

"You can call me Tucker." I smiled again, ignoring her lame attempt at scaring me away. And I couldn't help wondering why she so desperately wanted to be all alone. I certainly didn't like being single. Four months of moping around were enough for me.

She sighed and looked down at her hammer. "You're not supposed to be here, Tucker."

I wasn't sure what she meant by that. Here in the woods? Here with her? Here in this stupid town? She was probably right about all three of those things, yet…here I was. I shrugged. "Where am I supposed to be then?"

"Anywhere but here." She absently tapped the hammer against her thigh a few times as she glanced at the bags of food.

"It's a little too late for that, I can't eat all this alone."

She scrunched her mouth to the side in thought.

"Plus, I can fix that for you." I nodded to her air-conditioner.

She still didn't respond.

This wasn't a hard decision. She was sick. There was no way that she was in the mood to cook tonight. Plus I was offering her free repair services. I was going above and beyond. "You know what? You're right. You are crazy…" I knew I had her where I wanted her because a line in her forehead I didn't know existed suddenly appeared. "…because you care about fixing your air-conditioner even though it's freezing out. No wonder you're sick."

She frowned. "I'm trying to fix the heater."

This time I did laugh. "That's not your furnace. That's the air-conditioning unit."

She sneezed. "Ugh. I've been out here for thirty minutes trying to figure out how to open up the wrong thing?" She sneezed again.

"Let's get you inside."

She didn't move, she just looked back down at the bag. "There's really too much for you to eat alone?"

"I probably have enough food here for four people honestly. I went a little overboard because I didn't know what you like." The smile on her lips was small, but it felt like a win for me. "What do you say?"

She sighed. "No."

What? Seriously? "I didn't want to hang this over your head, but technically you did steal from a detective earlier. You can get into all sorts of trouble for that."

"You *gave* me your jacket. I didn't rip it off your back."

"True. Scratch the petty thievery. But dinner's getting cold. And I'm good at distinguishing between an air-conditioning unit and a furnace. What does a guy have to do to win you over?"

"Okay. Fine." She pinched her eyes closed like she immediately regretted her decision. "You can stay." She opened up her eyes again and pierced me with an intense stare. "But you have to fix my heater because the repair guy can't come for two days and..." her voice trailed off when she sneezed again. "And this isn't a date. Just give me three minutes." She put up three fingers like she was talking to a child and then ran up to her house, her hammer gripped tightly in her hand.

My eyes gravitated back to her ass. She was wrong. This was most definitely a date. A fake one. Absolutely, 100 perfect fake. *So stop staring at her ass.*

CHAPTER 7

Violet

What the heck did I just agree to? I sneezed as I wiped down the counter once, twice, three times until every remaining spot of flour was gone. But a clean counter didn't help. The rest of the kitchen was a mess. The rest of the house was even worse.

Zeke and I had spent most of the day playing hot lava, which entailed pulling off all the couch cushions and pillows and putting them on the floor to hop on. I had melted in the lava way more times than Zeke thanks to my constant sneezing in between jumps.

"Mommy." Zeke pitty-patted my leg. "What are you doing? It's your turn to make it through the lava course."

"I'm just..." I let my voice trail off. *Screw it.* I tossed the washcloth back down on the counter. My house was a disaster. And freezing cold. Zeke was dressed in his snow-pants and layered up in a few sweaters. The only reason I had agreed to let Tucker in was so that he'd fix the broken heater. Who cared what he thought of my house? This wasn't a date. I wasn't trying to impress him. We both knew why he was really here. He was fishing around for information. And my lips were sealed. And I was only going to open them to eat the food he had brought. If I hadn't been exhausted, I would have turned him away.

I tucked a dreadlock behind Zeke's ear. "You know my friend who brought us doughnuts earlier? Well…he brought dinner for us too."

Zeke's eyes grew round. "More doughnuts for dinner?"

"No, not doughnuts." Honestly I didn't know if that was true. He may have brought doughnuts for dinner. He was a cop after all. It may have been the only thing he ever ate for all I knew. "I don't know what he brought, we'll have to see when he brings it in."

"Doughnuts!" Zeke took off toward the front door.

Abandoning my lame attempt at cleaning up my house, I followed my son.

Zeke threw open the door and yelled "doughnuts" to a very confused looking Detective Reed.

He looked at me and then back at my son.

I assumed he knew I had a kid. I had told him I didn't live alone. And he had known my name without me offering the information. He had clearly done some digging on me. But the way he was looking at Zeke made me think he wasn't very good at his job. Because he sincerely looked surprised. Or maybe I had this all wrong. Maybe he wasn't digging at all. And this was a *real* date.

Which meant that letting him come in was a terrible, awful idea. I put my hand on Zeke's shoulder and stared at Detective Reed. I was about to tell him to go when he crouched down in front of my son.

"You know," he said. "I didn't bring doughnuts this time, but I did bring dessert. How about we eat dinner first and then you can have that?"

"Or...we could have dessert first." Zeke looked at him hopefully.

"Or we could have dinner first."

Zeke sighed. "Fine. But we have to get away from the lava fast or else we won't be able to eat anything because we'll be dead. Hurry, your feet are burning!" Zeke started to hop from foot to foot like his feet were on fire.

"You better hurry! Or the lava will get you!" I grabbed the take-out bags from Detective Reed's hands and watched Zeke pull him toward our family room.

Zeke looked so happy. It made me realize just how much I was failing as a mother. He never had friends over. It was always just the two of us. I knew some of the kids at school picked on him, but did he not have any friends? Or was he just embarrassed to have them come here? Or maybe his friends' parents wouldn't allow their children to come play here. All three options stung.

His laughter drifting from the family room eased some of the pain in my chest. We were happy just the two of us. We had been playing hot lava all day and laughing just as much as he and Detective Reed were. And I was a trooper because I felt like I was five seconds away from passing out.

I set the table for three, which was a first in this house. I tried to ignore the warning bells in my head. There was a detective in my home. One that seemed dead set on tying me to a crime I didn't commit. So why did I feel excited? It had just been too long since I had been around a single man. That was all. But it didn't stop me from tidying up the kitchen just a bit more.

I started to remove the take-out containers from the bags Detective Reed had brought. My fingers wrapped around a bottle and I pulled it out. It was just a simple bottle of Nyquil, but when I looked down at it, I felt the oddest sensation overcome me. My whole body felt warm, but it wasn't from my fever. He brought me Nyquil? I felt tears prickle the corners of my eyes. This morning Zeke had offered to make me pancakes. And now a complete stranger had brought me medicine for my cold? I wasn't sure I had ever felt more loved in my entire life. I immediately shook away the thought. Love? Detective Reed was just trying to butter me up. But my mind couldn't convince the rest of me. I felt…cared for.

"I thought you'd appreciate that more than a bottle of wine tonight."

I looked up to see Detective Reed leaning against the doorjamb. His shirt was a little off-center and his hair was askew. Zeke had probably jumped on him at some point during the game. And his cheeks were slightly rosy either from how cold it was in here or because he had been running around. He had also ditched his shoes somewhere because he was in his socks. He looked so comfortable and at home. I had never seen a more handsome sight.

"Yeah. Thanks." I cleared my throat because the words had come out weird and squeaky. "Thank you, Detective Reed, I…"

"Tucker." He smiled, making his appearance that much more handsome. "I'm off duty."

"Tucker. Right." I looked back down at the bottle. "I really appreciate this." It was sweet and thoughtful. I sneezed.

"Bless you. There's actually a box of tissues in there too."

My knight in shining armor. I grabbed one of the tissues and blew my nose. When I lowered the tissue, Tucker's smile looked even bigger. "What?" I touched my face, worried that I had just trailed snot everywhere.

"You have a little grease spot right there." He tapped his right cheek.

I grabbed another tissue and mimicked him, wiping off my left cheek.

He laughed. "No, opposite."

I could feel my face turning red as I wiped off the correct cheek. There was a lot of black residue on the tissue for it just being a tiny spot. My whole cheek was probably covered in grease. I continued to wipe it. "Is it gone yet?"

"Yeah. You got it." He cleared his throat and looked around the room. "Is your furnace in the basement? Just point me in the right direction, I should probably get started on it so you don't have to sit here shivering while you're sick."

"Let's eat first, before it gets cold." I gestured to the seat that was always empty at the kitchen island. For once in my life I was happy I loved to do everything in threes. Or else I wouldn't have a seat for him.

Tucker may have been expecting a romantic night for two, but an extra seat was all I had to offer him. I didn't even have a dining room table. I also had a son that he hadn't known about. And I was sick. Yet Tucker was still looking at me with a smile on his face. Like somehow this was his idea of a perfect night regardless of the weird surprises. I looked away.

"Zeke! It's dinner time!"

He came running into the room, sliding in his socks across the wooden floorboards. "You're both dead. Which means I get dessert first." He scrambled into his usual seat, the one in the middle, with a big smile on his face.

I sat down on the other side of him. "Nope, we're still alive." I sneezed again. "Sick, but still breathing."

He sighed like that was the most disappointing thing in the world.

I opened up the container closest to me and then closed it again. And opened it. And closed it. I started to do it one more time when Zeke put his hand on my wrist to stop me.

"Mommy, you're doing that *thing* again."

I pressed my lips together and set the container down. Normally I loved when he pulled me out of my funk. But in this one rare case, it felt like he had highlighted my issues to the whole world. I could feel Tucker staring at me, but I ignored it as best as I could. "Thanks, bug. You know what? You serve everyone." I slid the container toward him and handed him a serving spoon. "I'm going to have a bit of Nyquil."

I grabbed the bottle and turned my back to the two of them. Now I kind of wish he had brought a bottle of wine. Although, I hadn't had a drink in ages. I honestly couldn't remember the last time I'd had a drink. There wasn't any alcohol in the house. For all I knew, it would make my issues worse, not better. I twisted off the cap of Nyquil and took a huge sip instead of taking the time to measure it out. Hopefully this would at least help with my cold symptoms. I immediately sneezed after swallowing the sweet liquid. *Ugh.*

The two of them laughing made me turn back around. They both had dessert on their plates instead of the delicious chicken parm Tucker had brought. But in their defense, they both had adorable grins on their face that made it impossible to reprimand them. Plus the dessert looked pretty amazing too. It was some kind of ooey-gooey chocolatey goodness that I definitely would have chosen myself.

"You're going to be up all night," I said and kissed Zeke on the top of his head as I sat back down.

"So? It's a three day weekend!" He shoved a spoonful of dessert into his mouth.

"Three day weekend?" Tucker asked. "I feel like kids get off for holidays I don't even know about now. What is it this time? National Puppy Adoration Day?"

Zeke shook his head. "No, I just earned it.

Tucker moved his gaze to me but I looked away.

"This looks amazing." I grabbed the container of dessert and put some on my plate. "What is it?"

"Chocolate bread pudding. I hope you like chocolate."

I took a bite and held back a moan. "It's amazing."

"She loves chocolate," Zeke said. "She has a whole drawer of it in her bedroom that I'm not supposed to eat."

Zeke. I didn't even know that he knew about that. "It's dark chocolate. You wouldn't like it." I tickled his side.

His spoon clattered onto his plate as he fought a fit of giggles. "I love all chocolate too. Almost as much as hot lava! It's your turn, Mommy." He scooted off his chair.

"Zeke, you didn't even touch dinner."

"But the *lava*! It's coming into the kitchen. Look." He pointed to the clean wooden floor.

"Oh no," Tucker said. "We better get back to the rocks!" He slid off his stool, lifted Zeke off the ground, and carried him back to the family room.

"You too, Mommy!" Zeke called through his laughter.

I abandoned the food and followed them into the other room. Who needed a well-balanced meal when there was fun to be had? And I was feeling a lot better after downing more than a recommended dose of Nyquil. I hopped from cushion to cushion, pillow to pillow with them before collapsing on the cushion-less couch to catch my breath.

CHAPTER 8

Tucker

I wiped my hands off on the front of my jeans and then placed the wrench back into Violet's backpack full of random tools. Before I zipped it closed, I rummaged through the assortment. I wasn't exactly sure what I was looking for. But the whole time I had been fixing the furnace, I had tried to ignore the fact that her tools were in a backpack. What did it really matter? Tool cases were easy enough to carry around. She just wasn't handy. Clearly. Her furnace looked like it had been patched by someone who knew nothing about them. It was on the fritz. She'd be lucky if it lasted through the winter.

But what if they were in a backpack for a different reason? It would be easier to tramp through the woods with the weight distributed between two shoulders instead of one. Before tonight, I had wanted her to be guilty. I wanted to solve the case and keep my job or get a promotion if I was lucky. After spending a whole night with her though? I wasn't sure what I wanted anymore. I thought Violet had been bluffing when she said she didn't live alone. I hadn't been expecting a kid. One with the same hair color and eye color as his beautiful mother. I knew she was sick, but I still expected the whole night to be flirtatious. I hadn't expected…this. And I certainly hadn't expected to love it so much.

I zipped the backpack closed and then wiped my hands off on the front of my jeans. There wasn't anything suspicious in it at all. Just wrenches and screwdrivers of various sizes. As far as I could tell, there wasn't anything suspicious in the entire house. I had taken every opportunity I had to look around. And on top of that, Violet really didn't seem crazy to me. All night long she had only done one odd thing and I might have missed it if her son hadn't pointed it out.

The only thing out of place here was her. I still had no idea why she would live out in the middle of nowhere in a dump. A cold dump. The house was crumbling around her. It didn't really feel that way though. Her and her son's laughter could make any room feel warm. He was an adorable kid.

I heard a creaking noise upstairs and glanced at the basement ceiling. Violet was walking somewhere. It felt like this was my chance to catch her doing something, anything suspicious. I pulled the backpack over my shoulder and ascended the basement steps as quietly as possible.

There was no need to look around to find where she had gone. I could hear her and Zeke's voices drifting down from upstairs.

"I know it's a special weekend, but that doesn't mean a special bedtime. It's late, little dude."

"But *Mom*. We never have anyone else to play with. Five more minutes?"

He drew out the word mom in the cutest way. But I was more focused on his words than how he said them. They didn't have anyone else. I figured it was just the two of them, but I hadn't asked. She didn't wear a wedding ring and Damien had confirmed that she wasn't married. But it was hard to believe that someone would have left the two of them behind. They'd be missing out on too damn much.

"You're not going to convince me tonight. You already got dessert for dinner. It's bedtime."

I stared up the stairs. I felt drawn to them, like I wanted to be up there tucking him in too. Like maybe they needed me.

"I like your friend," Zeke said.

"Yeah. He's very nice."

I cringed. Nice? That wasn't how I wanted her to think of me. *How do I want her to think of me?*

"Will he be back?"

There was a long pause. "I don't know. Maybe."

Her voice had at least sounded hopeful there. That hope spread to me. I wanted to come back. I just wasn't sure if it had anything to do with the case anymore.

I heard the floorboards creek upstairs and moved away from the steps. Eavesdropping wasn't exactly a good way to get invited back. I retreated into the kitchen.

Violet walked in a minute later, looking anywhere but at me.

"The furnace is all fixed. You'll be able to take off all your layers in no time." *Screw me.* I had inadvertently just implied that she could get naked soon. For a second, I thought maybe she missed it, but then her cheeks flushed.

"Thanks. Are you hungry? I can warm up the food you brought."

I wasn't really hungry. But there was an awkward tension hanging in the air between us. She still wasn't looking at me and all I wanted was for her to make eye contact. Now that Zeke was asleep, neither one of us knew exactly what our dynamic should be. The hot lava game had been distracting. It had been easy to focus on Zeke, but now that all my focus was on her? I couldn't look away from her. The flush of her cheeks. The curves of her hips.

"Or…" her voice trailed off. "It's pretty late. Maybe…"

"I'm hungry." I didn't want tonight to end yet. I hadn't asked her any questions at all.

She tucked a loose strand of hair behind her ear. "Okay, just give me one minute."

"Do you want to watch a movie or something?"

"I don't have a TV. But we can eat in the family room if you want. It's more comfortable. I just need to pick up the cushions…"

"I got it. You heat the food, I'll clean up the other room."

She smiled like it was the nicest thing she'd ever heard.

I left her alone and started picking up all the pillows and cushions in the other room. By the time I was done, she was walking in with two hot plates of food.

She sat down on the couch all the way on the end, like she wanted to be as far away from me as possible. She balanced her plate on her lap and took a bite.

I sat down only one cushion away from her and took a bite too. The chicken parm hadn't survived well in the microwave. The coating was soggy and the meat was a little rubbery. I was about to make a joke about it when she broke the awkward silence.

"I don't know how to thank you for this. And the furnace. We probably would have frozen tonight if you hadn't stopped by." She laughed like what she'd just said wasn't a big deal.

"I'm sure a repairman would have come out if I hadn't. It was no problem."

She sneezed. "No one could come for two days."

"What? That's ridiculous. You should have called a different company."

"I called five. And I'm sure they do come out quickly for most people. Just…not for me." She took a bite of chicken and sighed like it was the most delicious meal she'd had in ages.

If only she knew what it tasted like when it had been fresh. "Why not for you?"

She took another bite, and for a minute I thought she was going to ignore my question. But then she set down her fork and knife and looked up at me. "Because no one wants to come all the way out here." She scrunched her mouth to the side. "That's a lie." She laughed. "I'm sure they wouldn't mind that. It's me. I told you earlier…I'm the crazy lady on the hill. Everyone avoids me like the plague."

"I don't think you're crazy."

"You don't know me very well." She tapped her fork against her plate a few times before looking back up at me.

"I have a feeling I've gotten to know you better than most of the people you're referring to."

"You're really not from around here, are you?"

"No. I was transferred to this department about a year ago." I didn't want to talk about me. I wanted to know more about her. "Zeke mentioned earlier at dinner that you were doing that thing. What was he referring to?" She had been opening and closing one of the takeout containers continuously. Like she was stuck in some sort of trance.

She put her fork back down. "I have a little bit of a nervous OCD thing. Well, not just when I'm nervous...it's also when I'm upset, agitated, anxious, and nervous."

"You said nervous three times."

"Yeah. It's especially bad when I'm nervous. But really whenever I feel at all uncomfortable." She tapped the side of her plate.

I watched this time. She tapped it three times and then stopped. Then she proceeded to do the same thing with the next finger. "Are you uncomfortable right now?"

"No." She pressed her lips together. "I think you make me nervous, Detective Reed."

"Tucker."

"Right. Tucker." She continued to tap the side of her plate. "Why are you here?" She didn't give me a chance to respond. "I can pay you for the furnace."

"I'm not here for your money. I just wanted a chance to really talk to you."

"You mean to question me? I've already answered all your questions."

I set my plate down on the ground and moved closer to her on the couch. And I swore I heard her gulp. "Your son is adorable."

She smiled. "He is. He's funny and brilliant and so sweet. I couldn't have imagined a better son into existence."

"And his earned day off?"

She shrugged her shoulders. "One day isn't a big deal."

"It's almost the weekend."

"Kids need a break every now and then. Just like adults."

She was right, she did always answer my questions. But not the way I wanted her to. She was hiding the truth from me. I thought about the conversation I had overheard. Zeke had said they never have anyone else to play with. "Does he enjoy school?"

"He loves learning."

"And his friends?"

She put her plate down on the ground beside mine. When she leaned back against the couch, she closed her eyes.

I should have been studying her face. Trying to figure out what she was hiding. Instead, I found my gaze wandering lower. She was so close that I could smell the sweetness of her skin. I wasn't sure if it was soap or perfume, but she smelled like a field of spring flowers.

She pulled her legs up on the couch, not caring when her knees graced my thigh. Her breathing started to slow. For a moment I thought she was asleep, but then she broke the silence.

"The other kids pick on him. It's not fair that I make him go to school when I hide out here. And that's the whole problem. It's my fault that he gets teased." She wiped beneath her eyes and then tucked her head more against the pillow. "I'm a bad mother. I'm the reason he doesn't fit in. It's all my fault." She wiped beneath her eyes again.

Her words broke my heart. I wanted to reach out to her and give her a hug. But I was worried that once we touched, I wouldn't be able to control myself. I was already distracted enough by her knees against my thigh. *Look away from her. Tell her you need to go. Leave.*

"Are you married?" I asked, instead of listening to any rational thoughts. I knew she wasn't. There was no ring on her finger. And Damien had already told me she wasn't. But I still wanted to hear it from her.

"No." Another tear fell, like she had loved and lost. Or maybe she was still upset about what she had told me about Zeke. "I'm not married. That was never in the cards for me."

"What about Zeke's father?"

"He didn't want anything to do with him."

How? How was that possible? "His loss."

She smiled and a small moan escaped her lips. "Yeah. His loss." Her breathing became more shallow. And then she snored. A cute, adorable little snore. It was probably because she was sick.

"Violet?" I whispered.

She didn't respond.

All night long she had been running around playing with her son. If she thought she was a bad mother then she was insane. And if she missed Zeke's father at all, she was even more insane. I immediately regretted the thoughts. Insane wasn't the right word. Violet wasn't crazy, despite the rumors. She was kind. And sweet. And beautiful.

She snored again and I smiled.

For just one night, she deserved to be cared for. I leaned forward and lifted her into my arms. She was lighter than I expected, the layers of clothes she was wearing adding a little more bulk to her lean frame. I carried her down the hall and up the stairs. The second floor was more fixed up than the first. I walked into what I assumed was her bedroom. When we first met she had said she was fixing the place up. Maybe she was handier than I had given her credit for. As soon as I thought it, one of the floorboards at the base of her bed squeaked beneath my foot.

I kept walking and laid her down on her bed. My body begged me to climb in bed beside her. Instead, I pulled the covers over her. I wanted her to invite me into her bed the first time. I didn't even care that my mind was already jumping to that conclusion. Violet wasn't crazy. And she wasn't an arsonist. I doubted she could kill a fly. Everything about her nature screamed that she was innocent. Did she have secrets? Sure. But she was just reserved, that was all. And I was coming back tomorrow. And the next day. And the next, until I broke down her walls. I wanted to know everything about her.

I walked back in the direction I had come from. The floorboard squeaked again. I stopped and looked down. It almost looked like it hadn't been laid properly. I bent down and tried to shift it back into place, but the whole piece of wood lifted into my hands.

Shit. I was about to place it back where I had found it when I realized there was a box hidden beneath the floorboards. I glanced at Violet sleeping and then crouched down. This was snooping. I didn't have a warrant. And beyond that, I wanted her to trust me. She hated the rest of the people in this town. I didn't want to be one of them.

And yet…I picked up the box. I couldn't help it. My curiosity had gotten the better of me. I lifted the lid and opened up one of the letters inside. A love letter.

Vi,

Meet me at the lake after practice. I have a surprise for you.

Forever and always,
Joel

I picked up another note and scanned it.

Vi,

Study session tonight? I need to look at your Calc notes, mine suck.
Forever and always,
Joel

They were all high school nonsense and signed the same way. Promises of forever. I tossed the notes back in the box. It was none of my business, but I wanted to know if Joel was Zeke's father. And how "forever and always" became "never and goodbye." He seemed to love her. So why would he leave when she needed him the most?

Violet snored, pulling me out of my thoughts. I closed the lid of the box. I wanted to put Joel's name into the system and see what I could find. I wanted to know what kind of man would abandon his beautiful family. But I wasn't going to do that. Violet was slowly opening up to me. Maybe she'd tell me about Joel soon. And Zeke's father, if they weren't the same person.

I turned to put the box back where I had found it when my eyes landed on something I never expected. A pistol. Right there under the floorboards. I looked back at Violet sleeping and a chill ran down my spine. All night long I had been captivated by her, completely ignoring my suspicions from a few days ago. But Violet wasn't as sweet and innocent as she seemed. She wasn't a damsel in distress in dire need of someone to take care of her. She could clearly fend for herself. After all, people that couldn't even kill flies didn't own guns.

CHAPTER 9
Violet

I woke up with a smile on my face, and for the life of me I couldn't remember the last time that had happened. My nose was still stuffy, but my throat and head hurt less. I took a deep breath and ignored my sniffling noise. I felt good. I felt alive. And I felt warm. Very, very warm.

The sun streaming through the blinds was somehow warming me from head to toe. The sunshine felt amazing on my face, like it was the first rays of springtime instead of the impending winter. I slowly opened my eyes and glanced at the alarm clock by my bed. It was only six in the morning. The sun must have woken me early.

I looked at the blinds and my good mood faded. I always closed them before bed. Always. After I double checked that all the doors were locked downstairs. And then triple checked. Because it was the only way to ensure that intruders wouldn't come bursting into my home. I couldn't remember doing any of that last night.

And I...I looked down at my layers upon layers of clothing. I definitely always changed into pajamas before bed. I never just collapsed in bed without going through my usual routine. It was a routine for a reason.

I groaned and pushed myself into a seated position. What the hell happened last night? I touched my forehead, expecting a sharp pain, a reminder of times when I drank too much in high school. But there wasn't one. I felt good and well rested and…betrayed.

Betrayed? The thought settled around me, making it hard to breathe. *Shit.* I shoved the blankets off of me. *No. No, no, no.* I climbed out of bed and ran out of my bedroom, down the hall, and descended the stairs. It had just been a dream. It had just been a wonderful, perfect, stupid dream. The only problem with that theory was that I never remembered my dreams. The other problem with that theory was that there was a note from Detective Reed sitting on my kitchen counter.

A detective had been loose in my house while I slept. I eyed the bottle of medicine on the counter beside the note. That son of a bitch had brought me Nyquil to make me pass out. Giving him free reign to snoop. Why had I let him in? What was wrong with me?

This was bad. This was really, really bad. He could have gone anywhere. Seen anything. I swallowed hard.

You do not lie about big things. My mother's words came back to me. *Big lies have big consequences.*

But for the first time, I wasn't thinking them to reprimand myself. Detective Reed came here under false pretenses, drugged me, and then did God knows what in my house while I slept. As far as I was concerned, his big lies would have big consequences.

I ignored the note, grabbed my cellphone, and dialed 911. I had warned him to stay off my property. This wasn't a game to me. This was my life. And my number one responsibility was to protect my son. Going to prison wasn't an option for me. I wouldn't let Zeke go into the system. He needed me.

"911, what's your emergency?" The dispatcher asked.

"Hi, it's not technically an emergency, but I want to file a complaint about..."

"Ma'am, this line is for emergencies only…"

"Right." I cut her off. "Well, I was drugged by one of your detectives and then he snooped around my house without a warrant."

"Ma'am, we can get an ambulance out to you right away. What is your location?"

"No, I don't need an ambulance." I started pacing back and forth. "I'm fine *now*. He drugged me last night and I just woke up."

"Ma'am, did the man who drugged you sexually assault you?"

"What? No." God, this conversation was pointless. "It's not technically an emergency. I just need to file a complaint."

"Then an emergency response is not required at this moment. But I will send an officer out to speak to you as soon as possible about your complaint. In the meantime, are you sure you're not in need of an ambulance to take you to the nearest hospital? The drugs in your system may…"

"I don't need an ambulance!" This woman was driving me insane.

"Alright then." She verified my address and phone number and then the line went dead.

Seriously? I said a detective had drugged me and snooped around my property and that was all the help I got? Local law enforcement wasn't going to be any help. They were going to ignore me like all the freaking handymen and end up sending someone young and inexperienced. And there was no way in hell that they were going to believe me. I was the crazy lady on the hill. I tossed my phone down on the kitchen counter beside Detective Reed's note.

I wanted to scream and throw things, but instead I took a long slow breath. My head was foggy. I needed to calm down for a minute and figure out what to do. But all I could think about was the fact that I was running out of time. I could hear the hands of a clock counting down in my head and I couldn't silence them.

I snatched the letter off the kitchen counter, trying to distract myself from the ticking noise.

Violet,

I had a great night with you and your son. You are a wonderful mother and Zeke is an adorable kid. Let me take you both out tonight so you can try that chicken parm when it's hot from the oven. I'll be by at seven to pick you two up.

-Tucker

Tucker my ass. He was Detective Reed. Our relationship was purely business related. He thought I blew up some random suburban home nearby. And he didn't know anything about anything. *I hope.* I looked around the kitchen. There was nothing here that incriminated me. But there was upstairs. In my bedroom where Detective Reed had most certainly been last night. I thought about the pistol hidden beneath my floorboards. I needed to get rid of it. If there was even a small chance Detective Reed had seen it, police officers would be showing up arresting me instead of helping me.

I ran back upstairs and lifted up the floorboard. Everything still seemed like it was in place, but that didn't mean anything. I would have put the items back where they belonged too if I had been snooping.

Last night had seemed perfect. But it wasn't. It may as well have been a dream. Romance wasn't something I was interested in. A stranger infiltrating the home I'd worked so hard to fix up so my son could have a normal life? *Not happening.* Leaving said house for a meal surrounded by whispers and stares? *No, thank you.* I couldn't believe that he suggested going out to dinner. The thought was so awful it made me cringe. Detective Reed clearly didn't know me at all.

I lifted the gun out of the floorboard. No one really knew me. And they certainly didn't know what I was capable of. I'd do anything to protect my son. *Anything.*

I tried to clear my head. I tried to calm down. If Detective Reed had seen this, would it matter? He searched my house without a warrant. The case would be thrown out in court right away. I didn't watch TV anymore, but I had seen enough crime shows in high school to know the importance of a warrant. He'd be thrown off the force, I wouldn't be thrown into prison. But I didn't know how realistic TV shows were. What if they depicted that small fact wrong? If there was even a chance that I could go to jail for having this gun, I needed to get rid of it.

The pistol felt heavy in my hand. I had never fired it before. I had never fired any gun before. I turned it over and for a moment I saw red. Blood dripping off the handle. Down the barrel. Dropping in splotches on the ground. Blood was everywhere. I closed my eyes, willing the memory to fade.

When I opened my eyes again, the gun was clean, like I had just scrubbed it. There wasn't a single trace of blood. I took another deep breath. If I was lucky, maybe the memories would stop haunting me once it was out of the house. Not that something being out of sight ever really took it out of mind for me. I could still picture my stepfather holding it like it was yesterday. Taking his gun hardly seemed like a crime. I had just been protecting myself. I hadn't done anything wrong. But I was pretty sure that the more time that faded, the guiltier I'd look. My mother had warned me about lying. And it was about time this pistol ended up in the same place that all my secrets did.

CHAPTER 10

Tucker

I ran my hand down my face and then looked back at the screen. I had scoured every database, but the consensus was always the same. There was no gun registered under Violet Clark. Which meant she was in possession of an unregistered gun. Which meant I had a decision I didn't want to make.

It was still early, I had come in an hour before my shift so that Damien wouldn't be breathing down my neck. But I didn't know what else to search. I was completely out of ideas. Violet Clark was a ghost. No Facebook page, no Twitter account, no Instagram. Nothing came up under any Google searches either. I tried to search the mysterious Joel as well, but without a last name I didn't have much to go on. *Last name.* Maybe I had her last name wrong!

Most of the cops were out patrolling, but there were a few sitting at desks nearby. I walked over to the closest one. "Doyle, I got a question about a local for you."

"Big bad detective coming all the way over here to talk to us lowly folk," he said. "This must be good."

His friend snickered.

I hadn't set up the hierarchy here. I don't know why they gave me shit when I had done nothing but be nice to them. Ignoring their sarcasm was always the best tactic. "Have either of you ever met a Violet Clark? She has a son named Zeke and she lives on…"

"You mean the crazy lady on the hill?" Doyle's friend asked.

My blood started to boil. "She's not crazy."

Doyle's eyes seemed to bug out of his face. "She is. It's a fact. And why are you asking about her anyways? Some case that's too high level for us?"

"No. Personal reasons."

They both laughed.

"I just need to know if Clark is definitely her last name."

"Violet Clark. Always has been and always will be. If you know what I mean." Doyle laughed.

"Why?" I knew what Doyle had meant. But if he had the audacity to say it, I was about to punch him square in the nose. "I'm hoping you're about to say it's because she's incredibly independent and you could see her choosing to keep her name when she gets married."

"No. I meant because no one's crazy enough to marry that psycho bitch."

I clenched my hand into a fist. If I had any other options, I'd walk away. But I needed more information from this idiot. "Did either of you know her when she was in high school? She had a boyfriend…Joel something. Know his last name?" I could have asked Damien about it, but I swore to him I was off the case. He wouldn't answer my question even if he knew Joel's last name. I didn't have a choice here.

"Nah," Doyle said. "Heard he left town as soon as he found out his chick was nuts."

"You shouldn't talk shit about someone you don't know. Didn't your mom teach you any manners?"

"Don't talk about my mother, Reed, or we can take this outside."

I held up my hand. "Cool your loins. Thanks for the insightful conversation." He hadn't helped me at all. The only thing he had accomplished was pissing me off. But maybe that had always been his intention. I had at least learned never to talk to him again. *Judgmental asshole.* I started to walk back to my desk, but before I sat down, his friend caught up to me.

"I actually knew Joel in middle school. We lost touch in high school but his last name is Walker."

"Any idea where he is now?"

"Last I heard he was moving to LA to pursue screenwriting or something like that. Or was it acting? Can't remember."

The few love notes I had seen from him had been short and not exactly groundbreaking. I wouldn't have guessed he was into screenwriting. Acting though? Maybe. He had certainly pretended to love Violet and then left her out of the blue. "Do you still talk to him?"

"No. Like I said, we weren't even friends in high school. I assume he's still out there, but I haven't seen his name scrolling during any credits."

"Is he Zeke's father?"

He shrugged. "I really have no idea. I don't think anyone knows. She kind of disappeared after Joel skipped town. We all thought she went with him, but then we found out she was living in that shack she calls a house."

"Did she buy it? Or did she just start living there?"

"No idea. And I doubt that anyone cares. It had been abandoned for years. I'm sure no one's going to come a-knocking anytime soon. Rumor has it that the place is haunted."

It didn't feel haunted to me. Violet's home was warm and inviting. The place was full of love. "Does she have any other family?" Damien had mentioned that they had left too. I couldn't even imagine what it would be like if my family turned their backs on me.

"I didn't really know her. Sorry I couldn't be more help."

"It's fine. Thanks for the info about Joel." I thought he'd walk away from my desk when I sat down, but he kind of hovered.

"So is it actually about a case? I get it if you just didn't want to tell Doyle that."

"No, it's not." I didn't need anyone else getting into my business. I needed to figure this one out on my own. Especially since I was tiptoeing the line of professionalism. Or maybe I had already jumped over the line completely.

"So you're like…into her?"

"What if I am?" I didn't mean to sound so defensive, but the words came out like I was about to punch him in the face.

"None of my business. It's just…" his voice trailed off. "Her boyfriend and parents left around the exact same time. No one's really heard or seen them since. People think she axed them."

I laughed. "Yeah…I don't think so." But then I thought about the unregistered gun hidden underneath her floorboards. I couldn't imagine her slaying anyone with an axe. But a gun? She had hid the thing for a reason.

"Just be careful with her. I'm not one for rumors, but when you hear them so many times…you start to wonder if there's some truth to them. Like the whole dragon thing. If there are so many stories about dragons from different literature all over the world…you gotta wonder."

I glanced at his name tag. Officer Montgomery. I looked back up at him. I'd take anything a man who believed in dragons said with a grain of salt.

"I mean, she lives out there in the middle of nowhere. With no one around. All that land. That's a lot of places to bury bodies. A lot of places."

I shook my head. "You're letting your imagination get away from you."

"Well, let me know if you find Joel. Guess he could put the rumors to bed."

"I'll let you know when I find him."

"*If* you find him."

"*When* I find him."

Montgomery laughed. "Just don't get yourself killed." He nodded at me and walked back over to Doyle.

I tapped my fingers on the top of my desk. After my night with Violet, there hadn't been a doubt in my mind that she didn't deserve her nickname. She had a nervous OCD thing. It was barely noticeable. But there were so many more layers to her than that. She was sweet. And kind. I stared at my screen showing the lack of records for her pistol. And a felon.

I realized I was tapping my fingers, just like she had done last night. I started tapping keys instead, searching for Joel Walker. Unlike Violet, he did have a Facebook page. At least, I was pretty sure it was him. His account was private, but there was a picture of him standing in front of the Hollywood sign. Alive and well in LA, just like he was supposed to be. I debated whether or not I should send him a friend request. That would be weird, right? I stared at the image. It was taken from several years ago, but that didn't necessarily mean anything. I hadn't updated my profile in years either. I was rarely ever on Facebook. Maybe Joel was the same way.

Besides, Montgomery was hinting that Joel had never even made it to LA. This picture proved him wrong. I closed the browser and leaned back in my chair. Maybe he left because Zeke *wasn't* his. Not the other way around. I wished I could just ask Violet about it, but I couldn't exactly bring up that I knew about Joel without revealing that I had snooped around her house last night.

What I needed to do was hear about all the rumors circulating about Violet. Maybe I could piece together some kind of truth if I heard everything. Sally Bennett popped into my head, the nosy neighbor I had met at the crime scene the other night. Might as well go straight to the source. I put her name into the database so I could find her number.

"Morning," Damien said and slapped my shoulder as he walked by me.

I exed out of the browser, but probably not before Damien had seen my screen. *Shit.*

He parked himself in the desk across from mine and propped his feet up on it. "I tried to call you last night to see if you wanted to get drinks but your phone went straight to voicemail. Where were you?" He raised both eyebrows like he was hoping for something scandalous.

"Sorry, it must have died. I was just at home watching the game."

"Huh. Funny you should say that, because I drove by your house and your car wasn't there."

I stared at him. "Are you stalking me now?"

He leaned forward. "You were with Violet, weren't you?" He angrily whispered at me.

I could have lied, but he'd see right through that. "Yeah, but it's not what you think."

"You swore you'd drop the case, man."

"I did. I wasn't there because of the case." Half a lie was better than a whole one.

"Then why were you there? I told you she was nuts."

"And why do you think that? Tell me the exact rumors so I can figure it out. As far as I can tell, she has a nervous OCD thing. That's it. That doesn't make her crazy. And saying that she's crazy with no proof to back it up means nothing to me."

"I'm not done talking about last night yet. I asked you to call me if you went to her house. You went in without backup. Her crazy is clearly running off on you."

She's not crazy. "It's cute that you were worried, but I don't need you to babysit me, Damien."

"Clearly you do."

The click of the captain's heels made us both pause our whisper yelling match.

"There's a distress call," she said. "Who wants to take it?"

Damien and I both looked at each other. There were cops out on patrol right now. Why was she asking the ones here?

"Torres. Reed. Great, thanks for offering. I'll text you the address. Feel free to take your time, it's not an emergency." She turned on her heel without waiting for a response.

Apparently she wasn't asking the cops sitting around. She was targeting us. It was like she was trying to get us out of the office for a while. "What the heck did you do to her?" I asked. "She has us handling cops' work." I went to grab my jacket but my hand came up empty again. I needed to either buy a new coat or ask Violet for mine back.

"I didn't *do* anything. She's probably pissed at you. You do realize she has access to our search history, right?"

Shit, this probably was about me. "Do you think I should talk to her?"

"No you shouldn't talk to her. You should cut this crap out."

"I told you, I wasn't at Violet's house to talk about the case. We were having dinner."

"Dinner? Jesus Christ." He looked up at the ceiling like we were both about to be smote. "Why can't you date a nice, normal, non-suspect woman?"

I ignored him as we climbed into my car. There was a cold front coming and instead of the heat kicking on, we got a blast of frigid air. I was glad I had gone to Violet's last night, despite all the warnings, and despite the pistol I had found. The thought of her suffering through this cold without a working heater made me mad. I still couldn't believe that repairmen were scared of her too.

"Where are we heading?" I rubbed my hands together, trying to get them warm.

"It's your lucky day. We're going to your girlfriend's house."

"What happened?" It felt like my heart was ricocheting around my chest.

He looked back down at his phone. "Apparently she was attacked or something."

There was a reason why rumors shouldn't be trusted. Just the thought of one of them escalating to violence was terrifying. And I had no doubt in my mind that the distress call was related to some idiot who believed whispers instead of reality. It didn't matter that Violet had an unregistered gun. She was a good person. She didn't deserve this shit. I made up my mind in that second that I wasn't going to report her for having an unregistered gun. There was no question about it. We had been on one date and I already felt protective of her. I shoved the car into drive and slammed my foot on the gas. If someone had hurt her, I was going to kill them.

CHAPTER 11

Violet

I tilted my head and inhaled the sweet smell of cologne that still clung to the collar of Detective Reed's jacket. He smelled like heaven. I silently cursed at myself as I pulled it off. Tucker was no heaven. He was my living hell of a nightmare. I hung up his jacket and forced myself not to breathe in his scent again, even though it was tempting.

What it came down to was that meeting Detective Reed had accomplished two things. It had turned me into a thief and back into a liar. I bit the inside of my lip. He had also made me remember what it was like to be looked at without fear. But the first two things outweighed the last. I didn't care if people thought I was crazy. It was better that they did. I hated snoopers more than anything, and Detective Reed was a terrible snooper.

Whatever officer showed up later would be getting this jacket with instructions to give it to Detective Reed. I never wanted to see his face around here again. He was no longer welcome in my home. I planned on never speaking to him again. It wasn't like I owed him anything. *He fixed your heater. Brought you breakfast. Brought you dinner. Played with Zeke. Shut up, stupid reason!* I owed him nothing because he was a liar too. He pushed his way into my life only to what? Take everything I held close to my heart away? No one would take me away from Zeke. He needed me just as much as I needed him. I'd do anything to keep him safe. To keep my secret.

The worst part was that I felt duped. For some idiotic reason, I thought Tucker might actually like me. I shook my head. Not Tucker. Detective Reed. Last night was a moment of weakness while I was sick and…drugged. My emotions couldn't be trusted. I took a deep breath. No one in their right mind would like me. I didn't even like myself. And I didn't need a man in my life to point out my own shortcomings. I was self-aware enough to know my own flaws. One of my worst ones? That my heart was too big for my own good. Too trusting. Too caring. Too naïve.

I took another deep breath, trying to clear my head. I needed whatever cop that came here to believe me. Being upset hadn't helped my case over the phone. A clear mind was a must. The last thing I needed was for this cop to just roll his eyes and write off my concerns because I was the crazy lady on the hill. Detective Reed had invaded my privacy. He had crossed all sorts of lines. He was…*handsome, kind…God.* I buried my face in my hands. He was an asshole.

It was as if my mind was at war with itself. One more breath in. And out. Again. And again. Three times. I closed my eyes and repeated the process. Again. And again.

"Mommy, what are you doing?"

My eyes flew open. I knew what I must look like. I had just been running around out in the cold for half an hour. My nerves were shot. I was always worse when I was upset. I ran my fingers through my hair, trying to pretend everything was fine. But then I did it a second time. And a third. "Nothing, little dude. Ready for some breakfast?"

Zeke squinted his eyes at me. "No, what's wrong? We were so happy last night."

I tried to swallow down the lump in my throat. Weren't we always happy? Just the two of us? He was getting more perceptive of my nervous ticks. He was good at calling me out. But right at this moment, counting to three was the only thing that was helping me calm down. I bit the inside of my lip three times, hoping he couldn't tell.

Zeke pulled his pet lizard out of one of the many pockets of his cargo shorts. "You can borrow Lizardopolous to pet instead of biting your lip. He'll make you better."

"Zeke, what have I told you about carrying him around in your pockets? You could hurt him."

He didn't listen to me. He just thrust him into my hands and then ran out of the room.

I didn't like Lizardopolous. His little beady eyes freaked me out, like he was always watching me. The only reason I had allowed Zeke to get him was because Zeke's eyes were adorable when he looked up at me with that pleading little face. I looked down at Lizardopolous. *Ugh.* A gross little lizard wasn't going to make me better. But I wished it would. Because I didn't want my son to think that I needed something to make me better. I was fine. But my pep talk felt like a lie. I hadn't felt fine in a long time.

A car door slamming made me lift my head. "Zeke? Can you take him back?"

Zeke didn't respond.

"Zeke?"

Nothing.

So I did what I had just told Zeke not to. I pulled on Detective Reed's jacket and tucked Lizardopolous into one of the pockets. To make sure he was safe, I zipped the pocket up before shoving my feet into boots and opening the door.

I ran straight into someone. No, not someone. Detective Reed. I knew it before I even looked up. The smell from his coat was all around me now, invading my air supply.

"Are you okay?" He gripped both sides of my face. "Is Zeke okay?"

I wanted my skin to hate him as much as my mind did. Instead, I melted into his touch. And I hated how weak that made me feel. For just a moment, I tried to savor this feeling. I tried to hold on to what it was like to be cared for. And then I shoved my feelings aside and did what needed to be done to end this before anything got worse.

"No thanks to you." I pushed him off of me.

"What?"

He looked truly confused. And upset. And I had no idea why he was going on with this charade like he actually cared. The game was up. And he won. He made a fool of me. "Seriously, they sent you?" The force he worked for was completely inept.

"And me," said another detective standing at the bottom of my front porch. He walked up the steps and put his hand out for me to shake. "Detective Torres. It's nice to finally meet you, Mrs. Clark."

The way he spoke to me made me even madder. Damien Torres. I had seen him around town. Everyone knew everyone around here. And if I knew his name, he most certainly knew the rumors about me. He knew I wasn't married. He knew everything. "*Miss* Clark. But we both know that you already knew that, Damien." I didn't offer him my hand.

"Tucker has told me all about you, but he failed to mention that you're a little feisty. I can see why...because that's usually more my type." He winked at me.

The fact that Tucker had told him about me stung even more. Just laughing at me behind my back like everyone else in this stupid town. "Well I hate to ruin your day, but neither of you are my type. At all. So you can both turn your asses around and get off my front porch."

"Whoa." Detective Torres lifted his hands to his side. "Ma'am, we received a 911 call that you were under duress. We're only here to help you..."

"I don't need your help. Or anyone else's. That call was a mistake. I'm perfectly capable of taking care of myself without the help of two meatheads. I'm not going to ask you again. Get off my property."

"Are you threatening us, Mrs. Clark?" Detective Torres asked.

He was trying to make me lose it. He was trying to see if the rumors were true. I bit the inside of my lip three times.

"Would you stay out of this?" Detective Reed said in a tone that even made me feel like telling him every one of me secrets. He turned back to me. "Violet what happened? The dispatcher said someone attacked you..."

Attacked? They really hadn't listened to me at all. "No one attacked me. Like I said, the call was a mistake. So you can both just go."

"I'm not going anywhere until you tell me what happened. Did someone try to hurt you?"

The way he was acting so innocent made me want to cry. I felt tired and defeated. "Yeah, and you succeeded. In humiliating me in front of your friend too. You've had your fun like everyone else. Please just leave me alone."

He shook his head. "What are you talking about? I'm here because you called the police…"

"On you! You looked around my house without a warrant, Detective Reed. You took advantage of me. We both know why you were here last night. And whatever you were looking for? I hope it was worth it." I knew it wasn't. The pistol was long gone. He had nothing.

He shook his head again like he couldn't comprehend what I was saying. "I didn't snoop around your house."

I was good at spotting a liar. After all, I was one. "Don't bother lying. It doesn't matter anyway. But drugging me?"

"Whoa." He sounded just like his dumb friend.

And his dumb friend had the audacity to laugh. Like my whole life was a joke to them. I blinked back my tears, keeping my emotions locked inside.

"Wait in the car, Damien," Detective Reed said.

I was surprised to see Detective Torres nod. "Good day, *Miss* Clark. See you around."

We both knew he wouldn't. But then I thought that maybe he meant it a different way. Like he *knew* he'd be seeing me again soon. Like I was in some kind of trouble. I glanced past him and the car down to the lake. How could they possibly know?

Detective Reed took a step toward me, too close for comfort, pulling me out of my thoughts. "I didn't drug you, what the hell are you talking about?"

"The Nyquil."

"Okay? It's just Nyquil."

Liar. "I freaking passed out just like you wanted."

"The alcohol component in it isn't even enough to get an infant drunk. I wanted you to feel better, I wasn't trying to get you unconscious."

"There's alcohol in it?"

"Yes."

"Well, I don't drink!"

"Okay well…I'm sorry. I didn't know that. But it's hardly…"

"You looked around my house." I wanted him to stop lying. I wanted to hear a confession. I needed to know if I was about to be taken to prison.

I watched his Adam's apple rise and then fall. "And I didn't find anything."

I wanted him to admit it, but I never actually expected him to. Wasn't that tampering with evidence or something? He just confessed to a crime. I glanced over his shoulder. Detective Torres was in the car, well out of earshot. No one would take my word over a detective's.

The only problem was that I couldn't tell if what he said was a lie. He seemed sincere. If he really hadn't found anything, I was lucky. And I needed him out of my life before he did uncover something that would ruin me. "I'm glad I gave you and your buddy something to talk about." I unzipped his coat and shoved it into his hands. "But if I ever see you anywhere near my property again…so help me…I'll…" What? Kill him? The image of the blood dripping down the handle of my stepfather's pistol made me feel strangled. "Just leave me alone."

"Violet, I had a good night with you. A great night. I'm sorry that I looked around your house. I just needed to put this little voice in the back of my head to rest so I could give us a real shot. But like I said…I didn't find anything. I know you're not involved in that explosion. I know you're innocent."

God, he didn't know me at all. But my mind didn't focus on the word "innocent" in his spiel. It had focused and attached itself to the word "us." I wasn't sure why it hurt so much to hear me be part of a we again. But it did. Like a slap in the face from my past.

"Let me take you and Zeke out tonight. Let me make it up to you. I swear it has nothing to do with the case. I just want to get to know you better."

"It's too late." My response really had nothing to do with him. It had been too late for years now. No one could help me fix the mess I had made. No one could pull me out of it. And love? Love was not an option for a monster like me.

"Violet." He reached out for me, but I took a step back.

"I don't go out on dates. I don't date period. And if I ever did change my mind…I certainly wouldn't date you." I wondered if he could spot a lie as easily as I could. Because I was full of them this morning. But it didn't really matter. I'd never open the door for him again. I wouldn't answer his calls. He was out of my life. I let my eyes meet his once more. And for just a moment I got lost in their warmth. In their sorrow. In their hope. I had the strangest sense that his eyes were a reflection of my own. That he knew my pain. That maybe he really could save me.

But he didn't say a word. He didn't call me out on my lies. He didn't see that my pushing him away was actually me begging him to say. I wasn't sure I had ever felt so alone as I did in that moment with him. Truly and utterly alone.

I dropped his gaze. My thoughts were right before. It was way too late to be saved anyway. I opened up my front door again and closed it behind me. I wasn't sure why, but I held my breath. Like I needed to hear him retreating, leaving me, like everyone else had. I wiped away the tears on my cheeks as I heard the car door slam and the tires on the gravel. He was gone. Out of sight, out of mind. *I hope.* I bit the inside of my lip again and again and again.

Zeke came running into the room. "Mommy, where is he? I want to try to teach him a new trick."

For a second I had no idea who Zeke was talking about. Was he referring to Detective Reed like a dog? I stopped biting the inside of my lip when I tasted blood. And as soon as I stopped the nervous habit, my mind cleared, and it came rushing back to me. *Shit.* I looked out the window, but Detective Reed's car was already gone. His jacket along with him. And Lizardopolous.

CHAPTER 12

Tucker

"Sooo..." Damien's voice trailed off as I sped down the winding trail in the woods.

I ignored him. There was nothing to say. I wanted to blame him, but *I* blew my shot with Violet. Damien wasn't the reason I was angry. Although his demeaner toward her certainly hadn't helped. I had gone to her house last night with the intention of snooping around. But I hadn't really ended up doing that. Sure, I had looked around the basement while I was fixing her radiator. And I'd casually looked around the first floor. But I had quickly abandoned the fact that I was at her house on business. It had turned into a real date. Apparently a one-sided one, but still.

The fact that I had carried her to bed and stumbled upon a loose floor board that happened to be hiding an unregistered gun? I hadn't been snooping. Except for the fact that I could have ignored it. I could have walked out of that room and she could have still trusted me. Clearly she knew what I had seen. Clearly she didn't believe my lies. And why had I lied? I could have just told her that I saw the gun and didn't care. Why had I fucked everything up for no reason?

"She seemed really into you, man," Damien said with a laugh.

"Can it, Torres."

"Torres? You must really be pissed at me if you're using my last name. What did I do?"

I chanced a glance at him during a turn. "Mrs. Clark? Pretending not to know her? Oh and then there was the fact that you hit on her right in front of me." I turned my attention back to the narrow path.

Damien laughed. "I forgot how hot she was. I couldn't help myself. If anything I was giving you a compliment."

"Commenting on her looks isn't giving me a compliment. It's...sexist and demeaning."

"Sexist? Don't tell me you're turning into a feminist on me."

I clenched my hands on the wheel.

"She has you wound around her little finger and she doesn't even like you, Tucker. What the hell are you doing wasting your time with a chick like that?"

"She does like me. We're just having a disagreement."

"Seems a little early for couples counseling. And you didn't exactly deny the fact that you're whipped."

"I can't be whipped. We're not technically in a relationship."

"Even worse for that couples counseling thing then. You can't even work things out in the honeymoon stage." He whistled. "Imagine actually being on a honeymoon with that loon."

"Can we please just drop this?"

"I'm only getting started. Forget your lack of relationship. Did you really look around her house without a warrant? What the hell were you thinking?"

"I was there on a date."

"So it had nothing to do with the fact that she's your prime suspect in a case that you promised me you gave up?"

I didn't say anything.

"Are you at least going to tell me what you found in her house?"

"I wasn't looking around."

"Fine. Let's just pretend for a second I believe you. Which I don't. Did you really drug her? That's crossing all sorts of lines."

"Of course I didn't drug her. I brought her Nyquil because she wasn't feeling well."

"That's adorable. And also super crazy…sorry, I mean weird. Is that a better word for her? It's weird that she called the cops on you for being adorable."

I shook my head. "Apparently she never drinks. It hit her harder than she expected. She thought I was trying to knock her out so I could look around her house."

"Hmm. Maybe she's less crazy than I thought. Because that's the same conclusion I'd come to. You know…because that clearly was what you did."

"That's not what I did."

"Sure." Damien picked up my jacket from the center console and started playing with the zippers on it. "She may be weird, but she has great taste in jackets. Can I have this?"

"No you can't have it. That's my jacket."

"Oooh she bought you a present? That was fast. Maybe she's secretly loaded."

"I loaned it to her. She returned it. End of story."

Damien laughed as he tossed it back onto the center console. "That really is the end of the story, because it sounds like she doesn't want to see you again."

I know. But that wasn't going to make me stop trying. I just needed a chance to explain.

"Anything I can do to make you feel better about your new breakup?"

I felt him tickle the side of my stomach. "Tickling me is definitely not going to make me feel better."

"Good. Because I'm not going to tickle you." He continued to tickle me.

"Stop touching my stomach!" I laughed.

"I'm not touching you, Tucker."

I laughed. "Stop!" He was full on tickling me now. But when I looked over he was just sitting in the passenger's seat staring at me like I had lost my mind. I glanced down at my stomach and saw a small blob moving beneath the fabric of my shirt. And I screamed at the top of my lungs. It was so piercing that it hurt my own ears.

For some reason, my scream made Damien scream, until we were both screaming and staring at each other instead of at the road.

I slammed on the brakes. The car slid on the leaves on the road and almost did a 180. I jumped out of the car before it even came to a complete stop.

"Kill it!" Damien yelled as he ran up beside me.

I started hitting my chest and stomach as the blob ran around beneath my shirt. And then Damien started beating me with the handle of his pistol.

"Ow! Stop it!" I jumped out of his way, reached up beneath my shirt, and grabbed on to something slimy. *Ugh.* I pulled it out from under my shirt and threw it to the side of the road before I even got a chance to look at it.

Whatever it was landed in a pile of leaves and skittered into the underbrush. Leaves crunched in a path as it ran away from us.

"What the hell was that?" Damien asked. He was patting himself down, looking to see if there was anything on him.

"Some kind of reptile? How should I know?"

Damien smoothed his shirt back into place and then started laughing. "You should have seen your face."

"You should have heard your scream."

"Mine? You sounded like a wild banshee."

"How do you think that thing got in my car?"

"I don't know. But let's get out of here. Nothing good ever happens in these woods." He patted me on the back before walking to the car.

I looked at the spot where I had thrown the creature. What the hell was it? And how did it get on me? I shuddered. My cellphone started to buzz in my pocket, startling me again. I quickly denied the call when I didn't recognize the number.

Violet's house was warm and inviting once you were inside. But Damien was right. These woods were unsettling. It almost felt like I was unwelcome. Like someone was telling me to get out. To run away while I still had a chance. I shook my head and climbed back into my car.

CHAPTER 13
Violet

Of course Detective Reed wasn't answering my calls. I had threatened him. I had practically begged him to never speak to me again. But two minutes later, avoiding him was no longer an option. He had Lizardopolous. I had to get my son's pet back. It was his best friend. *How did I let this happen?*

I looked back down at my cell phone. Maybe I had called the wrong number. I tried to picture the business card he had given me before I burned it. No, I definitely had the number right. I knew I did. *Shit.* I felt myself gripping the phone tighter. I should have driven after him right when I realized what had happened.

"Mommy he needs breakfast! We have to find him!" Zeke pounded on the bathroom door.

"Okay. One sec, little dude." I flushed the toilet even though I hadn't peed. Pretending to need to use the bathroom was the lamest excuse ever to hide from my son. But I didn't know how else to make the phone call without Zeke realizing what I had done. I already felt bad enough.

"You know what?" I said as I came out of my hiding spot. "Maybe he's in the kitchen waiting for breakfast. Let's go look there." I was stalling. I knew what we needed to do. I just really really didn't want to have to.

"He doesn't eat in the kitchen. He eats in his aquarium. You *know* that. It's *your* rule."

"Then let's recheck his aquarium. He's gotta be around here somewhere." Lies, lies, lies. *I'm a horrible person. Just tell him the truth. Go fix it.*

"What if he ran away?" Zeke looked up at me and his eyes were all watery like he was seconds away from crying.

I didn't have any other options. I had to tell him the truth. This was a great learning lesson about how you shouldn't put animals in pockets. A lesson that I needed to teach myself apparently. "You know what? Maybe he jumped onto Detective Reed when he stopped by. Maybe he has him." God, Zeke's adorable little face made it impossible to tell him the truth. I didn't want him to look disappointed in me. Blaming it all on Detective Reed was definitely a better plan.

"Then let's go get him back!" He went to the door and grabbed his coat and mittens. He ran outside without his boots.

"You have to put on shoes, Zeke!"

He ran back in and shoved his feet into his favorite rain boots. "Come on, Mommy. Mr. Reed doesn't know it's feeding time. Lizardopolous needs food or he'll starve."

Surely he wouldn't starve if we fed him a few minutes late. Right? But I didn't really know. The agreement Zeke and I had when I allowed him to get a pet was that it was 100 percent his responsibility. Regardless, we did still have to go get the lizard back. "Okay." But I didn't move. I felt paralyzed. I didn't want to go to the police station. For some reason, I was afraid that I'd walk in and never walk out. Going there was basically a confession. It was turning myself in. *I can't do this.*

"Pleeeeease."

I looked down at his adorable little face again and nodded. "I'm coming." Of course I was going. I knew exactly where Lizardopolous was. He was safely in Detective Reed's jacket. They were probably both perfectly safe at the precinct by now. I'd be in and out of there super fast. It would be fine. I grabbed my light jacket off the hook. Everything was fine.

But my heart was racing. I lived out in the middle of nowhere for a reason. I didn't want anyone looking too closely at me. Walking into a place filled with cops was the absolute last thing on my list.

Zeke grabbed my hand and pulled me to the door.

I didn't have a choice. This wasn't about me. It was about Zeke. And I'd do anything for him. I pushed my thoughts aside as the cool autumn air hit my face. By the time I reached my old pickup truck, I felt calmer. I was a woman on a mission. All I needed to do was repeatedly tell myself I'd be in and out super fast. Again. And again. I pulled out onto the main road.

"Why didn't you invite Mr. Reed in?" Zeke asked. "He probably had doughnuts, or Danishes, or something else yummy."

I couldn't help but laugh. Sugar was the second most important thing to Zeke, after Lizardopolous. "You know how I feel about guests coming over."

"But he came in last night. And it was fun."

"Yeah." I exhaled slowly. "It was fun. But it was a one-time thing because I wasn't feeling well." Saying it was a one-time thing out loud made me feel a sense of sorrow I didn't understand. I barely knew Detective Reed. Not seeing him anymore should be easy. So why did the thought of it put a pit in the bottom of my stomach? *It wasn't a real date. It was all a lie.* My heart couldn't afford to fall for another liar.

"I think it should be an everyday thing. He liked you, Mommy. He didn't look at you the way other people do. He was nice."

I swallowed hard. It was impossible to protect my son. He was too observant for his own good.

"So can we invite him over again for dinner? I want to play hot lava. Maybe he'll be better this time."

I laughed. Detective Reed had tried his best last night, but half the time we were playing he had been dying slowly in hot lava. "Maybe some other time, but not tonight." By that I meant absolutely never ever again. It just wasn't possible.

"But…*why*?"

"Because I said so."

Zeke folded his arms across his chest. "It's not fair. Mr. Reed is my friend. Why can't I ask him to come over? You don't even have to play with us."

I didn't answer him as I made the final turn. He knew I liked our privacy. We had already talked about this dozens of times. It's why he had been able to guilt me into getting him a lizard in the first place. I pulled into one of the empty spots in the parking lot and cut the engine.

"We're going to go get Lizardopolous back, and then you're going to spend the rest of the weekend making sure he's okay. He's probably had quite the ordeal. He hasn't been out of our house in years."

"Fine." He said it in the utterly unsatisfying way that only a five year old could muster the attitude for.

I unbuckled my seatbelt and hopped out of the truck. The door squeaked on its hinges as I slammed it shut.

"I've never been inside a police station before," Zeke said as he put his hand into mine. "Do you think it's like the cop shows?"

"What cop shows?"

He looked away from me. "Nothing."

"Zeke Clark, have you been watching TV without my permission?" I pulled him to a stop right outside the entrance.

"Everybody in school has Hulu. It's not fair that I'm not allowed to watch when everyone else does."

"So you got it without my permission?"

"No?"

"*Zeke.*"

He didn't answer.

"If all the kids in your class decided to run into oncoming traffic would you join them?"

"No. But that's stupid. Hulu isn't stupid. It has all the shows in the whole world on it."

His statement was truly and utterly false. There was no way that it had every show in the world on it. *I think.* Honestly I didn't know enough about it to be sure. "We'll talk about this when we get home." I could only think of one thing at a time if I wasn't going to lose my nerve. I opened up the door of the precinct and we both walked in.

Unlike the air outside, the air inside the police station was stifling. Every instinct in my body was telling me to run. But the little hand pulling me up to the front desk made me focus.

"Hi," I said to a very disgruntled looking man. "I'm here to see Detective Reed."

The man looked up at me. "Is he expecting you?"

"We're friends," Zeke said. "I'm Zeke and this is my mommy and we're looking for our lizard."

The man at the desk leaned forward so he could see my son. "A lizard, huh?"

Zeke nodded. "Mr. Reed was at our house earlier and my Mommy thinks my lizard accidentally went with him. He doesn't know any better…he's a lizard."

"Well then," the man said with a smile. He seemed much happier to be talking to my son than me. "I'll let him know that you're here, young man." He lifted up the phone on his desk and held it to his ear. A few seconds later he said, "There's a Zeke at the front desk here to talk to you." He paused and lifted his gaze back to me. "Yes, his mother as well. They say they're friends of yours." He hung up the phone. "He'll be right out. You two can take a seat over there."

"Thank you very much," Zeke said and walked over to the chairs against the wall.

"Cute kid," the officer said. "He looks just like you."

I smiled, even though it felt forced. Zeke had my eyes. And hair color. And almost everything else. But every now and then I saw his father in a facial expression. Those fleeting moments gutted me. "Thanks. Do you know about how long it will be till he comes to…" my voice trailed off when Detective Reed came pushing through a door behind the front desk.

His eyes landed on Zeke and then drifted to me. "Is everything okay?"

There was something about being away from my house that made me focus on him more than my surroundings. I could hear the concern in his voice. I could see it on his face.

He actually cared about me and my son. And I felt a little like an ass. But only a little. Because he had been way out of line.

I cleared my throat, but before I could say anything, Zeke ran over to him.

"Lizardopolous is missing and Mommy thinks maybe you accidentally took him?"

"Lizardopolous?" He raised both eyebrows.

I was relieved to see that he was confused. That probably meant that my son's lizard was still safely in his jacket pocket.

"My pet lizard. I know he's really fun but I need him back. He's hungry. But you can come over and play with him later." Zeke stuck out his hand, waiting for Detective Reed to deposit the lizard in it.

He opened his mouth and then closed it again. Now I was worried that he didn't look surprised enough to hear about the lizard. Although, he did seem to be at a loss for words.

"Can I speak to you privately?" I asked. "Please?" God, if anything happened to that lizard I didn't know what I was going to do.

"Yeah…just…" he looked over his shoulder. "You can both come with me. How would you like to see where I work, Zeke?"

"Yes!"

"Great. Right this way." He opened up the door he had just come through.

I made my way around the front desk. I barely looked at Detective Reed as I walked through the door he was holding open for me. What was I supposed to say? *Sorry for acting like an ass, but you deserved it. Now give me my son's lizard?* But again, as I walked past him, I got the sense that he truly did care. I just wasn't sure how that made me feel.

He gestured toward the desk that was across from Damien Torres.

It felt like everyone in the precinct was staring at me. Especially Damien. He was probably analyzing whether or not I was capable of setting a house on fire. Which was stupid. Anyone was capable of that. All it took was a few matches and a gallon of gasoline. It didn't mean that I was guilty.

"This is awesome!" Zeke said and jumped into Detective Reed's chair. He started clicking on the computer's mouse. The little devil was clearly better with computers than I ever realized. And at stealing credit cards. And at lying. *Just like his mother.*

But I was just relieved that Zeke was distracted for a moment. I leaned forward, ignoring the smell of Detective Reed's sweet cologne. "I need to talk to you away from Zeke," I whispered into his ear.

For a moment he didn't respond. Or move. We both just stayed close, our arms brushing together, my lips only a few inches away from his ear.

I didn't have time for whatever weird game he was playing. I grabbed his arm and pulled him away from the cluster of desks. "I put Zeke's lizard in your coat pocket. I forgot that I was about to give you your jacket back and…anyway, I need Lizardopolous. So where is your coat?" I looked over his shoulder and saw it slung across the back of his work chair. I started walking back over to it, but he grabbed my arm to stop me.

"Uh...bad news on the lizard front. I...well he..." He let go of my arm and ran his hand down my face. "I didn't know what it was. I threw it into the woods."

"You what?" My voice came out high pitched and weird. *Oh no, Lizardopolous!* He'd never survive out there alone. The nights were getting frosty.

"I had no idea what it was. It got loose in my car and started crawling all over me."

"So you threw it into the middle of the wilderness? Lizards aren't bred for these conditions. He's going to freeze to death. Zeke's too young to learn about death. What were you thinking?"

"What was *I* thinking? I'm not the one that put him into a pocket of a coat that didn't belong to me." His eyes darted down my body in the most unnerving way. "Speaking of which...don't you own a winter jacket?"

"This isn't about me. My son's lizard is moments away from death and you...where? Where did you throw him?"

"I was a few minutes out from your house."

"Can you show me exactly where? We need to go get him right now."

He shook his head. "I don't know. It all looks the same out there to me."

"You can't think of anything specific? Like a certain kind of tree? Or a bend in the road?"

"I'm sorry, Violet. There's no way that we're going to find him. As soon as I threw him, he scurried off pretty quickly."

What kind of unobservant detective was he? My mind was going a mile a minute. How was I going to fix this now? I hadn't given myself a chance to consider that Lizardopolous wouldn't be here. *Damn it.* There was too much ground to cover with no leads. Lizardopolous was officially gone. "Then you have to replace him."

"I don't even know what *it* was."

"It? That thing you're calling it was my son's best friend, Detective Reed."

"Tucker. Please, just call me Tucker."

The way he said it combined with the way he was smiling at me made me gulp. Even though we were surrounded by a bunch of cops, the moment suddenly felt intimate. It had been a long time since the stares hadn't bothered me. But when I was looking into Detective Reed's eyes he was the only person on my mind. Even if I was pissed at him. "We are not on a first name basis."

"We've shared a meal, conversation…I've even carried you to bed. I'd say we are on a first name basis."

"You're failing to mention the fact that you violated my privacy."

"And if you'd give me a real chance to explain…maybe over that dinner tonight?"

Again, this moment was too intimate. He was too close, his breath invading my air supply. When his eyes drifted to my lips my knees felt weak. What was he trying to do to me? I cleared my throat and took a step back. "I'm not here for me. The only reason I came was to get Zeke's lizard back."

"Then let's go get him a new lizard right now. I'd do it myself, but I don't know enough about lizards to tell if it will even look the same."

I hated how he kept calling Lizardopolous it. Sure, I had done it a few times when I was annoyed with the little guy. But there was supposed to be frost tonight and Detective Reed had basically murdered him. "I can't just leave Zeke here by himself." God, this was a disaster.

"There's nowhere safer than a police station. Damien will watch him while we're gone."

I glanced toward Damien, not that I was actually considering his suggestion. I could feel the eyes of all these judging cops trained on me. Probably trying to figure out why I was here. Wondering what on earth I was finally confessing to. "No." I wasn't going to leave my son here in the midst of all this negative energy. I'd never give them a chance to turn my own son against me too. "I'm not leaving him here."

"Well, he's going to school on Monday right? I can pick you up in the morning once he's gone and we can head to the pet store together to find a suitable replacement."

"Monday?" I bit the inside of my lip. How was I supposed to distract Zeke for the rest of the weekend? But I also didn't see a better option unless I wanted to sneak out of the house when Zeke was sleeping. I didn't feel comfortable with that. I shook my head, feeling ridiculous that I didn't see the very obvious solution right in front of me. "Thanks, but I'll just go on Monday by myself." I turned to Zeke. "It's time to go, Zeke!" I'd keep pretending that his pet was lost in the house. Maybe I could do some much needed cleaning while I was pretending to search for Lizardopolous. Not that any more house guests would be stopping by. Six years seemed like a good amount of time between visitors.

"I'm only asking for five minutes of your time, Violet. Let's get an early lunch right now with Zeke too. My treat."

I plastered a fake smile to my face. "I appreciate it, I do. But you're better off not talking to me. Just ask your partner."

Zeke came running over to us. "Mr. Reed, have you ever used your gun? How does the database of wanted criminals work? Have you ever caught a bad guy?"

"Time to go, little dude." I lifted him up even though he was way too heavy for me. I had a feeling that he'd refuse to leave if I didn't literally carry him out.

"But I have a bazillion questions," Zeke protested. "I want to know how to catch a bad guy."

"Then we'll just watch a show about it when we get home, okay?"

Zeke's turned his attention back to me. "Does that mean I can keep Hulu?"

"Sure." Watching some shows this weekend might be just the distraction he needed from the disappearance of Lizardo-polous.

"Violet," Detective Reed said.

I glanced over my shoulder once at him. He looked hurt. And it wasn't fair for him to put that emotion on me. If he was actually pursuing me, there was something clearly wrong with him. No one would like me if they weren't broken themselves. And I could barely keep up with my own problems, I didn't have time to fix him when I couldn't even fix myself. I pushed through the door without responding and headed outside so I could breathe again.

CHAPTER 14

Tucker

My nights had been lonely since my split. But my days off had been lonelier. I had no one and nothing in this town. It wasn't just loneliness that made my thoughts keep drifting back to Violet, though. There were plenty of things I could do to fill my time that didn't involve her. I kept thinking about her because she was alluring. Smart, sensitive, feisty, drop-dead gorgeous, and off limits. A man could only be told to stay away so many times. I had to respect her decision even though a simple explanation could fix everything. *Maybe.* I wasn't sure at this point if she'd ever believe me. But no matter how many times I told myself to let it go, I couldn't. Thoughts of her consumed me.

I grabbed my phone as I headed outside. There were a few texts from Damien, most likely nagging me to go out with him tonight. But I saw enough of him on my days at work. I slid the phone into my pocket as I climbed into my car.

Today I was working on my side project and I had a meeting with the neighborhood gossip, Sally Bennet. After talking to her I could hopefully put any suspicions I had of Violet completely to rest. If I thought she was innocent, it would be a hell of a lot easier trying to explain why I had looked around. I shook my head as I put the car in reverse. There wouldn't be an explanation. Violet would never allow one. And a part of me understood that. If someone had looked through a bunch of my personal belongings, I'd be pissed too. But I hadn't done that.

By the time I reached Sally's house, I had thought a lot more about my apology to Violet than the case. I put my car in park outside Sally's. It was only a few doors down from the house that exploded. I climbed out of my car and stared down the street. All that remained was rubble and caution tape. I didn't know how far along the FBI was on the case. For all I knew, it was closed. My big break was slipping through my fingers while I was hung up on a woman that wanted nothing to do with me.

Before I even reached the front door, it flung open. Sally was standing there with a big smile on her face, clearly excited about everything she was about to learn from me instead of the other way around.

"Come in, come in," she said. "I just put a tea kettle on the stove. And I made some cookies. I hope you like chocolate chip."

"Yeah, that sounds great." I walked into her house. It was pretty much exactly what I'd expected. The walls of the foyer were covered in flowered wallpaper. I glanced into the living room to one side. Nope, not just the walls of the foyer. The hideous wallpaper was everywhere. There were also strange little collectibles on every available surface. They ranged from little dolls to what looked like glass animals of all varieties. There was even a penguin that was at least three feet tall by the fireplace. All of it was odd, but I found that placement particularly weird. Penguins didn't like fire.

"Right this way." She led me into her kitchen. The wallpaper continued in here, but fortunately the collectibles stopped.

I sat down in the kitchen chair she gestured to. It squeaked underneath me so I stayed unnervingly still. I could have asked her a bunch of personal questions to make this more natural. Like how long she'd lived in town. And whether or not she had a husband. But I honestly didn't want to be in here any longer than I needed to. It was stuffy. I felt as if the flowers in the wallpaper were leaning toward me, staring at me.

I cleared my throat as she busied herself with the tea. "Sally, how long did you know Adeline Bell?" I studied her face as she turned around.

"As long as she lived in this neighborhood, which wasn't for very long. I'm always the first neighbor to welcome new homeowners on this street. I was over with a plate of these same cookies the minute she pulled up." Sally placed the plate of cookies in front of me as well as a cup of tea and a stack of napkins with kittens printed on them.

I ignored the cookies and tea and stared directly at her. "When she pulled up? I thought you said she was married?"

"Yes, she was married. But I never saw her husband. He traveled constantly. A housewife with no husband to care for every night? The poor thing must have been bored out of her mind. I mean…maybe not such a poor thing if she burned her house down." She stared at me expectantly.

I wasn't playing this game of give and take with her. "Did she have any friends in the neighborhood?"

"Besides me? Hmm. Well, there are a few other women the same age as her in the neighborhood. Charlotte, Rosie, and

Phoenix. But I never got the sense that Adeline particularly liked them."

"And why would you say that?"

"I'm good at reading people, Detective Reed."

"So what did Adeline do that led you to believe she disliked these women?"

"Well, on several occasions I literally saw her hide from them. Or she wouldn't answer the door when I knew for a fact that she was inside. She rarely ever came to the civic association meetings. And there's a neighborhood book club that she refused to attend as well."

"Did she like you?"

"Of course. Everyone likes me. Cookie?" She slid the plate toward me.

I lifted one off the plate so she'd focus. "And you mentioned the first night we met that Adeline had blonde hair."

"Yes."

"Are you sure?"

"Yes? Why, what color does everyone else think it is?"

"I thought maybe it was more of a brown."

She stared at me. "You're mistaken, Detective Reed. She was a natural blonde. A beauty. That's how she got that wonderful, sweet, handsome gardener to enter a scandalous affair with her. Speaking of Ben Jones…how is he doing? No one around here has heard a word. We're worried sick."

I didn't bother correcting her. The detective's name was Benjamin Harlow, but he had been undercover here. It was bad enough I had told her his real name once. I didn't need to do that again. I was trying to keep this whole thing as under wraps as possible. The last thing I needed was Sally showing up at the hospital with a bouquet of roses for a Ben Harlow instead of a Ben Jones. And she was derailing the topic. Ben was a dead end. I wasn't here to talk about him. "He's unresponsive."

She gasped and put her hand over her mouth.

I was as upset as her. If I could just talk to him, I could piece a few things together. As it was, I was stuck with Sally.

"Then why haven't they let me visit him? I go almost every day but no one will let me see him."

"They transported him to DC."

"Why on earth would they transport him there? This is where he lives. You must know something."

Something that she can tell everyone in town? But the woman truly did look upset. "He was placed in a medically induced coma. No one knows for sure if he'll recover."

"Dear me." She shook her head. "You should eat your cookie. It will make you feel better about all the terrible things that keep happening here."

I took a bite as she started to talk and then stopped mid-chew. Terrible things? Plural? I swallowed, ignoring the jagged corners I hadn't fully chewed. "What other terrible things?"

She leaned forward slightly like she was about to tell me something top secret. "Someone's been stealing my lawn gnomes."

For the love of God. "Did you file an official complaint at the police station?"

"Of course. But they won't even put a patrol car outside my house. It's rubbish."

"Sally, if I could ask you a few more questions about Adeline. Were her eyes green by any chance?"

"No." She shook her head. She looked disturbed by my sudden change of topic.

"I have a few other questions about someone I hope you know. Violet Clark."

Sally raised her eyebrow at me. "Brown hair. Green eyes. Ah. You're not asking about Adeline at all. You're asking about Violet."

"Is there any chance that they're the same person?"

She shook her head like I was an idiot. "Dear, I knew both women. They aren't the same. At all, really. When Violet was little she was so full of life. A sweet little thing. Life's been hard on her. But Adeline? She was always very cold."

"How has life been hard on Violet?

Sally lifted her teacup and took a sip. For a moment, I thought she was going to keep her lips sealed for once in her life. But then she grabbed one of the cat napkins and dabbed her bottom lip. She leaned forward like she was about to launch into the story of all stories.

"I used to babysit Violet when she was little. Like I said, she was so full of life and a wonderful little girl. Nothing at all wrong with her. Her father died a few years after they moved here, and you know how the death of a parent at such a young age can be detrimental to the mind? Well, she seemed okay. Not good, but as you'd expect after such a loss. Like she was putting on a brave face. I still babysat her on occasion. But looking back on it now, maybe she was more distressed than I realized. Kids are smarter than you think. I still wonder if there's something I could have done to help..." her voice trailed off and she shook her head, lost in her own story.

"When her mother remarried shortly after...Violet started to grow more sullen. I thought it had just taken her a while to process the fact that her father was gone. Like that brave face was suddenly just gone. I tried to talk to her mother, but she barely ever answered the door. And whenever she did...she called me nosy. I never got to babysit the little girl again. But I'd see her around the neighborhood. She seemed okay. Her smiles were rare, but still there occasionally. I thought she was good. Until suddenly she wasn't anymore."

The chair beneath me squeaked. I realized I had practically scooted to the end of it. I waited, but Sally seemed like she was done with her story.

She started humming as she lifted her cup back up.

"What about between when you thought she was good and when she wasn't anymore?"

"I stopped babysitting her when she was ten years old. I couldn't tell you for sure what happened to Violet. Only things I've heard."

"Well, what things have you heard?" I never realized how hard it was to prod a gossiper into gossiping.

"Hmm." She placed her tea cup back down. "I've heard a lot of things. People can be cruel."

If Damien wasn't such an asshole I'd already know about all the rumors. But he was adamant about me dropping the case. After Violet had shown up at the precinct he had gotten even worse. I couldn't even glance at my phone without him looking at it over my shoulder. "Do you mind telling me what people have said?"

"Well, take it with a grain of salt. You know how rumors are."

Was she seriously warning me about rumors? She was the queen of them. "Of course."

"Let's see. Some people think that her odd behavior started when she failed the SAT's and didn't get into the college of her dreams. Some think it's because her boyfriend dumped her and moved across the country. Or that her nervous ticks drove him away. Or that it happened after her mother and stepfather died, but I know that's not true because she moved out to the woods before that happened. And those are just the kind rumors."

"Her mother and stepfather died too?" *Poor Violet. She was surrounded by death and tragedy.* I tried to ignore that Sally was referring to Violet's OCD as odd behavior. Plenty of people had that. It wasn't a big deal at all, and I barely noticed it when I was with her.

"They passed away shortly after they retired out of state. Tragic. The poor girl lost her boyfriend and family all in the same year she found out she was with child."

It was tragic. She had no one to help her. She must have felt so alone. "Do you know who Zeke's father is?"

Sally shook her head. "I'm assuming it was her ex-boyfriend. What a jerk for leaving her all alone to fend for that child. But I swear I only see Violet in Zeke. He looks just like she did at that age. Without the dreadlocks of course." She smiled and shook her head.

An awkward silence settled around us.

I placed my hand around my cup of tea, suddenly cold. "You said those were the kind rumors. What about the ones that aren't kind?"

Sally sighed. "That she murdered her boyfriend, stepfather, and mother in cold blood and has been hiding out in that dilapidated house ever since, biding her time until she strikes again. Or possibly hiding out there to help prevent herself from killing again. Regardless of the reason, rumor has it that all her victims are buried underneath the floorboards. Maybe there's even more bodies than just the three."

I waited for her to laugh. Or…something. The officer I had talked to the other day had said the same kind of thing. All the warnings from Damien. Is that really what most people thought? How? How could they possibly think that? No wonder she wanted to escape from all the prying eyes. Violet wasn't a murderer. Despite the fact that she tried to be strong for her son, she seemed as delicate as her name. A violet lost in a sea of cruelty. "You don't believe that?"

"She's disturbed. No one would live out in the woods if they were right in the head."

"She doesn't live out in the woods. She has a house."

"One that doesn't belong to her. That house has been falling apart out there ever since I was a child. I'm telling you, she fled her house and ran off to the woods just as fast as Adeline Bell did. If Adeline Bell is guilty of something, I believe Violet is too."

My blood felt cold as I listened to her. "You knew her when she was little. What do you really think is true?"

"I think something happened in her childhood home that no one knows but her. Something that caused her smiles to disappear at a young age. Something that caused her to eventually lose it. Something terrible."

I realized I was holding my breath. My exhale sounded ragged. I held my cup even tighter. What the hell did she mean by that? Was she trying to give me a clue without actually saying anything at all? "Sally, if you know something that happened, you have to tell me."

She shrugged. "I don't know what happened. But as I said, terrible things happen in this neighborhood. Speaking of which, can I file another complaint with you about my missing gnomes?"

I took a slow, deep breath. This woman couldn't be trusted. I shouldn't listen to anything she said. But her words were jarring. "You have to wait to hear back from the county." I placed my cup down on the table and stood up. I was done talking to this woman. I wasn't going to listen to lies. I was going to get to the bottom of all of this and put everyone in their place. Violet deserved someone in her corner. "Which house did Violet grow up in?"

"Oh, I figured you knew. It was the house that blew up."

I knew this was all related! I could feel my heart racing. I was so close to solving this thing.

Sally started laughing. "I'm sorry, I'm just kidding, Detective. You should have seen your face! We're sharing ghost stories, and I thought it would be funny."

Damn it. I tried to keep a straight face. Honestly, it was kind of funny. What were the odds of that happening? "Which house did Violet grow up in, Sally?"

"Right next door. Rosie's house. I mentioned her earlier. She's one of the women that Adeline was definitely not friends with."

"Thanks for your help, Sally."

"Any time. And Detective?"

I turned back toward her.

"Take these for the road." She shoved the plate of cookies in my hand.

I had no idea when she had the chance to put plastic wrap on them. She was like a housewife ninja.

"And be careful out on the streets."

Right. Because it's a dangerous neighborhood. Only, it wasn't. The only dangerous women here were the ones that spread gossip instead of trying to seek the truth. They were the ones hurting people, not the other way around.

***

I knocked on Rosie's door and waited. And waited. She was probably at work, despite Sally insisting that she was home. It was mid-morning. Most people without my crazy schedule that could afford a house like this had a 9 to 5 day job. I glanced down at my watch and then knocked again.

Finally a woman with curly blonde hair and glasses opened the door. Her cheeks immediately turned rosy. She was the epitome of her name. Her hair was in a messy bun and a pencil was sticking through it. She was wearing baggy sweatpants and an even baggier t-shirt.

"Hello?" She tucked a flyaway hair behind her ear.

"Hi, Rosie. I'm Detective Reed." I stretched my hand out to her.

Now instead of flustered, she looked flat out concerned. "Detective?" She put her hand out after an awkward pause and shook mine. "Is there something that I can help you with?"

"Yes, I have a few questions for you. Could I come inside so we can talk?"

She pressed her lips together, probably going over all the TV shows that said not to let cops inside your house. Her fingers tightened ever so slightly on the doorknob. She was nervous. I was freaking her out. I needed to put her mind at ease.

"You're not in any trouble at all. I promise. I have a few questions about your neighbor Adeline Bell. I was actually just discussing the same questions with Sally next door."

"Oh. Okay. No problem at all. I'm happy to help in any way that I can." She held the door open for me. "I'm sorry, I would have changed if I knew someone was coming over." She adjusted her baggy shirt as if it helped her appearance at all.

"My apologies. I should have called ahead." I stepped in before she had a chance to change her mind. "I hope I didn't catch you at a bad time." What I was saying was pleasant, but I wasn't acting pleasant. I was staring everywhere but at her. Her house was a similar layout to Sally's, but the floorplan seemed way more open. More modern. If the houses in this neighborhood were all the same age, Rosie had done some major renovations. She also had much better taste than Sally. There were no tchotchkes or wallpaper in sight.

"Not at all. I'm an author. I look like this because I've been stuck in a writing cave for the past month."

That made me look back at her. "A cave?"

She laughed and tucked another loose strand of hair behind her ear. "Figuratively. I just mean that I'm on a roll. Too busy to shower." She laughed. "Um…can I get you something? Or…" She seemed at a loss for words for someone whose job it was to write them.

"I'm good. Really, I just want to know if you were close to Adeline? I heard you were about the same age."

"I don't know if anyone was that close to her. She was a very private person."

"Do you think she could have done that to her own house? Or do you think someone else did it?" I had given up on the possibility of Adeline being Violet. Even though there were no pictures of Adeline, Sally seemed positive they weren't the same person. It was one of the only things I believed that came out of her mouth. Which meant I wasn't really here about the case. I was here about Violet.

"I guess anything is possible."

"Right. But what do you think?"

"I couldn't say. She didn't seem violent to me, if that's what you're asking."

Neither did Violet. Sally insinuated that something had happened in this house though. Something bad. "Did you renovate when you moved here? Or was the floorplan already like this?"

"We knocked down a few walls. But I promise it's all up to code."

I ignored her and walked toward one of the rooms off the foyer. I ran my thumb along a deep gash in the molding around the double glass doors. "What happened here?"

"That was there when we moved in. This is some of the only original molding left down here. We converted the living room into my office and put in a few doors. But the molding is the same. I thought the mark added character. I assume it was the previous owner's dog or something."

It didn't look like just any ordinary animal scratch. It was too deep and thick. The mark was also too high, unless the dog was some kind of giant monster breed. I let my hand fall back to my side and then noticed a similar marking in the wooden floor. The gashes didn't necessarily mean anything bad had happened here like Sally had suggested. Furniture being moved around the house could have nicked the wood like this. I tried not to shake my head. But the gashes were so deep. Like something was driven into them with a lot of force. But what? And why? I looked back up at Rosie. "Did you ever meet the previous owners?" *Violet's mother and stepfather.*

"No. We were new to the area and moved here from out of town. We fell in love with this neighborhood and this was the only house for sale. It had been vacant for quite a long time, apparently."

"Why was that?"

"The community just seems really tight-knit, which we thought would be a nice change of pace from..."

"Not why you fell in love with the place. Why was the house vacant? Such a prime location...surely there was a reason."

"I'm not one for stories. All I know is that we love it here."

She was literally a writer. How could she not be one for stories? This woman was the opposite of Sally. It was refreshing and frustrating at the same time. "Do you remember the previous owners' names?"

"Their last name was...Jones I believe? Or Johnson or something pretty common with a J. Definitely Johnson. I'd have to look up their first names. But I have the document somewhere if you'd like to wait."

I shook my head. "No, that's okay." I was hoping their last name would be Clark. The house must have been through a few owners since Violet lived here. But that didn't mean there wasn't anything here to find. The gash in the molding was unsettling. Like someone had hit it with something sharp. And I doubted it was an accident. My mind was leaning toward a struggle. Alarms were going off in my head. I imagined whatever had made this mark slicing through skin instead. What had happened here? "Have you remodeled the upstairs too?"

"Only the master bedroom and bathroom. The rest of the bedrooms and hallway bathroom haven't been touched. They're our next project."

"Do you mind if I take a look around upstairs?"

"Um…why?"

"We believe that Adeline was good at hiding stuff."

Rosie gasped. "In other people's homes?"

Sure. "Yup." I wasn't trying to scare her, but I needed to look around those rooms. One of them had belonged to Violet when she was younger. I needed to see if there were any more signs pointing toward violence in the house. And what better place than a childhood bedroom?

"By all means then. I don't even think she was ever in my house though."

"She was a very sneaky woman." I honestly didn't know anything about Adeline. Or care. It was like the upstairs was calling to me. Like there was a secret waiting to be found.

Rosie nodded.

"I'll be right back then." I turned and walked up the stairs, even though I felt like running. The room at the end of the hall caught my attention right away. There was a huge window, spilling light into the hallway. When I walked closer, I realized it was a view of the woods out back. I pushed the door open further. Violet loved the woods. Was this why? I walked closer to the window. In the backyard I could almost make out a trail leading straight into the woods. It would be easy to follow that later. For now I only had a few minutes to scour this room.

I stepped away from the window and started looking around. There was nothing unusual jumping out at me. No more gashes in the door frames or floor. *The floor.* I thought about the loose floorboard in Violet's current bedroom. I got down on my hands and knees and started feeling around for floorboards with a little give to them. There weren't any at the foot of the guest bed in the room. But Violet's furniture probably hadn't been arranged the same way. I continued to crawl around on my hands and knees. Two planks of wood in front of the bedroom door were worn out. Almost like something had been dragged across the floor. I glanced to the left, the worn wood continuing until all of a sudden it stopped. Something had been repeatedly moved back and forth in front of the bedroom door. A dresser or desk maybe? A makeshift barricade.

Violet had been scared of something. I thought about the rumors swirling around town. She needed help and no one was there for her. I crawled over to where the wood continued to fade. And that was when I found it. A board with a little wiggle to it. I pried it open and stared down into an empty hole. *Nothing.* My excitement immediately vanished. Violet had hidden something here, but she had taken it with her. *Damnit.* Another dead end.

I was about to throw the floorboard back down when I felt an indent on the bottom of it. I turned the board over in my hands and stared down at the carvings inside of it.

There were tally marks. Dozens of them. No, hundreds of them. She was counting something. Or counting down to something. A chill ran down my spine. Maybe she was counting down the days until she took action. The days until she murdered her whole family. Because the only thing more alarming than the tally marks etched into the wood were the words carved in the very center.

"The only escape is death."

CHAPTER 15
Violet

I pulled my warmest sweater over top of a long-sleeved shirt. Maybe I'd pick up a new coat while I was in town today, if I could handle walking through the whispers for that long. Sometimes I'd drive an hour away just to avoid the gossip. Leaving town always felt liberating. I could walk around without anyone staring or pointing.

But I didn't have that luxury today. While Zeke was at school I needed to go to the exact same store we had originally gotten Lizardopolous from. I had no idea what kind of lizard it was, but I knew where in the store we had found him. Plus, if that didn't work, I had the receipt. It wasn't detailed with the species, but hopefully the shop owner would be able to tell me what kind of lizard I had bought if I couldn't find it myself.

Backup plans always made me feel better. But today's plans hadn't helped calm me down at all. There had to be a suitable replacement or I was royally screwed. Doubling down and lying to my son all weekend? There was no going back from that.

I had even snuck outside a few times and searched for him at night. And called for him, which was ridiculous. The little lizard didn't know his name. He was a lizard. Zeke and I had also destroyed the house "searching" for him.

Today could have gone a little smoother if I had at least gotten an early start. I had learned to go shopping as early as possible if I had to do it in town. Grocery shopping was one of those things. Food spoiled when you drove around with it for an hour. But I hadn't gotten an early start. I had been cleaning up the mess we'd made all weekend in our fake search. It wouldn't have taken that long, but I wasn't doing well today. Physically I felt fine. But I couldn't seem to stop counting. I had stood in front of the couch fluffing the same damn pillow 96 times. I had practically beaten the thing to death.

I knew I was just nervous about going out. But the longer I waited the worse it would be. My logic hadn't stopped me from deciding to clean the house instead of leaving, no matter how much sense it made. Once I started something, I had to finish it though. So the house was finally spotless hours later. And I was ready to go. I stared at my reflection in the bathroom mirror. Ready to go just after I washed my hands three more times.

Stop it, Violet. I took a deep breath. My hands were clean. Everything was clean. Soon there would be lunch traffic. There was nothing worse than people in a rush during lunchtime. But my body wouldn't leave the bathroom.

Get a hold of yourself. You'll only be gone for thirty minutes tops. Lizardopolous 2 will be at the store just waiting to be adopted. *If you hurry. Someone else might snatch him up if you don't hurry.*

My pep talk worked. I was out of the bathroom and down the stairs in record time. I started humming, distracting myself from the feeling of doom in my stomach. "Going to get Lizardopolous," I sang as I slipped on a pair of boots, gloves, and a hat. "And Zeke's never gonna know the difference." I shook my hips as I closed the front door behind me. "And he'll live happily in ignorant bliss."

I hoisted myself into my truck and stuck my key into the ignition. It sputtered lifelessly and made a terrible churning noise.

My stupid cheery song disappeared from my mind in a flash. "Shit!" I screamed at the top of my lungs. "Fucking fuckity shit!" I slammed my hands against the steering wheel. God, I had finally forced myself out of the house and now my truck wasn't going to start? What did I do to deserve this torture? I turned the key again and it made the same terrible sputtering noise. "Damnit!" I slammed my hand against the wheel again. And again. And again.

I didn't have time to call a repairman who wouldn't come. Or a tow truck. Or any of that. *You could call Tucker.* I ignored the voice in my head. But it was like the voice was on repeat, saying it over and over on a loop. Like I was standing there fluffing that stupid pillow for half an hour straight again. *Fine, universe. You win, you ungrateful, hideous ogre.*

I climbed out of my truck and slammed the door as hard as I could. It closed slowly, its hinges squeaking with rust. I couldn't even slam the door properly. Piece of junk. I kicked the tire and then silently cursed when it hurt my toes.

I tried to take a few deep breaths, but nothing would calm me down. Before I could back out, I pulled off my gloves and typed in Tucker's number. Hopefully he'd pick up this time. If he had answered my call a few days ago, all of this could have been avoided. I pressed the phone to my ear. It rang several times and then the voicemail kicked on.

I was pretty sure I was about to have a panic attack. I couldn't keep lying to Zeke. I needed to get Lizardopolous 2 today. *Now.*

The voicemail beeped, signaling it was time to leave a message.

"Hey, Detective Reed." I didn't try to lather my voice in fake honey. I said it exactly how I was feeling. Like I wished I was calling anyone else in the world but him. And that my morning wasn't going well. And that I was on the verge of tears because everything around me was falling apart. Including me. "I changed my mind. Not because I want to see you again, but because my shitty truck won't start and I have zero other options for a ride. But I need you to call me back right now. And I don't mean that figuratively. I mean it literally. Like right this second." I started pacing. "We have to go immediately or I can't go at all. It's almost lunchtime and I can't be out during lunch. I don't know what your schedule looks like, but maybe you could take an early break or something? Just…get here or else...." The voicemail beeped, cutting my message short.

Get here or else? Seriously? That made it sound like I was threatening him. I debated whether or not I should call him back. But as I went through my message in my head I started to panic. I hadn't left my name or number. I hadn't even mentioned the pet store. He'd have no idea who was calling. I dialed his number again and held the phone back up to my ear. It went to voicemail again.

"I wasn't threatening you," I said after the beep. "I got cut off. I was going to say, get here or else it'll be too late and we'll have to wait until tomorrow. Which can't happen, because Zeke is already suspicious of my lies. This is Violet by the way." *How many Violet's does a detective know?* "Violet Clark. Call me back if you get this before eleven, otherwise don't bother. But you owe me. Please. I need you."

I need you? I hung up before I said anything else stupid. Why on earth had I said that? I didn't need him. I wanted nothing to do with him. Now he was going to get that message and get all sorts of weird ideas about my intentions.

This day couldn't get any worse. I sat down on the cold ground and leaned my back against the tire. Tears started to stream down my cheeks before I even realized I had started crying. I was officially losing it. It wasn't just the fact that I was nervous about going into town. Or that I got stuck in my head this morning. Or that my car wouldn't start. It was more than that. All the lies were tearing me apart. Lie after lie after lie.

Big lies have big consequences. I heard my mother's voice in my head.

Lying to Zeke about his pet was protecting him. It was a white lie. A small nothing lie. But that was the problem with lies. They stacked on top of each other until they became one big unbearable lie. I felt like I was drowning in my own secrets.

CHAPTER 16

Tucker

The farther I went into the woods, the colder it got. The trees started to blot out the sun in longer increments. But I didn't think it was the chill in the air that was causing me to shiver. It felt ominous out here, just like Damien had warned. And I was cursing myself for not bringing him with me.

The Adeline Bell case had hit a dead end. But there was something else to find. I could feel it in my bones. Maybe Damien would be willing to help me with a case that we hadn't been officially excused from. But I already knew what he'd say. That there was no case and I had lost my mind. It was possible he was right. And I was on even thinner ice with the captain. It was my fault we'd gotten that dispatch the other day to Violet's house. I felt like a grounded teenager.

Just thinking about that made me shake my head. Being grounded was the least of my problems when I was a kid. But Violet? She hadn't felt safe unless she barricaded her bedroom door with furniture. She thought death was the only escape. But from what? What was she counting down the days to?

My phone started ringing in my pocket. I ignored it as I continued to follow the trail. It wasn't paved in stone or anything fancy, but it was worn with use. Years and years of footsteps. The only things that hid it were the colorful autumn leaves. The orange, red, and yellow should have made the trail look happier. But nothing could make being out in the middle of these woods less menacing.

I kept my head down, staring at the path. Until suddenly it ended. I could feel the sun on my face again. The canopy of trees had separated. I looked up and stared at the lake in front of me. It smelled like snow. I couldn't remember the last time I had thought that. Probably when I was a kid wishing for a snow day. But there was something so peaceful here by the lake. The ominous feeling was gone. Everything was just still and silent. There were pieces of ice along the edges. The whole thing would be frozen soon.

My phone rang again, cutting through the silence. I pulled it out of my pocket and denied the call from an unknown number. I just wanted a minute. One minute to myself. Was this how Violet felt when she came here all those years ago? That this was an escape easier than death?

I thought about the letters I had found in Violet's current home. Her ex had asked her to meet him out by the lake. She had probably stood right here with him.

Or maybe I had it all wrong. Maybe that wasn't even her room. For all I knew, she had siblings. Maybe she never came out here. Maybe her ex had been talking about a different lake. I wasn't sure how many lakes there were around here though. Especially in walking distance from Violet's old house.

My phone made a beeping noise, signaling there was a new message. I pulled my attention away from the lake. There were two missed calls and two voicemails. I lifted my phone to my ear as I stared out at the lake. *What are you hiding, Violet? What happened to you?* No matter what I tried to tell myself, it felt like I had been in her room. It felt like she had carved those words into the floorboard. It felt like something horrible had happened in that house, just like Sally had said.

"Hey, Detective Reed." Violet's voice sounded on the message. She sounded pissed. I listened to the rest of it and laughed. My laughter echoed across the water. She had basically threatened me. Get here or else? All she had to do was ask. I'd been dying for another chance to explain myself.

I clicked on the other voicemail. It was her again. Apparently she thought I wouldn't know who was calling. How many Violet's did she think I knew? But I smiled at the last line of her message. *I need you.*

None of the woman I had dated in my past really needed me. Maybe because I usually kept my hookups casual. My job had unusual hours. It was hard to have anything serious. But there was something comforting about the fact that Violet needed my help. That she trusted me enough to ask for it.

I turned my head and looked toward the hill in the distance. I could just make out Violet's house through the trees. After another week of leaves falling I'd be able to see it perfectly. Her home was really close to her old house. If something was scaring her there, why didn't she move farther away? She could have gone anywhere. But she stayed. Why did she stay?

There were millions of questions I wanted to ask her. I looked once more out at the lake before turning around and walking back towards her childhood home. I'd have all afternoon with her. I'd convince her to go to lunch, despite her ramblings about not wanting to be out around noon. Maybe she'd finally open up to me. I just had to make sure I didn't let something slip that she hadn't told me herself yet.

I debated calling her back to let her know I was on my way, but that would just give her a chance to change her mind about me coming over. Besides, she was right. I did owe her. I had killed her son's pet. *Maybe.* It was possible that the lizard was still alive. Although I doubted it would survive after the first snowfall, which could be tonight.

I picked up my pace. I just wasn't sure if it was because I was excited to see Violet or eager to get out of the woods. But I knew that the lake was important to Violet. It might have been a safe haven for her growing up. I didn't love the fact that she used to frequent it with her ass of an ex-boyfriend, but that didn't mean new memories couldn't be made there. Better ones. I wondered if I could use a little of the information I knew about her to get back in her good graces. It didn't feel like cheating to me. Violet was a tough nut to crack. I'd need all the help I could get to make her fall for me.

The thought made me stop right in the middle of the woods. *Fall for me?* Was that what I wanted? I looked down at the worn path beneath my feet. Violet was all I could think about. She was all that I wanted to think about. I took a deep breath of the fresh air. For once in my life it might be nice to be needed.

***

I closed my car door and made my way up to Violet's front porch. The rest of the woods were a little creepy. But here? I was drawn to this place. Her home was warm and inviting, as long as she wanted me there. Today was my chance to prove to her that I belonged there too.

"You came."

I turned around before my foot hit the first step. Violet was sitting on the ground by her truck. Her eyes were red like she had been crying. And I realized it definitely wasn't her home that I was drawn to. It was her. All I wanted to do was put my arms around her and take away whatever pain she was experiencing. But I was still on her shit list.

"I was told I had to come…or else."

She gave me a weak smile. "Threatening cops seems to be my new favorite past time." She turned away and quickly wiped beneath her eyes, like she could hide the evidence of her tears.

I didn't want her to hide from me anymore. I started to walk over to her. "Car trouble?"

"Everything trouble." She stood up and brushed the dirt off her ass. She was wearing a pair of jeans that hugged it perfectly. And a sweater. Just a sweater even though the temperature was dangerously close to dipping below freezing.

When she had been at the precinct a few days ago, I'd asked her if she owned a winter jacket. She had ignored my question. But she clearly didn't. I watched her pull her hat a little lower over her ears. And I realized I didn't really know anything about her. Just the whispers of a town that hated her. Did she even have a job?

I started to unzip my jacket.

"I'm going to stop you right there. I'm not going to steal your…" she sighed as I wrapped my coat around her shoulders.

"It's fine. I was overheated anyway." I wasn't. I could see my breath as I spoke the lie. It was fucking freezing out here.

"You were just sick. You gotta take it easy, Violet, or your cold will come back." I had no idea how long she had been sitting out here waiting for me.

She sighed in the most contented way. "There's a little boutique next to the pet store where I bought my last coat. Maybe we can stop in there after we pick up the replacement lizard? If you don't mind...my truck isn't working again or I wouldn't have asked."

"I don't mind." I glanced at her truck. I could fix appliances around the house, but I honestly didn't know a thing about cars. I'd call Damien later to come check it out. He'd be able to get it started.

She started walking toward my car. "We have to hurry. The stores get crowded around lunchtime."

"And?" I unlocked my car for her.

"And I don't play nice with others." She opened up the passenger side door and climbed in without another word.

She didn't play nice with most people. But I was pretty sure I was wearing her down. Her eyes were glued to her window when I got in the car.

"What happened to your last coat?" I asked as I started the car and drove down her driveway.

She didn't turn her attention back to me. She just stared out the window at the passing trees. "I lost it a few days ago."

"You lost it? Where?"

"I don't think you'd believe me if I told you."

"Of course I'd believe you."

She finally turned to me. Both her eyebrows were raised, like she thought what I said was the most ridiculous thing she'd ever heard. I knew why she was skeptical. This was my chance to clear the air with her. Before I could open my mouth though, she started talking.

"I don't think you've believed anything I've said since we've met. But I get it. No one trusts me." She looked back out her window. "And you certainly wouldn't believe how I lost my jacket."

"I'm sorry, Violet. You have every reason to be upset with me. I tried to tell myself I was so focused on you because I thought you were linked to the case. But I think we both know that wasn't why I kept coming around. If anything, I was just trying to make sure you were in the clear. I never wanted you to be guilty. I just had to make sure. It's my job."

"You pretended to like me so you could look around my house. And I was too sick to even realize what was going on. You took advantage of me."

"I messed up. But I never pretended to like you."

"Right." She was tapping her index finger against her thigh. "Look, I've had a really crappy morning, Detective Reed. Do you mind if we just drive in silence?"

This apology was not going the way I intended. "I meant that…"

"Please just stop. I didn't call you because I wanted to be friends or make awkward pointless small talk. I called you because I had no other options. Zeke needs a replacement lizard and you have a car. End of story. Turn right here."

I had felt good ever since I had gotten her voicemail. She had said she needed me. But I guess she just needed a lift. All I was to her was a chauffeur? I glanced at her before pulling out onto the main road. She was tapping her thigh faster now, like she was upset. This was a communication issue. A trust issue.

And I knew exactly how to fix it. I hit my turn signal, but instead of turning right, I turned left.

CHAPTER 17

Violet

Detective Reed turned left like the incompetent jerk that he was. I was still fuming from his lame attempt at an apology. I was embarrassed enough about the fact that I thought he liked me. He didn't have to rub in the fact that he didn't. His mother clearly hadn't taught him any manners.

"Where are you going? I said right."

He ignored me.

"The pet store is at the mall." I glanced at his dashboard to see the time. "Seriously, it's past eleven. It's going to be so crowded if we don't get there soon."

He didn't answer my very reasonable rebuttal to whatever the hell he was doing. I could feel the same hysteria rising like it had earlier this morning. "Please, please, please."

He didn't respond.

"Please, please, please." Houses started to blur together. "Please, please, please." I couldn't stop saying the words. Over and over and over again. "Please, please, please."

"Violet?" He sounded far away.

"Please, please, please."

He was pulling me out of the car. I felt the sunshine on my skin and the air I desperately needed filled my lungs.

"Violet, take a deep breath for me."

I inhaled so fast it felt like I was choking.

"I'm sorry. I wasn't trying to upset you. Are you okay?" His voice still sounded far away.

The word "please" was echoing around in my head but I swallowed it before it came out again.

"Violet, are you okay?" He ran his thumbs underneath my eyes, wiping away my tears.

Suddenly I could feel him everywhere, like I had just awoken from a dream. His hands were on my face. His breath was intertwining with my own in clouds from the cold. My back was pressed against the side of the car, sandwiching my body between him and the cool metal.

I finally found my voice. "I'm not having a good morning."

"Okay." His hands didn't move from my face. "I'm sorry. I should have just taken you to the mall like you asked, but I wanted to have a nice afternoon with you. I thought that maybe if we were even…" his voice trailed off. "I'm sorry. I didn't mean to upset you."

My mind had slowed down, but my heartbeat was still racing. I wished that everything we had shared up until this point hadn't been pretend, because there was no denying the fact that I liked the way his hands felt on me. I liked being sandwiched here. And he wasn't looking at me like I was crazy even though I had just had a nervous breakdown in his car. He was looking at me like I mattered. Like I mattered to him. I wanted to tell him everything. I wanted him to understand.

"It wasn't your fault," I said. "I got…stuck this morning. And sometimes when I start the day stuck it's hard for me to step out of it."

He didn't understand. I could see it in his eyes. How could I make him understand?

"I was upset all weekend about having to lie to Zeke. And sometimes it feels like I have too much on my shoulders and that makes my…compulsions worse. Doing things repeatedly calms me down. Specifically in sets of three. But when I'm really upset, I do it over and over again. Always in multiples of three but sometimes it's hard to stop." I was blabbering on and on. It felt like I was having another episode, but that wasn't it. He was just making me nervous holding my face like this. I was about to start talking about how I had basically murdered a throw pillow this morning when he fortunately broke the silence.

"Are you okay now?"

"I think so." *It's easier when you're here to calm me down.* "I'm sorry…"

"You don't have anything to apologize for. It was my fault, I should have just done what you wanted me to."

"A change in plans wouldn't have mattered to a normal person."

"Normalcy is a little overrated, don't you think?"

I couldn't count how many times I wished I could go back to the way I was when I was young. Before I started having this problem. All I wanted was to blend into a crowd again. But when he was holding me like this, that desire mattered a little less. If he didn't mind that I wasn't normal, did it really matter so much? Maybe all I really craved was being loved again. I liked that he showed up today. It had been a long time since someone had shown up when I needed them.

It was okay if he didn't like me. Honestly, it was easier if he didn't. But it would be nice to have a friend for once, someone to talk to.

His hands fell from my face as he took a step back from me. It was as if he suddenly realized that the way he was holding me was awkward. That I'd read into it as something more. I felt my cheeks flushing.

"I'll drive you to the pet store now, alright?"

"Yeah." I took a second to soak in my surroundings before I turned back to the car. We were out front of a row of cookie-cutter townhomes on the outskirts of town. I had driven past this street on my way to far away stores countless times. It was the last stretch of homes before you entered a new zip code. "Why did you bring me here?"

He opened his mouth then closed it again, before reaching into his pocket and pulling out a set of keys. "Here." He handed me the keys.

"You're letting me drive?" I laughed. "I trust you not to go on a detour again."

"They're keys to my house." He nodded to the townhome we were parked in front of. "Go look around at whatever you want. I'll be waiting right here to take you to the pet store when you're done."

"What?"

"I want to have a nice afternoon with you. So we need to be even. You were right, I looked around your house. I can't exactly undo what I've done, but I can give you the same opportunity. You get to look around mine without me there. It's only fair."

I looked down at the keys. "This is a weird way to apologize."

"You wouldn't accept my normal one."

I smiled at him. "Well, normalcy is overrated, right?"

He smiled back. "Exactly." He shoved his hands into his pockets and leaned against the car to wait for me.

I appreciated the gesture, I did. But I didn't need it. I could tell that he was sorry. And really, there was only one thing I needed to know in order to forgive him. "Did you find anything incriminating in my house?" I tried to say it lightheartedly, but it came out sounding a lot more like I had something to hide. Which made sense. I had a lot of things to hide.

He hesitated, but only for a moment. "When I carried you to bed, I stepped on a loose floorboard. I went to see if I could set it back in place, but it kind of came up in my hands."

"Okay." My heart started racing in my chest. *Please don't have picked up that floorboard.*

"I should have put it back down, but when I saw the shoebox hidden underneath it, I was just too curious for my own good. I saw some letter from your ex, I guess? Joel?"

"Yeah." He read my letters? It felt like my throat was constricting. "Joel and I dated in high school."

He nodded, like he already knew that. "I only read two I think. There wasn't anything personal in them. One mentioned meeting at the lake. That was it. I realized I shouldn't be looking at them so I stopped right away."

"Okay." I could barely hear anything but my own heartbeat. There was nothing incriminating about the letters. They just made me look pathetic for keeping them so long. But there had been a gun hidden right beneath that box. "And that was all you found?" Again, I sounded guilty. I searched his face for what he had seen, but I couldn't read him at all.

He shook his head. "I also found a handgun."

For a few seconds we were both quiet. I was waiting for him to say he checked and I didn't have a permit for it. He should be arresting me. But...he wasn't.

"It was my stepfather's," I said. "It would be registered under his name, not mine. I didn't know what to do with it after he died, so I just kept it. I don't have any bullets. I've never even fired a gun before. I don't know how to use it. But I disposed of it now, so there's nothing to worry about."

"I wasn't going to turn you in, Violet."

"Oh." I stared at him. *Why?* "It was illegal for me to have it, wasn't it?"

"Having an unregistered gun is illegal, yes. But if it was registered under his name then..."

"It was. His name was Henry Johnson if you want to check."

"Johnson?" He lowered his eyebrows slightly. "His last name wasn't Clark?"

"No, Clark was my father's last name. My mother took Henry's last name when they got married. But I didn't want it. Besides...he never officially adopted me anyway." I wasn't sure why I was telling him all this. "So...you can check the registration now. I didn't mean to do anything wrong."

"I told you it didn't matter. And now that you got rid of it? It really doesn't matter."

I nodded. He could have turned me in but he hadn't. When he showed up on my doorstep a few days ago, I felt like he was there to ruin my life. I had heard a clock ticking down in my head, counting down the hours until I wound up behind bars. But all he had done was help me. Again and again. I wanted to be able to trust him. I wanted to be able to rely on someone. I tossed his keys back at him. "I'm glad we cleared that up."

"Don't you want free rein in my house?"

"I don't need to look around to know what kind of stuff you have hidden in your drawers."

He laughed. "What is that supposed to mean?"

"You're a bachelor. It's all tissues, lotion, and dirty magazines." I climbed in the car and closed the door to the sound of his laughter.

In a few seconds he was sitting down in the driver's seat. "I really am sorry that I lied to you, Violet. Maybe we can just start over?"

There was no need to start over. I was getting used to him being around. I was getting used to him. Besides, rewinding time was impossible no matter how badly I wished I could. I knew that better than anyone. "I kind of like where we are right now."

"So you're not mad at me anymore?" He put the car back into drive and started heading in the appropriate direction this time.

"I was never mad at you. I understood that it was your job. I was just…disappointed."

"Wow, that is such a mom thing to say."

I laughed. But he didn't understand my meaning. I had meant that I was disappointed in myself, not him. People were inherently untrustworthy. A town outsider was no exception to the rule. Maybe the people here hadn't manipulated him yet, but they would. I'd enjoy our time together until that happened. Besides, it was probably only a few minutes away from happening. We were about to go to the mall. He'd see the way people whispered and pointed. He'd feel how horrible it was to be me.

"How often do you have episodes like that?" he asked. He said it so calmly that I barely registered the fact that he was fishing for personal information.

"Maybe a few times a month." I fiddled with the hem of his jacket. "It's usually only when I'm alone. Zeke is good at pulling me out of my head before I get lost in it."

"He's a sweet kid."

"Yeah, he is." Zeke was the one thing in my life I had done right. He was everything to me. "Thank you for not arresting me. I'm all that he has."

"It didn't even cross my mind to."

A comfortable silence settled in the car. I still didn't know why I wasn't in handcuffs, but I was happy that he trusted me for some reason. I stared at his profile out of the corner of my eye. He already had a five-o'clock-shadow growing along his sharp jaw line. He was beautiful. And apparently naïve, if he hadn't learned that everyone is inherently untrustworthy yet. For some reason, I didn't believe my own thoughts though. It was like he trusted me because he *had* lived. Like he had made his own mistakes. Like he was more like me than I could possibly know.

"So, what kind of lizard are we looking for?" he asked.

I snapped my attention back to the road. "I don't know exactly. He was orange and yellow with spots. Sometimes."

"What do you mean sometimes?"

"He changed colors a lot."

"And you have no idea what kind of lizard it was?"

"No, I made Zeke promise he'd take care of him by himself. I never wanted anything to do with the slimy little guy. But I have the receipt for him. And I remember the location in the store that we found him. I'm hoping there will be replacements in the same place."

"Right. How hard could it be?" He pulled into the parking lot of the mall.

I glanced at the time display on his dashboard before he cut the engine. It was only a few minutes until noon. This was going to be a disaster. "It's lunchtime."

"If you're hungry, we can grab a bite to eat." When I didn't respond, he leaned over the center console and grabbed my hand. "It'll be fine, Violet."

I didn't move to get out of the car. I just sat there reveling in the fact that he was holding my hand. It had been years since anyone had held my hand aside from Zeke. It felt…comforting. I realized I was holding my breath and slowly exhaled. "You don't understand what it's like. People can be so cruel."

"I'm a detective. I know perfectly well how cruel people can be. A few catty women are nothing to even worry about. Fuck them."

I smiled. He was sweet even if he was naïve. "If you knew what they said, you wouldn't want to be seen with me in public. Maybe I should just run in real quick and…"

"We need a lizard, a winter jacket, and lunch. I'm not waiting in the car. This is going to be fun, Violet. Just try to live in the moment."

Live in the moment? I could barely live outside my own head. "Right. But not lunch. There's no way I'm eating out." I let my hand drop from his as I unbuckled my seatbelt. I ignored the fact that my body suddenly felt cold despite his huge jacket. It was like his touch could warm my whole body. I held the fabric tighter around me as we walked toward the entrance to the mall. And by walked I mean I practically ran. Because I could already feel all the stares. I could hear the whispers. I wanted Detective Reed to be naïve, at least when it came to me, for just a tiny bit longer. He'd be manipulated soon enough. For just one afternoon, I wanted normalcy even if it was overrated. I desperately wanted it.

"I didn't realize you were a sprinter," he said as he caught up to me.

I laughed. "I never did any sports. My mom was pretty strict. I didn't do any after-school programs at all."

"Did you want to?"

I shrugged as he opened the door for me. The blast of warm air made me sigh. "I don't know, I never really thought about it because it wasn't an option."

He stayed close to me as we walked through the mall. He somehow seemed oblivious to all the people staring at us. "What happened to your parents?" he asked.

"My father died when I was really young. I barely remember him. My mom married Henry less than a year after my dad passed away. I thought it would make her happy again. It didn't."

"That must have been hard for both of you to lose your father when he was so young."

"I think it was harder on me than it was on her."

"Why was it harder on you?" he asked.

"She suffered from severe depression for as long as I can remember. My father used to be the only one that could make her smile. She wasn't really present most of the time because she was so doped up on drugs. Almost like she was numb. And when she was lucid, she wasn't very nice. So the dark days stretched for longer periods after my father died. But she had the meds to numb her. I had to feel the loss every day."

"I'm sorry, that must have been hard."

It only got worse. I didn't want to talk about my family. He was asking me too many personal questions. I pointed to the pet store in the distance. "Almost there." I started to pick up my pace, but he grabbed my hand to slow me down. When I pulled him to go faster, he stopped moving completely. And then we were just standing in the middle of the mall holding hands. "People are going to talk."

"If they have nothing better to do, then let them talk."

"You moved here for a reason. Whatever that reason, if you get mixed up with me it'll be ruined."

He lowered both his eyebrows. "Violet…"

"No, Brendan, stay away from her!" a woman shouted as she scooped up her son before he could get any closer to us. "You're going to get yourself killed if you run off like that." She glared at me as she bustled off with her toddler pressed close to her chest.

I had never seen her in my life. But she knew all about me. I could feel my face turning red. There was no explanation needed now. He had just seen firsthand the way people reacted when they saw me. "You don't understand what it's like here. It's not just catty women spreading rumors. They're…horrible,

Tucker. It's like a virus. I've never even seen that woman before."

He squeezed my hand instead of letting go. "I'm glad we're on a first name basis again."

"That's what you took away from what I just said?" I shook my head. "That's the whole point…we shouldn't be on a first name basis. You shouldn't be talking to me at all. Especially in the middle of the mall during lunchtime."

"What is it with you and lunch?" He started walking again, keeping my hand in his.

"It's crowded when…"

"No, I got it the first time you said it. But you're being ridiculous. There's nowhere else I'd rather be right now than here with you. If that makes me part of this town's gossip, that's fine. Lunch shouldn't be a forbidden word in your vocabulary. You have to learn to shake it off. What's that old saying? Sticks and stones may break your bones but words will never hurt you?"

I decided it was better to not tell him about that time someone cut my brakes and I almost careened into a tree. Or how my house became one big cracked egg on mischief night every year. Or that my son sometimes came back from school with bruises on the backs of his hands that literally looked like someone had hit him with a stick. And on top of all that? I disagreed. Words did hurt. Horrid rumors that followed you around for six years had a tendency to sting. I wasn't weak for feeling that pain. I knew what weakness was. I was weak in high school. But now? I was strong because I was still standing in spite of everything I'd been through.

It was easy for someone who had never been ridiculed to say I needed thicker skin. He didn't understand what it was like to be a pariah. I hoped he never would, despite the fact that he was being condescending. There were a lot of things in my life that were out of my control. But this one thing, I could prevent. I could make it so that he never knew what it felt like to be me. And it was easier to distance myself when I was pissed at him.

"Here we are." I pulled my hand out of his and walked into the pet store. I kept my arms folded across my chest so that Tucker wouldn't be able to grab my hand again and headed straight toward the back of the store. The closest aquarium needed my undivided attention.

Tucker cleared his throat. "So your stepfather and mother both passed away too, right?"

I didn't realize that his only two points of conversation were my parents and how small-town gossip was harmless. But I'd honestly rather talk about them than hear anything else about sticks and stones. "Yeah. The summer after I graduated from high school." I'd keep my answers short and to the point. I just needed to find the lizard and get out of here.

"That must have been hard too."

I stood up straight and peered into the top of one of the aquariums. "I was pregnant with Zeke at the time. It was hard to focus on so much all at once. So I chose to be excited for Zeke's arrival instead of mourning a family who never actually wanted me."

"I'm sure they wanted you."

I glared at him. He was putting his own judgment on a situation he knew nothing about again. "You never met them.

Trust me, neither of them loved me. I was just a reminder of my dead father for both of them. And that was the way that they treated me." I looked at the lizards in the next aquarium.

"I'm sorry. Expecting a baby when you were so young must have been hard all by itself. Was his father never in the picture?"

"He made it clear that he wanted nothing to do with the baby. So I wanted nothing to do with him."

"The ex that you have the letters from...Joel. Is he Zeke's father?"

I could still picture Joel asking me to go to California with him. All the promises he'd made. He hadn't meant a word of it. He'd never loved me. But sometimes it was easier to lie. If you lied enough, some days it was hard to remember the truth. "Yes. But Zeke doesn't know anything about his father and I don't want him to. It's always just been the two of us and he's never asked."

"So Joel knew you were pregnant and he just...left?"

"It's easiest to see someone's true colors when things get hard."

"You've kept the letters for all these years, though. Do you still have feelings for him?"

I stopped staring at the lizards. A lot of feelings swirled around when I heard Joel's name. Mostly ones of regret. But if he was asking if I still loved Joel? If he'd asked me a few days ago when I was standing at the lake, I might have said yes. But I wasn't so sure anymore. I was trying to fight the feeling, but I knew I liked Tucker too much to be in love with another man. Liking Tucker was the scariest feeling in the world. I didn't know if I could trust him. I stared into Tucker's eyes and felt this pull between us, something I wasn't sure I had ever felt with Joel. If I had ever felt it with him, six years without him had made me forget. Regardless, I knew it wasn't Joel that I missed. I missed the dream of getting out of this town. I had loved what Joel represented. Freedom.

"No. Honestly, I think I loved the idea of him more than I ever loved him."

"The idea of him?"

"He always had dreams of leaving this town. I wanted that too."

"Then why don't you just leave now?"

Sometimes I dreamed of moving to a big city and disappearing into a crowd. I'd be truly invisible in a city like New York. Most people moved to places like that to be found. But me? I'd blend into the nobodies and the washups.

Leaving wasn't an option now though. If I left, I wouldn't be able to guard my secrets. I'd be found out. People stayed out of the woods because they were afraid of me. If they were no longer scared of the woods, they'd find everything I had tried so hard to keep hidden.

"Zeke and I have roots here. I wouldn't want to just take him out of school." My excuse was incredibly lame. Tucker knew my son hated school. He knew that Zeke was teased endlessly. And he knew that I hated it here. I was freaking scared to leave my house around lunchtime because I didn't want to be seen. But I wasn't going to admit any of that to him. He already thought I was weak.

"Moving is tough. But a fresh start can be a good thing sometimes."

"Is that why you moved here?" I asked. "For a fresh start?"

"I was born and raised in a small town like this. I never expected to leave. But when my mother passed away, everything I looked at reminded me of her. I needed a change. It was like I couldn't move forward. I just kept thinking about how we should have tried something other than chemo. That maybe there was something else I could have done to save her."

I knew what it was like to live with guilt. "Stuck in the past." That was the story of my life. I moved to the next aquarium. "I'm sorry about your mother. What was she like?" It was only fair that I could interrogate him about his parents too.

"Incredibly strong. She raised me by herself."

She sounded like the complete opposite of my mother. Especially because it was so clear that Tucker had adored her. "What about your father?"

"Never in the picture."

"So you can't even control yourself when you see a single mother? You just have to step in and help them even when they're doing just fine on their own?"

"I have a lot of respect for single moms. But if you're asking if I creepily like to date single moms only or something like that? No." He laughed.

Everything he just said was loaded. Did that mean he wanted to date me? Hopefully not. For a few minutes there back at his house, I'd had this tiny shred of hope that we could be more. But it was short lived because it was ridiculous. I moved to the last aquarium. "Well I'm sure there are plenty of single moms around town to choose from if that's your thing. Maybe that woman who yelled at her kid not to come near me was a widow or something. She's probably right up your alley."

"Hey." He put his hand on my shoulder. "Did I say something wrong? I feel like we were having a good time just a few minutes ago."

I ignored the hurt look on his face as I shifted my shoulder so his hand would fall away. "If you haven't heard yet, I'm crazy. You should start listening to all those rumors that don't hurt strong people."

"Whoa." This time he put one hand on either of my shoulders and turned me to face him. "I never said you weren't strong."

"You gotta shake it off, champ," I said in a deep voice. "Sticks and stones may break your bones but words will never hurt you." I rolled my eyes. "It was a great pep talk."

"I didn't mean..." his voice trailed off. "I most certainly didn't call you champ," he said with a laugh.

I shoved his hands off of me.

"I'm sorry, I was never bullied growing up. I just remembered that old saying and said it. It was stupid. Of course rumors hurt people. Do you have any idea how scared I was when I got that dispatch call that you were attacked? I thought it had escalated to violence. I was terrified because I knew it was a very real possibility that you or Zeke were hurt."

I could feel tears welling in my eyes. I blinked them away so he wouldn't see.

"I think you're incredibly strong, Violet. You're amazing." He touched the bottom of my chin to turn so I'd meet his eyes.

I was in trouble. I'd tried pushing him away. I'd tried everything I could think of to save him from me. But he was still standing right there staring at me in *that* way.

"They don't have the right lizard," I said to prevent myself from saying anything stupid.

He glanced at the closest aquarium. "What about that one?" He pointed to one that looked nothing like Lizardopolous.

"It's *green*."

"I'm pretty sure that he was green when I saw him. He blended into the grass along the side of the road."

I shook my head. "He changed colors all the time but he was mostly yellow and orange." Tucker had no idea what he was talking about. "I should go talk to the owner. Maybe he'll be able to remember what type he was." I walked past Tucker, relieved to get a little bit of air. He was wearing down all my walls. Falling for someone wasn't in the cards for me. It was as risky as fleeing my home for the big city. I needed to remember that I had secrets for a reason. Secrets I needed to keep if I wanted to keep my son.

CHAPTER 18

Tucker

Watching my mother slowly die after months of useless chemo had been the hardest thing I'd ever done. The fact that there was nothing I could do to save her had killed me. I had never felt so useless in my life.

I hadn't meant to tell Violet about my mother. Just talking about her brought all the memories swirling to the surface. But it was so easy to talk to Violet. I wanted her to know why I had moved here. It felt like she was my fresh start. Originally I thought it was this town, but when I was looking at her, I knew that wasn't true. I had already broken the law for her. I should have turned her in for having an unregistered gun in her possession but I hadn't even considered it.

She was fighting whatever this was between us, I could tell. But I wasn't going anywhere. I was going to be there for her and her son. No, I didn't make a habit of dating single moms. Honestly I had never dated one before. Violet didn't even remind me that much of my mother. But I was drawn to her regardless. I felt like I was supposed to be here. Like I had come in just the right moment when she needed me.

I turned to look in the aquarium. I hadn't gotten a great look at Zeke's lizard when I was throwing it into the woods. But I knew it was green. There were a few possibilities here. I squinted my eyes at one of the lizards in the corner of the aquarium. He looked about the right size at least.

"Yes, it was two years ago," Violet said.

I looked up to see her and a man walking over to the aquariums. He was walking so far away from her in the aisle that it looked like he was about to run into the feed on the shelves.

It was shocking how rude the woman in the mall had been. She had basically made it seem like Violet was out to kill her child, which was ridiculous. This man was no different. They were all scared of her. Normal rumors about your looks or something like that would be hard to swallow, but they'd be bearable. But rumors that you were violent? The phrase sticks and stones may break your bones but words will never hurt you did not apply. I couldn't imagine what it was like for her to live here. No wonder she preferred not to leave the house. I wanted her to feel safe with me. I wasn't going to hurt her.

"I'm sorry, I don't remember," the store clerk said. "I sell dozens of them a week. Are you sure it was even me who sold it to you?"

"Yes, of course I'm sure."

The man responded with a shrug.

"Could you at least tell me which lizards are usually yellow and orange though? Ours was usually those colors."

"It all depends on what they're near."

"So you have no idea what kind of lizard he was?"

"I'm sorry. My manager will be in tomorrow if you want to talk to him."

Violet sighed. "No, I can't wait. Tucker, which one did you say looked like him?"

I pointed to the one I had just been looking at.

Violet leaned down to study him. "I should have paid better attention. I honestly have no idea if he looks anything like Lizardopolous."

The store clerk laughed. "Cute name."

Violet ignored him and stared at the new lizard. "We'll take this one," she said. "God I hope you're right." Her eyes met mine. "Do you think Zeke will be able to tell the difference?"

"Hopefully he'll just be happy to have him back."

She nodded her head. "I hope you're right." She watched as the man pulled the requested lizard out of the aquarium. "He's too young to learn about death, you know? I want to protect him as long as I can. He still believes in Santa Claus and the Easter Bunny. I don't want him to know how horrible the real world is."

"It's going to be okay. He won't be able to tell the difference." I didn't know for sure, but if we were both there to pretend this new lizard was the real deal, hopefully Zeke would believe us.

A few minutes later the clerk handed us a small plastic container with a brand spanking new lizard.

"Zeke's going to be able to tell," Violet said as we left the store. "He's really smart for his age. I just know he's gonna know."

I was carrying the new lizard or else I would have grabbed her hand to reassure her. "How about I be there when you tell him you found it? Kids believe adults. Especially when they're outnumbered."

She laughed. "That would be great if you could help convince him."

"No problem at all. I have the whole day off. Speaking of which, do you still want to look for a jacket? If you want to keep mine, it's fine, but I should probably get a new one then. Winter will be here before we know it."

"I'm not stealing your coat," she said with a laugh. "I'll grab a new one real quick while we're out. This was the boutique I was talking about." She ducked into the store before an approaching group of women could notice us.

I followed her in and looked around at the array of clothing. I lifted up the price tag of the shirt I was next to and tried not to let my eyes bug out of my head. Who could afford to pay this much for two pieces of material sewn together? I looked up to see that Violet was already trying on a jacket.

No one should look sexy in a poofy winter coat, but somehow she did. Or maybe the ridiculous price tags actually did make a difference. I watched her pull her hair out from underneath the fabric and turn to look at the mirror. No, it was her. She'd look good in anything. I watched as she looked at the price and had no reaction. Could she actually afford to buy clothes here? I had just been wondering earlier if she even had a job.

The plastic container moved in my hand. I look down to see the lizard clinging to one of the side walls. It was almost like he was staring at Violet too. "She's pretty, huh?" As soon as I said the words out loud I felt like an idiot for talking to a lizard. I walked over to Violet.

"That one looks good on you," I said.

She turned away from the mirror. "Thanks. I guess I'll get it."

For a second I thought she was kidding. I had been shopping with women before. They never bought the first thing they tried on. At least not before trying on a million other things and pretending they looked fat in all of it. "You don't want to try on any others?" There were at least two dozen more to choose from.

"Nope. I guess you can have this back now." She held out my coat for me.

I would have been worried that she was just trying to cut her time with me short, but she had already invited me back to her place to help convince Zeke that this imposter I was holding was the real deal.

"Need anything else while we're out?" I asked, not that I minded her calling me if she needed to go out again before her car was fixed. Which reminded me that I still needed to call Damien to come out and look at her truck.

"Nope," she said again.

I wanted to try to persuade her to eat with me. We were already in the mall during lunchtime. What did it matter now? I followed her to the checkout counter. "Want to get a bite to eat?"

"Nope."

"Is that your new favorite word?"

"Nope," she said with a laugh as she pulled out three hundred-dollar bills from her purse and handed them to the checkout girl.

That answered my question about if she could afford the clothes in this place. Who carried around that kind of cash? The detective in me couldn't help but have a nagging thought - someone that was ready to flee at any moment would carry around that much cash. Someone who was guilty of something. I tried to shake away the thought but my mind immediately went to another detective thought. Her mother and stepfather's last name was Johnson. That meant the house I had been searching earlier today had been vacant for several years before Rosie moved in.

Violet's childhood home was in a prime location in a great neighborhood. It should have been highly sought after. Unless there were more rumors that I didn't know about yet. Sally had said that something terrible had happened in that house. Even though her scale of terrible started at stolen lawn gnomes, it didn't mean it didn't include something actually horrible. Houses didn't just remain vacant for no reason. They remained vacant because no one wanted to move in.

Violet assumed I hadn't heard those rumors. I had. I watched her grab the bag with her new coat. She turned to face me with a smile. The rumors couldn't possibly be true. I dealt with my share of criminal masterminds and murderers in my job. Violet wasn't one of them. I could feel it in my gut. But I still needed to look up what had happened to her parents. I got the sense that she didn't want to answer any more of my invasive questions. And now that I knew their last name it would be easy.

"We're going out to eat," I said.

"No…we're going back to my place."

"I'm the one driving. And I'm also holding Lizardopolous 2 hostage." I lifted up the plastic prison. "You kinda have to do what I say."

She opened her mouth and then closed it. "You're holding him ransom?"

"Come on," I said. I started to walk out of the store backward.

"Why are you trying to torture me?"

"Lunch with me is anything but torture, I promise."

"Tucker, look out!" she said a second too late.

I collided with someone behind me and dropped the container Lizardopolous 2 was in. It fell to the floor and the top popped open. "Shit." I quickly grabbed him around the middle before he could scurry off like his predecessor. I wasn't going to lose another lizard. "I'm sorry," I said without looking up.

"Tucker?"

I recognized that voice. I looked up to see my ex, Julie. And I felt…nothing. I expected to feel something. After she had dumped me, I had moped around for months, according to Damien anyway. But seeing her again after all this time? There was nothing left between us. "Oh. Hi, Julie."

"Are you sure a pet's a good idea? You don't exactly have a lot of free time from what I recall." She glanced over my shoulder and frowned.

The lizard squirmed in my hand. I shoved it back into its container and popped the lid back on. I made sure it was completely secure before I stood up. "This little guy is actually for Violet's son. Violet, this is Julie. My ex," I added because for some reason this situation didn't feel awkward enough already. "Julie…Violet." Now it felt even more awkward because I didn't say what Violet was to me. I couldn't say girlfriend. And friend seemed harsh.

Violet didn't take a step forward to introduce herself. She just nodded and held the bag from the shop closer to her chest. It looked like she wanted to be anywhere in the world but here.

"We already know each other," Julie said. "Isn't that right, Vi?" She turned her attention back to me. "We went to high school together."

"Oh." I didn't know the whole story about what had happened to Violet. But I knew all her problems started in high school and that no one seemed to have offered her any help. Violet was clearly uncomfortable standing in the middle of the mall like this. And I didn't care to make small talk with my ex anyway. "Well, it was nice seeing you, Julie. If you'll excuse us, we were just heading to lunch."

"Together?" Julie looked even more surprised than she had when she first saw the lizard in my hand. "Tucker, can I talk to you for a second? In private?" she added.

"Like I said, we were just…"

"It'll only take a second." She wrapped her manicured hand around my forearm. "You don't mind, do you, Violet?"

"Of course not," Violet said. She glanced down at Julie's hand on my arm.

I pulled my arm away from Julie.

"I'm just going to look around in there for a bit." Violet pointed back to the store we had just come out of. She walked away before I had a chance to say anything at all.

"What the hell are you doing buying a lizard for crazy Vi's kid?" Julie hissed before Violet was even out of earshot. "What are you doing hanging around her at all? Are you insane?"

"I'm not having this conversation with you. You broke up with me, remember?" *After I caught you sleeping around.*

"Um yes, I remember. I did it because you never had any time for me. And here you are prancing around the mall in the middle of the day with a psychopath. What the hell, Tucker?"

"Violet isn't crazy."

"I think I know her a little better than you do. I freaking grew up with her. We used to be really good friends."

"What a friend you turned out to be."

"It wasn't my fault that she lost her mind senior year."

Violet could have used a friend. She lost everyone in her life. I shook my head. "I gotta go, Julie."

"That crazy bitch murdered her parents and ex-boyfriend. Are you trying to get yourself killed?"

"She didn't murder anyone. You shouldn't believe everything you hear."

"Right because her parents died in a boating accident down in Florida?" She put air quotes around accident. "And poor, sweet Joel just up and left for Hollywood before graduating? It's too convenient. Everyone from your life doesn't just suddenly disappear. I heard she cut them up into little bitty pieces and hid them under her floorboards."

I knew Julie and I weren't compatible. But I had no idea she was so coldhearted. Two women walked by whispering to one another and pointed at the store that Violet had just disappeared into. This whole town was coldhearted. I was done with this conversation. "This has been a very enlightening conversation. But if you'll excuse me..."

"Are you sure you're okay?" She put her hand back on my forearm. "Maybe we should get drinks tonight and catch up?"

"I have plans, sorry." I pulled my arm away from her.

"With her and her son?" She shook her head. "I'm worried about you, Tucker."

"We both know you don't care about anyone but yourself."

Her jaw dropped in an overly shocked expression. "I'm trying to look out for you. What are people going to think if they see you two together? Can you even imagine what they'll assume?"

"I don't care what people think."

"Well you should. She's bad news, Tucker. God, you're supposed to be a detective. Can't you tell when someone's not quite right in the head?"

I was done listening to this. "Have a good rest of your day, Julie."

"Please, Tucker. You can't date her. What will people say when they hear you went from dating me to her?"

"That I made a hell of an upgrade." I started walking back toward the store, being careful not to run into any assholes this time.

"Yeah, literally no one around here is going to think that. They're going to think you lost your mind too!" she yelled to my back.

I didn't see Violet anywhere in the store. I walked back to the changing rooms. "Violet?"

"I'm here," she said behind one of the doors.

I leaned against the wall by her changing room. "I'm sorry about that."

"Sorry about what?" Her tone was overly casual.

I looked at the door. "About the way she acted."

"You sound surprised. She's always acted that way around me."

I winced. "She said the two of you used to be friends?"

"No. I had a lot of *friends* in high school, but it turns out they merely put up with me because I dated Joel. When he left, they made that pretty clear."

"I'm sorry."

"I'm not. There's nothing worse than fake people."

I smiled, and then realized she couldn't see my face.

"So you dated Julie Sinclair, huh?" she asked through the door.

"For a little while after I moved here, yeah."

"Why'd you break up?"

"Because I didn't have enough free time to devote to her."

"Funny, because I'm having trouble getting rid of you."

We both laughed.

"Do your friends call you Vi?" I asked. That's what Julie had called her. It was the same name that Joel had written in his notes to her.

There was a long stretch of silence. "I don't have any friends."

"Would you mind if I call you that?"

"Are you asking to be my friend, Detective Reed?"

I smiled as I stared at the door. This was one of the best conversations I'd ever had with her. Why was it that it was easier to talk to her when we weren't face to face? "If I'm being completely honest, I don't have any intention of staying just your friend for very long. You got upset earlier when I said I wasn't pretending that I have feelings for you. That's because I didn't have to pretend. I like you, Vi. I've had a hard time not thinking about you ever since you opened your door in barely anything at all."

The lock on her door clicked and for a second I held my breath. I was picturing her opening the changing room door in nothing at all. But I wasn't disappointed when she opened it and she was wearing the exact same thing she had been earlier. She didn't even have any clothes inside to try on. She had just been hiding out. For some reason that made me like her even more.

"I don't like to eat out in public," she said.

"Okay. How about takeout then? We can eat it back at your place."

She nodded. "I'd like that."

CHAPTER 19

Violet

I opened up the door to put the takeout bag in the backseat, but there was a plate of cookies sitting on the seat already. A plate of very familiar looking cookies. I placed the bag down beside them and then joined Tucker in the front.

"I take it you've met Sally?" I gestured to the cookies.

"Yeah. I was questioning her this morning. She was one of the witnesses to that house fire."

"How is that going by the way?" I hadn't been questioned by anyone but Tucker. My worst fears had passed. There were no cops and dogs sniffing around in my woods. Everything had quieted down.

"The case?"

I nodded.

"I'm not really supposed to talk about it. But there isn't really anything to talk about anyway. I'm done."

"So…is it closed?"

"No, I'm just off it. The FBI took over."

"The FBI?" My voice came out a little squeaky. I was relieved that there weren't police dogs roaming the woods, but compared to the FBI, a few stupid animals and local officers were harmless.

He glanced over at me. "It's fine. We both know you had nothing to do with that fire. I'm sorry I ever doubted you. It was a bad case of being in the wrong place at the wrong time. I got a little obsessed with trying to figure out if you were linked because I needed to know that you weren't guilty."

"Right." It was true, I had nothing to do with Adeline Bell or her house. I'd never even met the woman. But that didn't mean I had nothing to hide. There were a lot of things I wanted to keep secret in the vicinity of the crime scene. "So you don't know anything that's going on with the case at all anymore?" I played with the zipper of my new jacket. Up down, up down, up down. At this rate I was going to break it before I even got home. I let go of the zipper and put my hands beneath my thighs so that I couldn't fidget.

Tucker shook his head. "Nope. My captain took me off the case."

"Then why were you questioning Sally?"

"There were just a few loose ends I needed to tie up on my end before I felt comfortable dropping it." He kept his eyes on the road.

"It's hard to know what's true and what isn't when it comes to Sally," I said. I thought that maybe he was interested in me because he hadn't heard the rumors. But if he had hung out with Sally all morning? He knew everything that people whispered behind my back. And what everyone said behind those people's backs. And so on. She was a sweet lady, but an awful gossip. I wouldn't have been surprised if she had been behind the initial rumors about me.

"So what actually happened to your jacket?" he asked.

The change of topic was a reprieve. But it was a little unsettling that he changed it. *He knows. He knows exactly what they say*. I cleared my throat. "Well, now that you're off the case, it wouldn't be as interesting to you. It's kind of my alibi."

He didn't say anything, he just waited for me to continue.

I wondered if he was being truthful about being off the case. Or even believing that I wasn't involved at all. I leaned my head against the headrest and stared at him for a moment. He didn't look like a detective today. He just looked like…Tucker. The guy I was slowly getting to know despite my best efforts. Probably despite his as well. "I was out by the lake when I heard the explosion. It scared me and I fell in." I remembered the feeling of my mother's hands on top of my head, keeping me under. "My jacket was weighing me down and I had to ditch it in order to get back to the surface." It had felt like someone was grabbing my ankle, trying to pull me deeper. Like all my secrets were trying to drown me. I took a deep breath. That feeling had been haunting me ever since.

Tucker laughed, unaware of my distress. "I thought you had just dyed your hair to get everyone off your tail." He shook his head. "Makes sense now. Why you were so wet."

Something about the way he said it made me swallow hard.

"No wonder you caught a cold. The lake was pretty icy when I was there this morning."

My heart rate kicked up a notch. "You were at *my* lake?" *Shit.* I was worried about random cops and dogs poking around in my business. I thought I was done worrying about Tucker.

"Yours?" He smiled at me as he made the turn onto the road that led to my house. There were no other houses, so it was basically a super long driveway. "It's public property, Violet."

"I know. But no one ever goes out into these woods."

"Because they're scared of you?"

"Yeah, I guess." *What do you know that you're not saying?* I started fidgeting with my zipper again. *Stop it.*

"Well, you're forgetting one important thing." He pulled his car to a stop next to my truck and cut the engine. "I'm not scared of you, Violet."

"Maybe you should be." It was a warning I hadn't even meant to say. But it was true. It wasn't very wise to listen to the word of one person over dozens of others.

He lowered his eyebrows as he stared at me. "I thought we were done pushing each other away?"

"I don't know how any of this works. I haven't been on a date in six years, Tucker."

"What are you so worried about?"

You seeing the real me. I shook my head. "I'm worried that I've become what they say I am."

"And what is that?"

"A monster." It came out as a whisper. For years I had wondered it myself. I had made some mistakes, just like everyone else. But they didn't make me a monster. Everyone deserved a second chance. I knew that in my heart. But it was like I had been waiting this whole time for a flip to switch inside of Tucker. Why didn't he see what everyone else saw? Sometimes I even saw it when I looked in the mirror. Sometimes I was worried that a similar switch would flip inside me and I'd repeat my mistakes. Again, and again, and again. The thought made me feel nauseous.

"You're not a monster, Violet."

"I know you've heard the rumors." I turned in my seat to see him better. "Just rip the Band-Aid off. What have you heard?"

"Nothing nice."

"You don't have to sugarcoat it. I've heard them all. I just…need to know what you've heard." Maybe I was wrong about Sally. Maybe she had learned to keep her big mouth shut after all the hurt she'd done.

"The basic consensus is that you cut up your family and ex-boyfriend into little pieces and hid them under your floorboards."

Wow. "I actually hadn't heard that last part." I exhaled slowly. "That's new." And how utterly ridiculous. The smell would be horrible.

"When I still thought you were involved in my case, my first thought was that I had found something hidden in your floorboards." He laughed it off. "But you've never even fired that gun you owned. I know you're not capable of hurting anyone. Especially your own family."

"Because that would make me a monster." It came out as more of a question. I bit the inside of my cheek. Why did I ask him that? Of course murder made you a monster. Of course. Of course. Of course. The words echoed around in my head.

"Yes." He laughed. "Murdering your family in cold blood would make you a monster."

Of course, of course, of course.

"Violet." He reached across the center console and grabbed my hand. "I don't believe rumors. I believe you."

My mouth formed a smile but it felt a lot more like a grimace. "We should probably eat before it gets cold."

He nodded and let go of my hand. I sat there and watched as he unbuckled his seatbelt and stepped out of the car. I took a deep breath before I got out, in hopes of clearing my head. He believed me. For now. I needed to remain calm or else I'd start to look crazy. It was hard to trust a crazy person. I climbed out of the car.

"Seems like Zeke likes when I bring dessert." Tucker grabbed the plate of cookies and balanced it on top of the plastic container holding Lizardopolous 2. "Maybe cookies will distract him from what this lizard looks like."

I grabbed the takeout bag. "I hope so."

***

I placed the last plate in the dishwasher and glanced back outside. Tucker was still standing next to Damien, who was leaning under the hood of my car. Tucker was moving his hand around animatedly as he talked to his friend. It looked like he was arguing with him about something. I had clear tells for when I was upset. I started doing everything in threes. Most people could hide their mood a little easier than me. But Tucker didn't know that anyone was watching him. And I had a feeling that he was upset right now. The only question was why.

I wiped my hands off on the front of my jeans and kicked the dishwasher closed with my foot. All I wanted to do was eavesdrop, but I was trying to do the whole trust thing. I tossed the dish towel on top of the dry rack.

Lizardopolous 2 was safe in his predecessor's aquarium. Our fake story for how he came home was solid. Zeke would most certainly avoid the whole conversation about death for at least a little longer. The house was once again spotless. There was nothing else for me to do.

I glanced at Tucker out the window again. It was only nice to offer them a drink or something, right? Bringing them coffee on a cold day like this wasn't eavesdropping. It was being polite.

I opened up my cupboard. Coffee made sense, but Zeke would be home soon. Maybe I could make hot chocolate for all three of them. Was that weird? I drank hot chocolate with Zeke all the time, but I wasn't sure most grown-ups drank it. Especially those without children. *Who cares.* Tucker already liked me. He had made that pretty clear. Damien did not like me one bit. He had also made that very clear. A good cup of hot cocoa wasn't going to change either of their opinions. I pulled out the mix.

When I had two cups with the perfect ratios of milk and chocolate, I dropped a handful of marshmallows on top of them. Who could resist a steaming cup of hot chocolate with marshmallows? Sure, murdering your whole family made you a monster, but not liking this beverage? Extra monstrous.

I opened up the front door while balancing the two piping hot mugs in my hands. Tucker and Damien's conversation drifted to my ears and for some reason I froze instead of making my appearance known.

"It was foul play, I'm sure of it," Damien said.

Were they talking about me? Or some random case? I held my breath.

Tucker placed his hand on the side of the truck. "And I think there's more going on here than that. How has no one looked into this before?"

They could be talking about anything. Or anyone. Tucker had told me they were done investigating me. They were done with the case, period.

"You've been completed blinded by a nice pair of tits. I've arrested plenty of dimes. Just because she's hot doesn't mean she didn't do it."

I cleared my throat.

Damien jumped, slamming his head against the hood of the car. "Fuck."

"Sorry. I'm sorry." I quickly walked down my porch stairs. I didn't know what else to do. I couldn't just retreat back into my house without another word. They knew that I knew that they were talking about me. They had been, right? The best thing to do would be to pretend I didn't hear. Besides, my motherly instinct had kicked in and I wanted to make sure he was alright. "Are you okay?" I thrust both of the mugs in Tucker's hands and tried to examine Damien's head. I was surprised when he didn't pull away from my touch. There was already a welt forming at the base of his skull. "I'm so so sorry, Damien." I stopped touching him when I realized I was being weird. I wasn't this grown man's mother.

He rubbed the back of his head where my hand had been. "Yeah, I'm fine. You just startled me. Never sneak up on a man underneath the hood of your truck." He gave me a super charming smile. One that he probably only gave when he was trying to get a woman to forget he'd just done something stupid.

"You'll probably have a nasty bruise if you don't ice it right away. I have an ice pack inside I can grab. If you want."

"I'm almost finished out here. But I might take you up on that when I'm done. Is that for us?" He nodded to the hot chocolate.

"Yes." I smiled at Tucker as I took one of the cups back and handed it to Damien. I was actually getting along with his friend for once. It felt almost normal. Like we'd all been friends our whole lives.

"Is it spiked?" Damien waggled his eyebrows at me.

Never mind. We were most certainly not friends. Anyone who really knew me would know why I didn't have any alcohol around. But no one really knew me. "I don't actually keep any alcohol in the house."

"Why is that?"

I shrugged. "It's usually just me and Zeke. There's no need." That sounded better than the truth.

"Maybe the four of us could all have dinner tonight?" Damien asked. "I can bring the wine."

"Oh." I couldn't exactly tell him no. I certainly owed him after he'd spent all afternoon working on my truck. "Yeah. Sure, that would be great. Making dinner for you is the least I can do to thank you." What the hell was I doing? One detective in my house was bad enough. But two? *Two?* Had I lost my freaking mind?

"Perfect. I just need a few more minutes out here and then I'll go get cleaned up. Need me to grab anything else for tonight?"

I glanced at Tucker.

"Maybe we should do it another night," Tucker said.

"What? It'll be fun," Damien said. "Right?" He looked back at me.

"Absolutely." I thought about what they'd been talking about when I had first stepped outside. *Just because she's hot doesn't mean she didn't do it.* I'd need to keep a close eye on Damien tonight.

"This is delicious, Violet," Damien said after he took a sip from his mug.

The way he said it made me feel uncomfortable. Like he wasn't talking about the hot chocolate at all. Luckily the sound of Zeke's bus coming down the lane gave me something else to focus on.

The bus slowed to a stop and the doors opened. Zeke was staring at the ground as he started walking down the steps.

A window near the back of the bus squeaked open. "See ya later, Zeke the freak!" one of the kids yelled out the window as Zeke stepped off the bus. "Zeke the freak!" another squeaky little voice yelled. Giggles exploded from inside the bus.

The sound of their laughter made me feel like I couldn't breathe. God, why did kids have to be such dicks? All I wanted to do was storm up to the bus and unleash hell.

Zeke didn't even turn to look at who had said it. He just slouched forward even more. The doors closed and the bus started to turn around.

"Zeke?" My voice was so soft that at first I thought he hadn't heard me.

But then he looked up at me. For a second the sad expression on his face disappeared. Like I was the only one that could make him forget about his crappy day. Then he glanced at Tucker and Damien. He scrunched up his face like he was about to cry and ran straight to the house.

"If you'll excuse me." I ran after Zeke without waiting for a response. "Zeke!" I yelled when I opened up the front door. But there was no reason to yell. He was sitting in the foyer with one rain boot off, one on, and his coat and backpack thrown on the floor. His face was tucked into his knees and he was sniffling.

"Hey. Sweetie." I sat down next to him on the floor and pulled him into my side. For a few minutes I didn't say anything. I just held him until his tears slowed. "It's okay. It's going to be okay." I ran my hand up and down his back.

He didn't respond.

"Tell me what happened on the bus today."

He slowly lifted his tear-stained face. "No one would let me sit with them. The bus driver had to make a kid move so that I'd have a seat all to myself in the front. They yelled Zeke the freak at me the whole way home."

"And the bus driver didn't tell them to stop?"

"He did a few times. They didn't listen. And now Mr. Reed is going to think I'm a freak too. Just like everyone else. And we were friends."

"There's no way he'd think that. He's a grown-up. Grown-ups know better than to listen to dumb kids."

"But everyone else thinks I'm a freak. He will too."

"No, he's your friend. Friends are forever, Zeke."

"Is he your friend too?"

That question felt loaded. He was basically asking if Tucker would be in his life forever. How could I answer that? Instead, I just nodded and tried to change the subject. "And you know all those kids that pick on you? They're going to have pimply faces well into their thirties and work for minimum wage the rest of their lives."

"What's minimum wage mean?"

"It means they're stupid and won't have good jobs. So the joke's on them because you'll be rich and successful and have beautiful skin."

"But being a grown-up is far away. And I don't want all those things if it means right now has to suck."

That was a very fair point. "How about I start driving you to school?" The thought of doing that was dreadful. Leaving the house twice a day to face ridicule myself? Awful. But so worth it to save Zeke from one more second of it.

"Really?" He finally looked up at me.

"Really." I tickled his side and he smiled. "It'll be fun."

"Will it make you do that thing?" He tapped my shoulder three times. "I don't want you to do it if it'll make you do that thing."

"We'll figure it out together, okay, little dude?"

He nodded. "Thanks, Mommy." He hugged my side and now I tried not to cry.

I knew kids picked on him during recess. I had been to the school a few times about it already this year. But I hadn't known about the bus. He hadn't told me. I would have driven him sooner if I had known. And I couldn't help but wonder if he hadn't told me because he was worried about how I'd react. He was worried I'd get lost in my own mind. My issues were starting to weigh on my son, and I couldn't have that. I needed to talk to someone. I glanced at the door. I needed to let someone in.

CHAPTER 20

Tucker

"Zeke the freak," Damien said and shook his head. "Man, she should have named him something like Albert that rhymes with nothing." He set his cup of hot chocolate down. "But then his name would be Albert, so…"

"What the hell was that?" I asked.

"Kids being kids." He pulled the wrench out of his toolkit.

I was pissed about the other kids bullying Zeke, but that wasn't what I was referring to. "No I mean you flirting with Violet? And inviting yourself to dinner."

He lifted his head back up and smiled. "She was the one with her hands all over me. Now I can see why you're so obsessed. She's sweet. And she smells even sweeter."

I slapped him in the back of the head where he had hit it earlier.

"Ow! What the hell?"

"Before she walked out you were just talking about the fact that she was insane."

"Because I just did what you asked. I looked into her stepfather and mother. They disappeared without a trace and I gave you my honest opinion. No one even knew they were moving to Florida. People don't just decide to move and then vanish into thin air. The whole thing reeked of foul play."

"So you think she murdered her parents and now you're hitting on her?"

"I said she was a dime before she even came out. I was trying to see why you're so smitten with her and I get it."

He didn't get it at all. Yes, Violet was beautiful, but I didn't just like her because of her looks. There was something about her that I was drawn to.

"And tonight I can look around to see if there really are dead bodies hidden somewhere in her house while you make googly eyes."

"I already looked around. I told you that."

"But did you look for itty bitty chunks of bodies? Pieces of bones from decay?"

"There's nothing to find. Besides, if her parents really died under suspicious circumstances, why didn't the cops look into it?"

"They did. But technically they died in Florida. There wasn't much to look into here. And the Florida cops are...you know. Florida cops. They just deal with drugs and old people. Homicide isn't their forte."

"Is that why her parents' house didn't sell for so long? Because people think they died in it?"

He nodded. "No one wants to live in a haunted house."

"I was looking around it earlier today. There were these really deep gashes in some of the trim work that were apparently there when the current owners moved in. And in one of the bedrooms there were a few worn floorboards. It looked like furniture kept being put in front of the door, maybe to prevent someone from entering. I think she was scared of something when she lived in that house." I didn't tell him about the other floorboard. There was no reason to add to his suspicion by telling him that Violet did indeed like hiding things under the floor. Besides, the countdown etched into the wood was alarming. The quote more so. *The only escape is death.*

"You think it was already haunted? I know you're a little squeamish, but I didn't think you believed in ghosts, Reed."

"That's not what I meant." I looked toward Violet's house. "What if someone was hurting her?" I hadn't wanted it to be true. But I'd had all day to think about what I had seen. The signs were pointing toward abuse. What else would she be counting down toward but graduation when she could leave town with Joel? The quote etched into the wood made it seem like she was suffering. Someone could have been hurting her. She could have been waiting to escape. *The only escape is death.* But that theory didn't really fit the quote. She didn't seem suicidal or homicidal to me. I couldn't figure out why death had anything to do with her leaving town.

"Have you seen her naked yet?"

His question caught me off guard. "No." What did that have to do with anything?

He laughed. "Your game sucks. But whenever you do get her out of her pants, look for scars. People that were abused usually have proof."

That was true.

"Or I can get her naked if you're too much of pussy to do it yourself. I'd be happy to."

"Just fix her truck."

He leaned back under the hood. "So you really don't think she's guilty?"

"She wasn't involved in that fire. I'm sure of it."

"Does this mean you're actually done with the investigation that you were supposed to be done with last week? For real this time?"

"Yeah."

"So…you could just stop poking around. Leave her alone and move on with your life."

"I don't want to move on." I leaned against the truck. "I like her."

"But you clearly don't trust her or you would have just asked her about her parents and her old house yourself."

My first reaction *had* been to get him to look into it. But it was only because Violet had made it pretty clear she was done talking about them earlier. She was skittish. Another sign of someone who'd been abused.

"Done." He slammed the hood of the truck closed. "Good as new. Well, kind of." He stared at the beat-up truck. "A little rusty for brand new, but still good. I'm going to go shower and I'll be back for dinner. Anything else I should grab besides the wine?"

"She doesn't drink."

"It'll help her loosen up. Loose lips." He winked at me.

I thought about when she'd had Nyquil and didn't realize there was alcohol in it. She did talk more freely, but that could have been the fever. I wanted her to open up to me naturally. Not like this. Especially with Damien around all evening. "I doubt she'll have any. Sure you don't want to make dinner plans with whoever you're hooking up with right now instead?"

"Nah, I wouldn't miss tonight for anything. I've always wanted to see inside that house ever since I was little. The thing was always boarded up. It still gives me the creeps."

"You don't have to come back!" I yelled at him as he climbed into his car.

He flipped me his middle finger and pulled out of the driveway.

I shoved my hands into my pockets and looked at the house. I never should have asked Damien to pull her parents' case file. It just gave me more unanswered questions. The part that bothered me the most was that it was like Julie had said. Technically, Violet's parents had died in a boating accident in Florida. The case was closed but their bodies weren't found. On paper, they had officially drowned. Unofficially? They were still missing. But missing people that didn't want to be found weren't a top priority. Violet had made it clear she didn't like her mother or stepfather. So no one wanted them found.

To anyone else there was nothing to think about. Case closed. But what if she had done something? What if even a tiny piece of the rumors were true? I tried to shake away the thought as I picked up both mugs of hot chocolate and walked up to her house. I should just let it go. What did the past matter? The issue was that it was ingrained in me to keep looking.

Violet opened the door before I knocked. She must have seen me standing out here looking like an indecisive idiot. She stepped out and closed the door behind her.

"He's watching TV. I thought maybe you wanted to be there when I tell him we found Lizardopolous, so I haven't told him yet."

"I thought you didn't have a television?"

"We don't. He subscribed to Hulu without my permission and is watching it on the computer. He said everyone else in school has it." She shrugged.

It was pretty clear she hoped it would help him fit in better. Based on what I saw earlier, I'd say it wasn't working. "How is he doing?"

"Tough day at school. I think I'm going to start driving him." She looked nervous about the prospect.

"I could take him if you want." I had no idea what made me say it. I didn't even know when his school started in the morning.

"Oh. No, I couldn't ask you to do that. I mean, unless my truck is still shot."

"Nope, it's all better." I smiled at her.

"That's a relief. Thanks for calling Damien to come out. I'm not sure what I would have done otherwise. And I'm glad he's coming for dinner. When he refused to let me pay him I was worried he'd hang this over my head or something. It's the least I could do."

The way she was staring at me was making it hard to process what she was saying. Her eyes were captivating, but there was something else there aside from just beauty. It was pain. She was staring at me with so much pain. And I wanted to ease that for her. I wanted to erase what the people in this town had done to her. I wanted to fix it.

"Zeke is going to be okay, you know. Nicknames come and go. It'll pass, you'll see."

"Why, because when he gets older people won't be mean anymore? From my experience, adults can be pretty cruel too."

Her eyes stayed locked with mine. "I overheard Damien say he thought I was guilty."

Damien had been referring to her homicidal tendencies, not the case. I wonder if she'd heard the beginning of the conversation, but I didn't think so. She probably just thought it was about the fire.

"You didn't seem to disagree," she added.

"We weren't talking about the case," I said, trying to stall for a second.

"So Damien wasn't referring to me? How often are you completely blinded by a nice pair of tits?"

It took me a second to register the fact that she was joking. I found my gaze dropping to her chest before I could help it.

She laughed. "It's okay if he doesn't believe me. Maybe I can convince him tonight. But you said you believed me. You do, right?"

"I do. I do want to talk to you about a few things, though. Maybe when Zeke's asleep and Damien's gone?"

"What do you want to talk about?" She looked as nervous as she did earlier when she was talking about driving Zeke to school.

"Nothing serious." I shook my head. I wanted to ask her what happened in her childhood home. I wanted to be upfront about everything. "I just want to get to know you better. One on one."

"You know me better than most people already. But I'd like that."

We both stood on her front porch staring at each other for a few moments. The silence should have been awkward, but it wasn't. It was comforting.

"I'm going to go get the lizard. You remember the plan?"

"I've got it."

She grabbed Damien's empty mug from me and opened up the front door. I followed her inside and shrugged out of my jacket as she left me alone. And then I wandered into the living room where Zeke was parked on the couch with a laptop on the coffee table. He was halfway done his hot chocolate and had the plate of cookies on his lap.

"Found the cookies?"

Zeke looked up. "Mhm. Thanks, Mr. Reed."

"You can call me Tucker." I sat down next to him and took a sip of hot chocolate.

"Okay." Zeke smiled at me before taking a bite of another cookie.

"What are you watching?"

"I don't know, I don't even like TV." He closed the lid of the laptop. "I know you heard what the other kids called me. You don't have to talk to me if you don't want to. I understand." He stared down at his plate of cookies.

"If they don't know you're cool then it's their loss. I love hanging out with you."

"Really?" He looked up at me with so much hope on his adorable little face.

"Really. Kids can be dicks."

"What does dicks mean?"

Fuck. Cursing in my head made me curse in my head again. I needed to watch what I said around him. He was five. I cleared my throat. "It's a bad word, you shouldn't say it."

"But what does it mean?"

"It's like…" my voice trailed off. "It's an offensive term in reference to you know…" I gestured toward my lap. "A penis." What the hell was I doing? I was going to go to jail for pedophilia. I looked over my shoulder, worried that Violet would choose this exact moment to walk in.

"Oh. But the other kids aren't penises. They're just mean."

"I know. Just forget I even said it." *Please.* I took a huge sip of my hot chocolate, so I wouldn't say anything else stupid to the kid.

"You're cool, right?" Zeke asked.

I didn't really know what to say. I fit in well enough in school, but I didn't exactly have jock status with cheerleaders throwing themselves all over me. Now though? Being an adult wasn't really about fitting in. It was about being comfortable with yourself. I shrugged my shoulders.

"You drive a fancy car."

I did drive a nice car. I thought about earlier when I offered to take him to school. Would that help? Driving up to school in my Charger with me could add to his cool factor. Driving to school with his mother in her rundown truck was not going to help him, that was for sure. But Violet didn't want me to do it. Or she at least didn't feel comfortable asking me to do it. "What time does school start?"

"Eight-thirty."

I could probably swing that. Before I could open my mouth, Violet walked in holding the lizard.

"Surprise!" she yelled. "Tucker and I found Lizardopolous today!" She walked over carrying the slimy little creature and held it out to him.

Zeke didn't look nearly as excited as I thought he would. He looked at the lizard, back up at his mother, and then back at the lizard. "If you found him then where is he?"

Violet laughed. "Right here, silly." She held the lizard a little closer to him.

Zeke squinted his eyes at the creature. "That's not Lizardopolous."

"What? Of course it is. Tucker and I found him right in this room."

"That's right," I said. "He was under one of the couch cushions. He nearly made me pee my pants." *Why do I keep talking about penises?!*

"You found *that* lizard in *our* house?" Zeke looked genuinely surprised by this.

"Just like I said we would," Violet said.

"Weird. I wonder where he came from." Zeke grabbed him from his mother and held him close to his face to inspect him. "I'll call him Lizardnoceros.

"But, Zeke, it's Lizardopolous."

"No it's not. It looks nothing like Lizardopolous."

"That's because of the camouflage thing he does. When you put him back in his aquarium you'll be able to see."

Zeke shook his head. "Look at him, Mommy." He held the lizard in front of Violet's face. "He doesn't look anything like Lizardopolous. He's not even as big. He's only a teenager."

"He's probably just cold," I said. "Sometimes things shrink when they're cold." *What the hell am I talking about?*

"Lizardopolous never shrunk. And he had spots on his tummy." Zeke lifted him up to show us the new lizard's belly. "This lizard doesn't have any spots."

"But who else would it be?" Violet asked. "We literally found him right where you're sitting."

"I don't know. I'm not the grown-up."

Violet sighed.

"Can I still keep him?" Zeke asked. "If he wandered in here he doesn't have a home."

It was cute that he knew for sure it wasn't Lizardopolous but that he also didn't suspect we were trying to trick him. He really did believe our story.

"I still think it's Lizardopolous," Violet said. She sounded defeated.

"It's definitely not. But I like him." Zeke opened up one of the many pockets in his cargo shorts and started to put the lizard inside.

"Absolutely not, little dude. Take him upstairs before he gets loose again."

"Technically it would be the first time Lizardnoceros escaped. I only just got him." He hopped off the couch and headed toward the stairs anyway, though.

"That was a disaster," Violet said and sunk into the couch next to me.

"Really? I didn't think it went that badly. He didn't even ask about Lizardopolous or suggest that we look for him. Maybe he's just content with the new one."

"He's momentarily distracted by the new one. I'll probably wake up to the house ransacked because he spent all night looking for him again. It didn't solve anything. Today was a complete waste."

I tried not to let her words offend me. "Not a complete waste, surely." I put my arm behind her on the couch, without touching her.

"No." For a second her eyes fell to my lips. "Not a complete waste." She shook her head. "I should probably get started on dinner. Do you think ziti is okay? This was kind of sprung on me and it's about all I have on hand. I'd already planned on making it this week and I think I can stretch it for a few more people."

"That sounds perfect." When she didn't get up to start cooking, I took it as the sign I'd been waiting for. I slowly leaned in.

For a moment she didn't move at all. Her eyes traveled back to my lips and I swore I heard a sharp inhale.

But then there was a noise upstairs, like Zeke had dropped something heavy on the ground. Violet immediately ducked away from me. "I should probably get started on dinner," she said again like she hadn't just said it a minute ago. She started picking up the hot chocolate mugs.

"Would you like some help?"

"No, you can just, um..." her voice trailed off as she looked around the room. "Actually, yes. Do you know how to medium dice vegetables?"

"Do I know how to medium dice vegetables?" I said with a laugh. "Of course." I didn't. And I had no idea why I was pretending that I did. I assumed it just meant cut it up pretty small. I could handle that.

"Great." She shoved some crumbs from the coffee table into her hand. "Do you mind grabbing the plate of cookies? I can't believe how many Zeke ate. He's not even going to be hungry for dinner. It's just so hard to say no to him when he's upset."

I picked up the half empty plate. Her son had a pretty big sweet tooth. I did at that age too. "He seems pretty resilient to me. And who knows, in a few years maybe he'll be the star quarterback and all those kids that are making fun of him now will be sucking up to him. Was his dad good at sports?"

"Yes. I mean…no. I don't know."

I laughed. "Did he play anything in high school?"

She shook her head and turned away from me to clean the mugs. "No, he was in plays and stuff. He wasn't that interested in sports."

"Oh, right. But you said you were and that you weren't allowed to participate?"

"I doubt I would have made any teams. I was fast but not that fast. And I'm coordinated, but not that coordinated." She opened up the fridge and started pulling stuff out.

"And what are your interests now?"

She finally looked back up at me. "In sports?"

"No…I mean like what are you passionate about now?"

"Being a mom."

Her response made me smile, but it still wasn't what I was looking for. "Do you work?"

She arched a brow at me. "Being a mother is work."

"I know. It's the hardest job of all and also the most important." I did know that. My mother worked her ass off to give me the best of everything that she could. "But do you have another job? To make ends meet?" There were so many things about her that didn't make sense. She dropped three hundred dollars on a coat but drove around a beat-up truck.

She made homemade tomato sauce out of organic products, based on the labels and items she was moving to the counter, but she lived in a house that was practically falling down around her. Nothing she did made any sense.

"I don't have to work," she said as she grabbed a recipe book from a shelf and started to flip through the pages.

"Why is that?"

"I invest and stuff." She pulled her hair into a messy bun and started rinsing vegetables.

"Invest what?" Most people invested money that they set aside from their day jobs.

"My inheritance."

"Oh. I'm sorry." That made sense. She had lost her father, mother, and stepfather. "That was rude of me to ask."

"It's fine. It's no secret that I don't work. Can you imagine me going to work every day? I'd lose my mind," she said with a laugh.

"I'm sure you'd be able to handle it." I started to cut up the vegetables she handed me. "So were your parents wealthy?" I immediately regretted the question. Why was I pushing this? She had just told me everything I needed to know. Not that I was worried that she was running around town pulling bank jobs. But I had been curious about where all her cash was coming from. Before today, I thought maybe she needed a little bit of financial help. I had found myself wanting to be that help. Now that she didn't need it, I was curious about how much she didn't need it. Was she just rolling around in cash?

"No, not particularly. But I got a big fat life insurance check from my mother's death. Apparently she'd had a pretty substantial policy ever since she got married to my dad. He was worried about her mental health. He probably thought she might try to off herself at some point. Honestly, I was worried about that too when I was little. I'd been terrified of being left alone with my stepfather. The money was the one good thing my mother ever did for me. All I have to do is invest it properly and I'll be good."

She didn't need a man to take care of her, but I already knew that. I just wanted to be a part of her life. My ego was a little bruised though. The salary from my job was probably chump change to her. I was more focused on the fact that she said her mother was suicidal though. Maybe the peculiar cause of death had nothing to do with Violet at all. *Of course it doesn't.* I was 99 percent sure she wasn't involved in her stepfather's and mother's deaths.

"What are you doing?" she asked me. "You didn't even peel the onion."

I looked down at the cutting board. I hadn't been paying attention, not that I particularly knew what I was doing.

She laughed and pulled the knife out of my hand. "Here, I'll let you cut up the bread instead." She handed me a loaf of fresh Italian bread. "Maybe like half inch slices. Think you can handle that?"

"That's probably more my speed." I took the knife bread and watched in awe as she sped through chopping the vegetables. She was full of surprises.

CHAPTER 21

Violet

"Sure you don't want a glass?" Damien asked for what felt like the tenth time.

I had never been one to succumb to peer pressure. But my stomach had been in knots ever since he arrived. For some reason, I found myself wanting him to like me. He was friends with Tucker, and if Tucker and I ever became something then Damien would be a part of my life too. Thinking about it made my stomach hurt even more. What was I doing? I couldn't date a detective and be friends with another. That was asking for trouble. But going on the way I had wasn't an option either. I needed to open up to someone or I'd drown in my own secrets.

My afternoon with Tucker had been really nice. He was respectful, even though he was a little nosy about my past. He was trying to get to know me and I kept adding to my pile of lies. I heard Zeke's laughter filtering in through the other room. Tucker had told me he was going to try again to convince Zeke that the new lizard was Lizardopolous. Lying clearly wasn't working. Which just reinforced the fact that I didn't have a choice here. Tucker wanted to talk one on one tonight. I could just tell him a tiny bit and see his reaction. I'd confess one secret and see how he took it. That was harmless enough.

I looked back at Damien. "You know what? I'd love a glass."

He gave me the one he'd poured for himself and then went to the cabinet he'd seen me pull the glasses out from originally. He was certainly making himself at home already.

I took a sip. I hadn't had a drink since the last party I had been to in high school. The wine was bitter, but it was certainly better than cheap, stale beer. Maybe it would help with my compulsions. I didn't want Damien's negative opinion of me to be reinforced tonight. I wanted to fix it. And clenching my hand in a fist all night to prevent myself from tapping anything wasn't going to cut it. The nerves made me worse. If I remembered anything about drinking, it was that it made me feel less nervous.

"This is a lot nicer than I thought it was going to be," Damien said and looked around the kitchen.

I wasn't sure if that was a compliment or not, so I didn't say anything at all, I just took another sip of my drink.

"When I was little I used to throw rocks at the windows with my friends. We'd all run away, scared that ghosts would come out and chase us."

I laughed. "I did too. I was always kind of fascinated by the place." It was weird that we had something in common.

"I was always creeped out by it."

Well, maybe not that much in common.

"Is it true that you just rent it or something?" he asked.

The *or something* made me know what he was really asking. I'd heard the rumors that I lived in this abandoned house without a real claim to it. Just a psycho living out in the woods.

"It was the property of the state. I bought it outright." This was one thing I didn't need to lie about. The place had been abandoned for years and I got it for barely anything. I was pretty sure the state would have given it to me for free if they could have.

"Oh. I didn't realize that."

"Yeah." I shrugged my shoulders. "People like to assume things instead of asking me. They'd rather not talk to me at all."

He rested his elbows on the kitchen island and leaned a little closer to me. "I'm sorry, Violet. I've been one of those people."

"I don't blame you. Sometimes it's easier to be part of the masses."

"Ouch." He put his hand over his heart. "I guess I deserved that one."

He did. But pointing it out wasn't a very nice thing to do as a host. "I didn't mean anything by it. I really appreciate you fixing my truck. Really, you're a lifesaver."

"It's more of a patch. You'll probably need a new car within a year at the most."

I couldn't get rid of my truck. That wasn't an option. "Are you sure?"

"I'm sure you could spend a bunch of money on Band-Aids, but it would be a better investment to get a new one. Which I realize sounds insane because a car is a really shitty investment. But it's better than pouring money down the drain."

I shook my head. I'd pour any amount of money down the drain to keep it. A rundown truck in the driveway would be suspicious. But as my main method of transportation it just fit in with everyone's opinion of me being a crazy woman in the woods.

"If you need someone to come to the dealer with you, I'm pretty good at negotiating." He gave me a charming smile.

It was the second time today that it felt like he was hitting on me. The way he looked at me made my whole body feel cold. "No, I think I'm good with my truck. Thanks for offering though."

He shrugged. "Well, if you ever need me to take another look I can. Speaking of which, I think you had an ice pack with my name on it." He rubbed the back of his head.

God, I was such an ass. He wasn't hitting on me, he was probably just concussed. "I'm really sorry about that. I shouldn't have surprised you while you were under the hood." I grabbed the ice pack from the freezer and held it out to him.

"Do you see a bump or anything?" he asked instead of taking it.

I walked up behind him and ran my fingers through his hair at the base of his skull. "It does look a little purple." I pressed the ice against his skin.

"Ah, that feels so much better." He lifted his hand and put it on top of mine.

"You're not dizzy or anything are you?" I probably shouldn't have let him drive around this afternoon without asking him that first.

"No, I don't think so."

"Nauseous or anything?"

"No." He smiled. "Just hungry."

I sighed. "Okay, good."

"Is dinner almost ready, Mommy?" Zeke asked as he ran into the kitchen.

"In a few minutes. Want to help set the table?"

He didn't reply, he just pulled one of the stools over to the counter so that he could climb up and reach the plates.

Tucker joined us in the room and the air suddenly felt stifling. He was staring at my hand underneath of Damien's with a look full of protectiveness. I loved that look. I immediately removed my hand. "I was making sure he wasn't concussed," I said.

Tucker shoved his hands into his jeans' pockets. "Concussed. Really?" He was staring at Damien.

"What?" Damien shrugged. "I could have been. At least someone cares enough to ask." He kept the ice pack on the back of his head.

"Are you convinced we found Lizardopolous now?" I asked and flicked one of Zeke's dreadlocks out of his face as he set the table.

"No, I'm convinced that Tucker isn't as good of a detective as he thinks he is."

I laughed. "You're right about that." As soon as the words fell out of my mouth, I regretted them. Everyone was quiet for a second. I had been referring to the fact that Tucker had been the one to insist that the new lizard looked like Lizardopolous, but I couldn't exactly explain that in front of Zeke. What I said made it seem like I was guilty, and Tucker wasn't smart enough to catch me. The silence was killing me.

"He is a pretty shitty detective," Damien said with a laugh. "He's almost been fired a few times."

"What's shitty mean?" Zeke asked.

God help me. "There's no cursing in this house," I said. "Don't you repeat that, Zeke, it's a bad word that grown-ups use when they're being inappropriate."

"Oh, like dicks?"

I blinked once. Twice. Three times. "What did you just say?"

"Dicks. It means penises. No one's supposed to say it but I guess people do when they're naughty."

I laughed. I couldn't help it. His explanation was kind of adorable. People say it when they're naughty? Probably true. "Don't say that either, little dude. Pinky promise me." I held out my hand to him.

"But *Mom*. Why do they get to say shitty dicks and I can't?"

"They're not allowed to say it either. They're going to promise me too. Right, Tucker? Damien?"

"Sorry, Violet," Tucker said and then he elbowed Damien when Damien didn't reply.

"Yeah, sure, cross my heart or whatever," Damien said.

"See. They're not saying the bad words either."

Finally Zeke wrapped his pinky around mine. "Fine," he said. He made it seem like it was a huge sacrifice when he had clearly only just learned the words today.

"So..." Damien said in a lame attempt to change the subject. "What kind of flooring is this?"

That was the weirdest segue ever. I looked down at the kitchen floor. I'd opted to refinish the wood in the house instead of replacing most of it. But I had no idea what kind of wood it was. It was re-stained a dark color that didn't look anything like the originals. "I'm not sure. It's the original flooring of the house but it's refinished."

"Oh. It's nice."

"Thanks. I feel like I was on my knees for weeks trying to figure out how to do it."

Damien smiled and I had no idea why. But I didn't have time to ask him, because the timer started beeping. I was relieved it was time to eat. The sooner dinner was over the sooner Damien would be gone and Zeke would go to bed. I needed that alone time with Tucker. I needed to tell him I didn't think he was a bad detective. He was a good one. His first instinct not to trust me had been right. I was guilty, just not of what he had originally thought.

"Is everything refinished, or did you have to tear any of it up and replace it?" Damien asked.

I liked talking about home remodeling. This was going to be an easier dinner than I anticipated. "I didn't have to tear anything up. The house was in much better condition than I ever could have hoped."

"How 'bout that." He kept looking at the floor like he didn't believe me.

I must have done a really good job with them.

But when I caught Tucker elbowing him again out of the corner of my eye, the compliment went out the window. Why was he really asking about my floors? I took another sip of wine before starting to serve the ziti.

Damien and Tucker had saved the seat between them for me, which made me uncomfortable because I could feel them both staring at me. Although the way Damien was staring at me was different. It felt like he was looking for answers instead of looking at me.

There were only three stools so Zeke sat cross-legged on the counter. I knew it was ridiculous, but luckily no one commented on it. And Zeke looked like he was having the time of his life. He had a million questions for Damien and Tucker. Everything about cases and random detective work in general. At this rate, I wouldn't have been surprised if he wanted to be a detective one day. Which would be ironic. Because then it would be his job to catch people like me.

I let Damien refill my glass of wine once it was empty.

"I actually have another bottle in the car. I grabbed two just in case. I'll be right back." He excused himself from the table.

"You don't have to drink that if you don't want to," Tucker said when he heard the front door close.

"It's actually really good." Honestly, the more I had of it the more I liked it. I didn't believe in taking medicine for my issues. But this seemed like an easy fix when I was in a pinch.

"Can I have some?" Zeke asked.

"Nope." I reached across the counter and squeezed his knee. "It's a grown-up thing."

"Awww, but, Mom. Everything's a grown-up thing."

I laughed. "Not true, little dude. None of us get to eat while sitting on the counter like you."

"That's true. Are there any more cookies?"

"Eat more ziti instead."

"*Fine.*" He grabbed the serving spoon and plopped more onto his plate.

"I'm sorry about all of Damien's questions," said Tucker.

I really hadn't thought anything about them until I saw how upset they had made Tucker. "I did spend a lot of time on the floors. It was nice to have someone notice. It seems like you thought it was an inappropriate question, though. Why?"

"Because of how people think there's bunches of bodies under our floors," Zeke said with a mouthful of food.

God. I was more horrified that Zeke had heard the rumor than I was that Damien was trying to trick me into confessing to something that wasn't true. I was embarrassed that my son had pieced the questions together and I was too blind to see it. Or too…drunk? *I don't know.* I pushed the glass aside. "Zeke, who did you hear that from?"

He shrugged. "I don't remember. A lot at school. It's not true, Tucker," he added. "I'd know if our house was haunted, I live here."

"I know," Tucker said.

"Zeke, what else have you heard?" I was horrified. I knew the kids teased him, but he'd never said they were spreading rumors about me too. About our house. No wonder he couldn't catch a break.

"I don't know."

Whenever he said that it meant he just didn't want to talk about it. He'd probably heard everything. Of course he had. The people in this town were horrible. "Okay, little dude." I squeezed his knee. I'd ask him about it later when we were alone. "But you know not to listen to rumors, right?"

"Yup." He took another huge bite of ziti. "Rumors are for shitty dicks."

"Zeke!"

He giggled.

Tucker started to laugh too.

I couldn't help but join them.

"I feel like you were making fun of me while I was gone," Damien said as he walked back into the room.

"Only a little," Tucker said. He winked at me as he placed his arm on the back of my chair.

I liked when he did that. It made me feel safe in the most comfortable way. I was thankful that he wasn't trying to put his arm around my shoulders or hold my hand again. That had been nice at the mall, but I didn't feel comfortable with him doing that in front of Zeke. It would lead to all sorts of questions, and I didn't have the answers. I didn't know what we were. It would all depend on how tonight went. Suddenly I was nervous for our conversation. What if he ran away too?

Damien topped off my glass without asking this time. I knew he was trying to do what I thought Tucker had tried to originally do to me. If I was indisposed it would be easy to search my place. Or maybe get a drunken confession. Tucker wasn't guilty of those things though. And maybe tonight would be easier if I just flat out asked Damien what he wanted to know. The only problem was that I wasn't sure I could give him the answers he wanted. I wanted to open up to Tucker tonight, not his friend.

He'll run. He'll turn you in. You'll lose Zeke. I grabbed the glass and took another sip. Liquid courage was a thing, right?

"Violet?" Damien asked.

I looked over at him. It seemed like he had been trying to get my attention for a while. "Sorry, what did you say?"

He smiled. "I was wondering if you ever hear from Joel anymore?"

"No. Not since high school." I could feel all three sets of eyes staring at me.

"Who's Joel?" Zeke asked.

"Just an old friend. Are you ready for bed, little dude?"

"No way. I want to hang out with you guys."

"But it's late and you have school tomorrow." I walked around the counter and pulled him off.

"But *Mom.*" He wiggled around in my arms. It was the second time tonight he had said my name in that way. Like I was torturing him.

"Come on. Let's go wash up. I'll be back down in a few minutes," I said to no one in particular. The wimp in me kind of just wanted them to both be gone when I came back down. The pessimist in me thought they'd both be pulling up floorboards when I reappeared. But I couldn't exactly tell them it was time to go to bed like I'd just told Zeke. I wasn't their mother.

After I finally wrassled Zeke into a pair of pajamas, I sat down on the edge of his bed. Despite his insistence that he wasn't tired, his eyelids were starting to droop.

I tucked the covers under his chin. "Hey, Zeke?"

"Mhm?"

"What other rumors have you heard? About me?" I smoothed his dreadlocks away from his face.

He yawned as he rolled over on his side. "That you killed my daddy."

Tears prickled in the corners of my eyes. Why would someone say that to him? He was just a kid. I didn't know how to reply to what he said. I was so tired of lying. "Zeke?"

His only reply was a light snore.

I leaned over and kissed his forehead. “I didn’t have a choice.” One of my tears landed on his cheek. I wiped it away. “I had to protect you.”

CHAPTER 22

Tucker

"You gonna try to nail her tonight?" Damien asked as I handed him a plate to dry.

"No." What the hell was he even still doing here? He had invited himself to dinner and now he just wouldn't leave. I needed to talk to Violet alone.

"Why? I thought you liked her."

He was being an idiot. I wasn't looking for a one night stand. Violet was too good for that.

"You're that bad in the sack, huh? Don't want to scare her away?"

"I'm still getting to know her."

"You can look for those scars if you get her naked."

I squeezed the water from the sponge and turned off the faucet. "Does that mean you agree with me?" I was trying to study Violet all day, but I didn't exactly know what to look for in abuse victims. She hadn't resisted my touch when we were in public. Honestly, she seemed comforted when her hand was in mine. I hadn't tried it during dinner because I didn't know how she felt about it in front of Zeke. It was one of the things I wanted to discuss tonight.

"I mean if her son can talk about dead bodies under the floor like it's the most ridiculous thing in the world…it kind of makes it seem untrue. But that doesn't mean that the bodies aren't somewhere else."

"I was actually asking if you thought maybe she was abused when she was little?"

Damien shrugged. "I don't know. She didn't seem to mind putting her hands all over me."

I had been pissed when I walked into the kitchen and she was doting on him. But I wasn't going to stoop to his level. "I thought you'd have it all figured out after your inquest."

He laughed. "I barely got to ask her anything. Zeke was the one leading the onslaught of questions."

"He's cute, right?"

"Yeah. He's got no fashion sense, but maybe you can help him with that when you become his new daddy."

I wasn't exactly sure what kind of reaction he was trying to get from me. I just ignored him again. "What do you think of Violet after the few questions you did get in?"

"Well, she seems sweet. But she's also a psychopath."

"She can't be both. She's one or the other. And you know she's not capable of hurting anyone. Look how she took care of you after you hit your head."

"Those two things aren't mutually exclusive, man. She's sweet like a psycho."

"What did she say tonight that led you to that conclusion? I thought you were having fun."

"I think being a detective is fun or else I wouldn't have gone this route. And how can you not see all the signs? All her answers are very calculated. I feel like you can't see it because of your rose-colored glasses. But she's…"

"What?" Violet asked as she walked back into the kitchen. "I'm what?"

"Vi..." I started but she held up her hand to stop me.

"What do you want to know so badly, Damien? Do you need me to rip up my floors to prove to you that the rumors are false? What? Just tell me what I have to do to get you off my back."

"I want to know if you killed Joel Walker six years ago," he said in such a calm voice that it didn't even sound like the horrible question that it was.

Jesus. I thought he'd start apologizing, but instead he acted in complete Damien fashion and dug his heels in.

"If I'm being honest, I wanted to. I loved him and he just...left. Everything he ever said to me was a lie. I hate him." It looked like she had more to say, but she pressed her lips together like she was trying not to let the words escape.

"So you gave in to the temptation?" Damien asked. "You axed him?"

She laughed. "I don't even know how to wield an ax. He's a piece of shit, but no, I didn't kill him. He up and went to Los Angeles. Ask any of his old friends. He'd been planning it for years."

"But he left before he even got his diploma. And no one's heard from him since."

"Because he doesn't have any family here. He was in the foster system. All he had was me."

"So you just expect me to believe that he left you? If you're the only person he cared about...why did he leave you?"

"Because he didn't love me."

"Then why did he leave before graduation? He could have waited a few weeks."

She folded her arms across her chest. "I haven't heard from him in six years. For all I know, he's dead now. But that doesn't mean I had anything to do with it."

"That doesn't answer the question, Violet. Why did he leave before graduation?"

"I don't know."

"I think you do."

"That's enough," I finally said. "She's already answered your question. She doesn't know why he left."

"She answered it, but she's lying. You're too blind to see it." He focused his attention back on Violet. "Joel Walker disappeared under suspicious circumstances and you're the only one who knows why. Why did he leave?"

She didn't say anything.

"Why, Violet?"

"Because I broke his heart!" She spat out the words like she hated them.

"You implied earlier that he broke yours."

"Can't two hearts break together?" She wiped a few tears away that had fallen down her cheeks.

"Yes. But usually one of the people doesn't go missing. What did you do to make him run so fast?"

One of her hands fell to her stomach and then she looked toward the stairs. "Zeke's five years old. How hard is this to figure out? Look, this has been a lot of fun, but it's late and…"

"He left you when he found out you were pregnant?"

Her hand fell from her stomach. "Yeah. I needed him and he ran. Just like you said."

I wasn't as blind as Damien thought I was. I wanted to believe Violet, but I was well trained in deception. There was more to this story. I could feel it in my bones. But I wasn't going to ask her about it in front of Damien. I wasn't looking for a confession like him. I just wanted to know the truth. I wanted to know how I could help her. "It's getting late," I said.

Violet nodded. "I'll show you both out."

Ouch. I deserved that. I had barely tried to stop Damien's questioning. It was hard when I was dying to know the answer too.

She brushed past us toward the front door.

"Sounds like no matter what you do, you'll be better than her ex," Damien said.

"If she'll ever speak to me again after tonight." We both followed her to the door.

Damien apologized for the accusations and then stepped out into the brisk night. I kept my hand on the door, trying to find the right words.

"You deserve better than Joel. And better than how I behaved tonight."

"At least you did the dishes."

I started to laugh, but it didn't look like she was making a joke, so I ended up coughing into my hand.

"Do you think I killed him?" she asked.

I stared at her. "No."

"You hesitated."

"I didn't hesitate. I was just processing the question."

"If there was a new case being opened against me, would you tell me?"

I wasn't sure how I kept digging myself into a deeper hole here. "There's no case. I just got curious about a few details of your life when I started looking into you. There's some things that don't really add up."

"So you've been looking into my past this whole time?"

"No." *Fuck*. "Yes." I shook my head. "This is what I wanted to talk to you about tonight. It's complicated."

"Get out."

"Vi..."

"Don't Vi me." She shoved my chest, pushing me toward the door. "You're not my friend, Tucker."

She was pushing me away, but all I could focus on was her fingertips on my chest. They were on the edge of driving me insane. We'd barely touched and I'd done nothing but dream of having her ever since we met. "Tell me what you really want."

"For you to get out of my house." She shoved me harder.

I was tiptoeing on a very thin line. But her eyes didn't match her words. She didn't want me to leave. I knew that she didn't. "Tell me to stay." I took a step toward her.

She stepped back, keeping the distance between us. "I overheard you and Damien talking outside earlier. And a few minutes ago. You're trying to tie me to something."

"I'm trying to stop the rumors."

"Liar."

"Me?" Was she kidding right now? "I'm trying to help you, but you won't give me anything."

"I didn't ask for your help."

I took another step toward her, and she took another step back.

She shook her head.

I wasn't sure if this was the best approach. She had already called the freaking cops on me once. But I was done playing games. One more step forward.

She retreated her last step. Her back was pressed against the wall.

It wasn't the chemistry between us she was shrinking away from. That much was clear from the way that her hand had formed a fist around the fabric of my shirt. She was practically pulling me toward her. She was just scared. It was all the what-ifs that surrounded our relationship. All the skeletons she had hidden in her closet. It would all come out. Every single lie. Every single secret. "You have to meet me halfway here." I tilted my head down toward hers.

"Knowing the truth might ruin your life," she whispered against my lips.

"Then ruin my life."

Her throat made a weird squeaking noise when I cupped the side of her face in my hand.

"I'm going to kiss you now. If that's okay?" I knew this situation was delicate. I had every reason to believe someone used to lay their hands on her without permission. I wasn't going to be that guy.

She didn't respond. Instead, she stood on her tiptoes and lightly brushed her lips against mine for a fraction of second before she attacked me in a kiss. There was no softness or insecurity behind her lips. The kiss was frantic. She was as desperate as me. Carnal. It was like she had been waiting for this moment her whole life.

I closed the final distance between us, pushing her back against the wall.

She moaned into my mouth in the most soul-crushing way. I wanted to swallow every moan that escaped her lips. I wanted every single one to be because of me. My fingers slid down the side of her neck. Farther. I pushed her sweater off her shoulder as I trailed kisses across the side of her jaw. "Just say the word and I'll stop." I wasn't sure I'd be able to stop even if she begged me. The taste of her skin was as sweet as the taste of her lips.

Luckily she didn't ask me to stop. Instead, she wrapped her arms behind my neck, drawing me closer. "Only stop if you're planning on breaking my heart. I barely survived the last time that happened."

"I'm not Joel. I'd never skip town when you needed me. I'd never be able to leave you." I wasn't sure what made me say it. I barely knew her. But I had been hit hard and fast. I was pretty sure I was addicted to her.

She nodded but it looked like she was about to cry.

There were warning bells going off in my head. I was not going to go farther than a kiss when she looked like that. "This can wait. We don't have to rush anything. I just planned on talking tonight."

"I'm so sick of talking." She buried her fingers in my hair, guiding my mouth back to hers.

I didn't want to second guess anything. I'd been torn with my feelings for her ever since we met. Guilty. Not guilty. Did it matter? I'd already lied for her once. I'd lie for her again and again if I had to. Her secrets didn't matter. I was already hooked. I grabbed her ass and lifted her legs around me. I captured another of her moans and dismissed the rest of my thoughts. All that mattered was that she wanted me. And God, I wanted her too.

CHAPTER 23

Violet

Last night was amazing. I stared at the rise and fall of Tucker's chest as he slept peacefully. He was amazing. Part of me thought I had dreamed him to life. I didn't just want *someone* like him, I wanted him. Only him. And that meant I needed to make sure I could keep him.

There were a lot of what-ifs floating around in my head. They were all part of the reason I had succumbed to temptation. I needed last night. I just wanted to be with him once before he knew the truth. Just once before he looked at me differently. I didn't know if what we had was love. But it would be tainted soon enough regardless. He'd only ever look at me the way he did last night before he knew the truth. Even if he stayed, it wouldn't be the same. He'd always wonder. *Please stay.*

I pulled on my robe and tied the sash as I stared down at him sleeping. Then I retied it again. And again as my stomach twisted into knots. The sun had barely risen. I had some time before he and Zeke got up. I was going to spend it wisely.

I glanced at him once more and tried to memorize the way his hair fell into his eyes as he slept. And the sharpness of his jaw. And his pecs. God, his muscles were a lovely surprise.

I thought I might have some sense of remorse about jumping into bed with him. But there was no hesitation. Somehow

Tucker and I made sense together. And I was thankful that I'd had some wine last night, or I may never have had the courage to find that out.

I tiptoed out of my bedroom and closed the door behind me. A cup of coffee was calling to me, but I didn't have time to worry about caffeine. I needed to prove my innocence of at least one thing before I confessed to all the other things I was guilty of. Today was the day I would come clean. I had to. I couldn't lie to Tucker anymore. I just couldn't.

I opened up my laptop and some random show started playing on Netflix. *Netflix? Seriously, Zeke?* Getting Hulu without my permission was bad enough, but getting a subscription to Netflix too? We needed to have a serious conversation about credit card theft. I paused the show so I wouldn't forget to come back to it when he woke up, and then I opened a new browser. I cracked my knuckles as the Google search bar loaded.

Come on, Joel. You owe me at least this one thing. It felt like he had stolen my whole life from me. All his dreams had become mine when we were together. And when he left I had never felt so alone. I typed Joel Walker into the search box.

There were a lot of Joel Walkers in the world. Hundreds on Facebook, LinkedIn, Twitter, Instagram. All the sites I didn't indulge in. I liked my privacy too much to be on anything like that.

It took me several minutes of browsing through all the results until I came to his Facebook profile. I expected to feel something when I saw him cheesing for the camera in front of the Hollywood sign. Anything. But there was nothing there. Six years was a long time. I had a whole new life. Certainly he did too. He'd made it. He got the life I would have held him back from.

I clicked on the image of his face and a box prompting me to either sign in or create an account popped up. Even if I wanted to, I couldn't peruse what had become of him. I leaned in closer to the screen. Joel barely looked a day older than when he left. It made the uneasiness return to my stomach. This could have been taken yesterday or six years ago. I stared at the image. If I made an account I might be able to see more. But even if I created one, I'd probably have to hit the add friend button to get more access, and that was a very bad idea. Requesting to be his friend on Facebook after six years of radio silence would be weird. He'd wonder what was going on. Or he'd just delete my request like it was no big deal. He'd bury any thought of me like he had so many years ago.

Either way, I didn't feel comfortable making an account. I sighed and exed out of the browser. I thought I'd be able to just look him up and find him easily. I wanted to be able to show Tucker that he was alive and well. If he believed that…maybe he'd believe the rest of my story too.

I tried to ex out of the Netflix video but ended up going to a details page of the show Zeke had been watching. I was about to close the whole browser when I saw the name J.J. Walker. He was a writer for whatever stupid cartoon this was. Joel's middle name was Jovi. It was a ridiculous middle name. Joel had been embarrassed the first time he told me about it. But I hadn't laughed. I'd been so madly in love with him that I even loved his silly middle name.

I typed "J.J. Walker sitcom writer" into a new browser. And there he was. Hundreds of pictures of him looking older than he had in high school. There was even an article about him published a few weeks ago. He was wearing black-rimmed glasses and had grown one of those trendy lumberjack beards. They both looked stupid on him. He was trying too hard to fit in.

J.J. Walker. He changed his whole identity for what? To prove he could make it out there? It was probably for some stupid publicity thing or something. But it felt like he was trying to stay hidden. From me, most likely. After all, I had broken his heart. Just not as much as he had broken mine. I stared at his picture. *Alive and well in Cali.* If my life had turned out differently, I could have been next to him in that picture. I could have a ring on my finger and maybe another kid by now.

It was like I was trying to force myself to feel something. I didn't want a ring from him. And I certainly didn't want a kid that resembled a homeless lumberjack. I had everything I'd ever wanted right here. I glanced toward the stairs. Zeke was my whole world. And Tucker was slowly becoming a part of our world. It was a lot easier to imagine a child that resembled him.

I shook away the thought. The last time I had told the truth, I lost everything. Part of me wanted to slam the laptop shut. The other part of me wanted to believe in second chances. This could be a good thing. Joel wasn't the man for me, that was a fact. But that didn't mean that Tucker couldn't be.

Or maybe telling the truth was a bad idea. Was that the lesson here? I had told Joel the truth and it hadn't exactly gone well. And now there was even more to the story. I took a deep breath. I didn't have a choice. I had been drowning in my lies for six years. There had to be a way out. If I was ever going to move on, I needed to come clean.

I stood up, carrying the laptop with me back to my bedroom. I climbed into bed with Tucker. Instead of poking his side to wake him, I pushed his hair away from his forehead. He looked so content sleeping. Not a care in the world. I wanted to curl up beside him and take refuge in the safety his arms provided. Our talk today would change things. Maybe it would bring us closer. More likely I'd be behind bars before dinner.

But he'd already ignored evidence for me once. I'd had an unregistered gun and he just brushed the whole thing under the rug like it was no big deal. But it was a big deal. I was pretty sure it was a felony. How many felonies could a detective ignore? I stared at his perfect face. Hopefully he could ignore a few more. I just needed a chance to explain everything before he reacted. Tying him up and putting duct tape on his mouth before he woke up was tempting. He'd have to hear me out if he couldn't escape. But that was crazy. The whole point was that I wasn't crazy. At least, not in the way that everyone thought.

My delete key flew off my laptop. I lifted it off my pillow. I hadn't even realized I'd been pulling on it. That was the only thing that scared me about myself. When I did things and didn't even know I was doing them. I took a deep breath. I was getting in my head, psyching myself out. There was no getting out of this. I had made up my mind to tell him. Once I made up my mind to do something, it was only a matter of time until it got done. I glanced around my bedroom. Just look at what I had accomplished here. This house had been falling apart when I bought it. Now the whole upstairs was beautiful.

Tucker shifted in bed, pulling my focus back to him.

I reached out for him again. This time my hand was shaking. The beginning of the end was near. I didn't want to believe it, but the thought seeped into my bones, settling there. I just hoped that I didn't have to do what I did six years ago. My heart couldn't take it. I lightly touched his shoulder. "Tucker?" I whispered.

He opened his eyes a crack. A smile spread across his perfect face. "Good morning, beautiful."

His words made my stomach flip over. His smile was contagious. I could feel the corners of my mouth turning up. "Good morning."

It looked like he was about to pull me back against his chest. I had already indulged last night. As tempting as it was to have him keep looking at me the way he was, it wasn't deserved. "He's alive." The words sounded harsh in the still morning.

"Who?" Tucker yawned as I shoved the computer onto his lap.

He slowly sat up and pushed the screen back a bit so it wasn't right in his face. "J.J. Walker?"

"Yeah, it's Joel. His middle name is Jovi. He must have changed his name to J.J. when he moved. He's trying to be a hipster now or something. But that's why no one could find him. They were looking for Joel instead of J.J." I pointed to the screen.

"This article is from a few weeks ago."

"Right." I turned my attention back to Tucker's face instead of the screen. "See…I didn't kill him."

"I didn't think you killed him, Vi." He finally lifted his gaze back to mine.

I loved when he called me that. I loved when he looked at me like that even more. "Everyone else thinks I did."

"And now we can prove that you're innocent. The rumors will stop."

In his sleepy state he was forgetting about the rest of the rumors. "Maybe."

His eyebrows lowered. "Or we can just skip town and start over somewhere new. We can have a normal life somewhere else."

"I thought normalcy was overrated?"

He smiled. "It is. But your reaction made it seem like you didn't want to stay."

Because you don't know everything yet. "Isn't it a little fast for a *we*?"

"I'm not some 18-year-old kid trying to add notches to my bedpost. Last night meant something to me."

"Did you do a lot of things you regret when you were 18?" *I did. I ruined my life. I sabotaged any chance of a life with you.*

He closed the laptop. "Enough. But I try not to live in the past. We all make mistakes. It doesn't mean we can't have a better future."

I wouldn't classify the things I had done as mistakes. Doing something once was a mistake. I hadn't just done it once. But I did regret it. Well, parts of it. I stared into his eyes. "You want a future with me and Zeke?"

"And whatever that new lizard's name is."

I smiled. "Lizardnoceros I think? I don't know where he comes up with these things."

"But yeah. I can picture a future for us. Can't you?"

I nodded without hesitating. I could. It was easy. He was already so good with Zeke. And he didn't look at me like I was a monster. *Yet.* It was possible that I could keep everything a secret for a little longer. But it felt like I was running out of time. With the FBI still sniffing around and Damien pressing things? It was only a matter of time before my secrets rose to the surface anyway. I needed to get out ahead of it.

He leaned forward like he was about to kiss me, but then pulled away before our lips touched. "Do you have a toothbrush I could use?"

I laughed. "Yeah. I have spares in the bathroom vanity. Help yourself. Actually, do you mind heading downstairs pretty soon? I don't want Zeke to know that you spent the night. It will lead to way too many questions."

"Not a problem." He slid the laptop onto the bed. "Do you think you will talk to him at some point? About us?"

"Yeah." *Probably. We'll see how the rest of the day goes.*

"In the meantime, I'll just pretend that we're still only friends." He winked at me and walked toward the bathroom.

He was only wearing a pair of boxers and I found my eyes wandering over the muscles in his back. I didn't realize how sexy a back could be. He turned around at the last second. He smiled when he caught me staring. "Zeke definitely looks more like you than Joel. He's a cute kid."

His words made my heart race. Sometimes it was like he already knew the truth. "Yeah."

Tucker smiled again.

As soon as the bathroom door closed, I opened my laptop back up. I typed "how soon is too soon to trust someone" into the search box. I needed to know if I was crazy for feeling this strongly about him so quickly. The last thing I wanted was to do to him what I had done to Zeke's father.

CHAPTER 24
Tucker

Violet was just as gorgeous in the early morning. Although, we didn't exactly wake up together. She'd been up for a while, scouring the internet for her ex. I felt like a dick for not showing her that I believed her earlier. I felt worse for not telling her what I'd done before sleeping with her. We were supposed to talk last night, but I stopped thinking when she put her hands on me. She was even more gorgeous when she was angry. Luckily, any trace of anger was long gone now. And I had until tonight to tell her about poking around her childhood home. It wasn't going to be a fun conversation, but I had to do it. I was too far gone. Even if I wanted to, I wasn't sure if I'd be able to reel in my feelings for her. I was in trouble with her.

I opened up one of the drawers in her vanity. Three tubes of toothpaste. Three containers of floss. Three lighters. Three hair brushes. It was obsessive to have three backups of everything. But I knew she had compulsions. She probably couldn't resist the purchases.

I pulled open one of the other drawers. I was expecting to see more bathroom supplies, not three sets of binoculars. Really high-tech ones. I had used a pair like this on a hiking trip once. I lifted a pair up and walked over to the window. After pulling the blinds open, I put them up to my eyes. Most of the leaves had fallen from the trees now, giving me a clear view of the woods. The lake in the distance glistened in the morning sun. It was a beautiful view. I turned my head. *Huh.* I lowered the binoculars. I could also clearly see the house that had blown up. It was easy to make out even without the binoculars. It was a perfect vantage point.

Which means nothing. I lifted the binoculars back up and looked at Vi's childhood home in the distance instead. Would she really want to leave this place? The trail from the back of her home to the lake meant something. But how could she love it here when the people were so cruel?

I lowered the binoculars. I needed to tell her I went to her old house. And I needed to flat out ask her what happened all those years ago. There was more to the story of Joel. But it was a relief that he was alive. It put that little voice in the back of my head finally at rest. Violet was a good person. I put the binoculars back where I found them and I pulled open the cabinet at the bottom of the vanity. There was a lot of toilet paper, stacked in columns of three. There were three of the same shampoos. Three conditioners. Three body washes. Three deodorants. Maybe a doctor could help her with her compulsions. Had she ever been to one? It was worth asking her about. Mixed with everything else I was going to bring up later, asking about a doctor didn't seem like such a bad idea.

I opened up the final drawer. Three backup toothbrushes. I pulled one out and wondered if only having two in there would upset her. I'd pick up another after work today. I closed it and quickly brushed my teeth and washed my face.

When I came back out of the bathroom the bed was empty. She had made it, removing any trace that two people had slept in it instead of one. I understood. It was going to be hard explaining it to Zeke. He asked a whole lot of questions about everything. His mind was like a sponge. He'd certainly taken to cursing like a sailor pretty easily.

I tried to be quiet as I made my way downstairs. Luckily it was just Violet in the kitchen. Zeke must have still been asleep.

"Do you have three of everything?" I asked as I sat down on one of the three kitchen stools.

She poured a cup of coffee and placed it in front of me. "It's good to have a back up for your back up. Just in case."

"Fair point." I wrapped my hands around the mug, happy for the warmth it provided. The old house was drafty despite the fixed heater. "Have you ever thought about seeing a doctor for your compulsions? I feel like they make medicine to help with them."

She put a few slices of bread in the toaster and proceeded to make a sandwich with two more slices. "I don't like doctors."

"No one likes doctors."

She finished the sandwich and put it into a plastic container. "I mean…I don't do doctors. I haven't been to one since Zeke was born."

"What about when you're sick?" I already knew the answer. She was sick when we first met and she just waited it out.

She shrugged. "I've taken Zeke to the pediatrician a few times. But I manage just fine myself."

"Do you always pack Zeke's lunch?"

"The food in the cafeteria isn't organic." She put the sandwich and an apple into a lunchbox. "You're full of questions this morning."

"We kind of skipped over our talk last night. And I need to ask some questions...I don't want you to think I'm a bad detective." She had joked about that last night. I hadn't taken it too seriously, but I didn't want her to actually think I was bad at my job. Even if I kind of was. Sometimes it was hard to find passion in a job that dealt with so many horrors. When I was with her, it was easy to forget all the horrible things I had seen. She was a breath of fresh air.

"I didn't mean you were actually bad at your job. I was referring to you being responsible for picking out that lizard. You clearly didn't get a good look at Lizardopolous. Zeke saw right through the imposter. But I guess in some other ways...you kind of are a bad detective."

She was making it hard not to be offended here. "In what other ways?"

"You've been flirting with your prime suspect."

"It's not my case anymore."

"Just because it's not your case doesn't make me innocent."

"We both know you're innocent."

She closed the lunchbox after putting in a bottle of water. "Do you think that maybe we can have that talk today?" She fidgeted with the lid of the lunchbox.

"I can come by for lunch." It was tempting to call in sick, but the captain was already breathing down my neck. I was trying to get off her shit list, not move my name to the top of it.

"That would be great." She nodded like she was trying to convince herself her words were true. The toaster popped, breaking the awkward silence. "Toast?" She didn't wait for a response, she just started spreading jam on it and slid me a plate.

"Is everything okay, Vi?"

"Yeah." She kept her eyes glued to her piece of toast. "We just have a lot to talk about."

She wasn't wrong. I'd somehow avoided all the awkward questions that would usually happen before I was intimate with a woman. Not to mention all the awful boundaries I had crossed by looking into her past. This afternoon would be my chance to come clean about everything. Or I could suck it up and do it now. I cleared my throat.

"Mommy! Mommy!" Zeke shrieked. His little feet pounded on the steps as he bolted down the staircase. "Lizardopolous came home! Lizardopolous came home!" He was holding his new lizard high in the air as he slid into the kitchen.

I didn't know what had changed his mind. Maybe he had a dream that his real lizard came home. Either way, I was glad to see he believed now.

"Oh!" Violet said and crouched down to look at him. "How about that. I told you once he started doing his camouflage thing you'd realize it was him."

"No. I mean he must have come home last night while I was sleeping. This is Lizardopolous. See? He has the tummy spots." He put him right in Violet's face and pointed out the spotted belly.

"Right. It's definitely Lizardopolous. He has all the right spots." She looked pleased with herself.

Zeke shook his head. "You're not getting it. The one you found wasn't Lizardopolous. *This* is."

Violet nodded. "Of course."

"I'm being very clear and you're just not getting it." He pushed Lizardopolous into Violet's hand, reached into his pocket and pulled out a second lizard. "Lizardnoceros," he said and lifted up the pocket lizard. "Lizardopolous." He pointed at the one in Violet's hand.

"Oh." Violet's smile turned into a frown. "He came back?"

Zeke jumped up and down. "Yes! He came home!"

"So you have two lizards now?"

"Yup!" Zeke grabbed the lizard out of his mother's hand and started to shove both the lizards into his pockets.

"Zeke. What have we talked about?"

"I don't know," he said. "We talk about a lot of things."

"Put the lizards back in your room. Now. I want to get going early so we beat the crowded drop-off line."

He nodded. "Okay. I'll be good. I don't want to ever have to take the bus again." He ran back out of the room, a lizard in each hand.

"How the hell did that happen?" Violet asked. "I thought you threw Lizardopolous into the woods?"

"I did," I said with a laugh. "He must have found his way back home."

"Now he has two of those awful little things. God." She started fidgeting with the lunchbox even more. She bunched her lips to the side like she was deep in thought.

It reminded me how she said sometimes she'd get lost inside her mind. I put my hand on top of hers. "It's fine, I'm sure he'll take good care of them."

"It's not that." She shook her head. "It's just...I kind of want to get him a third one now even though I hate them. Three would be better."

I could feel the stress oozing off of her. The way she was behaving was starting to wear off on me, stressing me out too. "You know what? How about you stay here and relax this morning. I'll take Zeke to school on the way to work." I'd offered the other day, but that was before we'd slept together. Surely she trusted me enough now.

"Really?"

"Yeah. I can even pick up another lizard before I come back if you'd like."

She shook her head. "No, I know that's ridiculous."

I didn't say anything. There were a lot of ridiculous sets of three things in her house, but it didn't feel like a good time to point it out.

"Were you going to show Damien the pictures of Joel?" she asked. "I want him to believe me too."

"Yeah, I can show him."

She removed her hand from beneath mine.

Last night had been great. This morning as well. But something seemed off now. I didn't know if it was something I did or the stress of there only being two lizards. "I really enjoyed last night, Vi."

"Me too." Her cheeks flushed in the sexiest way.

We were good. For at least a few more hours. Until she realized she was a little fast to trust me. I needed to do something grand. Maybe I'd stop and get her some flowers before lunch.

Zeke came running back into the kitchen.

"What do you want for breakfast?" Violet asked, turning her attention back to her son.

"I'll just eat cookies." He grabbed the plate from the counter and shoved one into his mouth in record speed.

"Zeke, I can make you toast. Or oatmeal. Or eggs?"

"No thank you, Mommy." He ate another cookie.

"You're going to turn into a pile of sugar." She grabbed the plate away from him a second too late. Zeke had already stolen a handful of them. He shoved one more into his mouth and put the rest into one of his cargo shorts pockets.

I wondered if it was the same pocket his new lizard had been in a minute ago.

"Are you ready to go?" he asked. He looked down at her slippers. "I thought you wanted to go early?"

"I'm going to take you, Zeke." I said.

"Really?" He sounded so excited. "Can we drive with the siren?"

"I'm a detective, not a cop. I don't have a siren."

"Oh." He still seemed excited. "That's okay. It'll still be fun." He grabbed the lunchbox that Violet handed him.

She crouched down to be at eye-level with Zeke. "Be good, okay, little dude?"

He nodded.

"I love you." She kissed the top of his head. "I'll pick you up later today."

He didn't respond. Instead, he hugged her. "By later do you mean late? Last time you picked me up you were late."

She closed her eyes. It looked like she was in pain. "I won't be late."

"Promise?"

"Cross my heart and hope to die."

The only escape is death. A chill ran down my spine as I remembered the engraving. Had she hoped to die at one point? She'd mentioned that she thought her mother might be suicidal. Maybe the engraving was about her. I'd ask her about it soon enough. I wanted a few more hours to remember how great last night was before I fucked everything up.

She kissed the top of his head once more before releasing him. Zeke ran toward the front door. We both followed, but I stayed back after he ran outside.

"Want me to pick something up for lunch?" I asked.

She shook her head. "I'll cook again."

"Are you sure everything's okay?" I reached out and lightly touched her cheek.

She melted into my palm, like our bodies were meant to be fused together. "Yeah. I'm just a little...tired. I woke up too early."

"Maybe take a nap then?" I smiled at her as I tilted her chin up. I had waited to join Zeke outside so that I could steal a kiss.

"Sounds good." She took a step back, letting my hand fall from her face. "I'm going to go do that. Thanks for taking Zeke to school." She walked away, leaving me standing awkwardly in the foyer.

Last night had been perfect. This morning, on the other hand, she was acting so distant. What was going on with her? I went to open the door, but she immediately came back into the foyer.

"Actually. I need your opinion on something. Do you think people can change? Like if you hated apples because they made you throw up once as a kid? You'd like...give them another chance right? Now that you're grown up? People can change. You might like apples now." She was scratching the inside of her wrist as she stared at me.

I could tell that there was a certain response that she wanted, but I didn't know what it was. Honestly, I didn't think people changed. I hated to think about all the people that got locked away and then repeated the same mistakes once they were free. It was ingrained in them to be on the other side of the law. But something simpler like apples? I wasn't going to shoot myself in the foot when it was clear she wanted a certain answer. The vaguer the better. "Maybe if I put some peanut butter on it or something to cover the taste? Then I could slowly acclimate myself."

"Until you loved apples again."

"To tolerate them perhaps. I doubt they'd ever be the same, but that's the theory, yes."

"I don't care about theories. I want to know if you think people can truly change?"

"Inherently?"

She nodded.

"No, not really. In my line of work it's a little hard to believe in second chances as optimistically as a normal citizen."

"Right." She started scratching the inside of her wrist again. "Okay, well have a nice day." Her voice was oddly high-pitched.

"I feel like you set me up for failure there," I said with a laugh. "What is all this about?"

"Nothing. We'll talk later. Just...don't say anything to Zeke yet."

I tried to think about how the questions had to do with Zeke. I knew she was referring to not telling Zeke about my relationship with her. But was her question about him too? Was she worried he'd always be bullied? I cleared my throat. "I won't. And you know what? I want to change my answer from before. I do think people can change. I mean, I was pretty different when I was little."

"Really?" She looked happy again.

I nodded. "I've made mistakes, I've grown…yeah, people can change."

The exhale that escaped her lips sounded like it held the weight of the world. "Yeah. People can definitely change."

"Zeke's going to be fine, I promise."

"Zeke?" She started scratching her wrist again. "Right, Zeke. I'm going to go take that nap." She leaned forward and kissed my cheek. "I'll see you in a few hours."

"Okay." It wasn't awkward when she left me standing there this time. But for some reason I still felt like I had just fucked something up. I shook my head and walked outside, closing the door behind me.

Zeke was standing by my car eating a cookie. He looked up as I made my way over. "We're going to be late. We should probably use the siren."

I laughed and unlocked the car doors. "I wasn't lying to get out of using them. I meant I actually don't have them.

We both climbed into the car.

"Oh." He stared at the dashboard. "But what does that do?" He pointed to the volume button.

"Ejector seats. So make sure to buckle up."

His eyes grew round. "Really?"

I nodded.

He immediately buckled his seatbelt. His feet didn't reach the floor and he was kicking his heels against the seat. He probably should have been sitting in the back, but he looked so excited to be up front. I'd drive slowly.

Before I even pulled onto the main road he started firing questions at me.

"Do you like arresting people?"

"I like catching bad guys."

He nodded. "What about bad girls?"

I laughed. "Being bad has no gender." I turned onto the main road.

"Have you ever arrested someone you wished you didn't have to?"

I thought about the busts I had made. I prided myself on putting people away that deserved to be there. The streets were safer because of the work I did. "No."

"You've never arrested anybody you loved?"

"I don't usually hang out with criminals, Zeke."

"Hmm." He turned to look out the window. For a second I thought he was going to stop asking questions. But then he turned back to me. "But what if someone you loved did something really bad? Would you arrest them?"

Honestly, I wasn't sure. It wasn't something I never thought about before I'd found Violet's gun. But I hadn't turned her in. Technically I was a criminal too. Nothing felt as black and white as it had a few weeks ago. "I think it depends on what they did."

"Do you love my mom?"

Shit. Violet had specifically asked me not to talk about this with him. I should have known he'd ask a question that would lead me into a hole just like his mom always seemed to. I cleared my throat. "We're just friends."

"Is that why you had a sleepover last night?"

"Why would you think that?"

"I heard her talking to you last night in her bedroom. She kept comparing you to God."

Oh, God, Tucker. I had loved when she moaned that. Now? Not so much. Zeke had rendered me speechless.

"It's okay. None of the kids invite me to sleepovers either."

"That's not…" my voice trailed off. How the hell could I turn this around? "It was a grown-up sleepover or else I would have invited you, little dude." I realized it might be weird that I just called him that. It was what Violet always called him. It felt like I was crossing some kind of line and making the whole situation worse. *Please don't ask me what we were doing in her bedroom.*

"It's okay. I was glad she didn't wake up in the middle of the night though."

It was something a mother might say about her kid. Not the other way around. I wanted to just be relieved that he didn't know what Violet and I had been doing. He didn't know anything about the progression of my relationship with his mother. That was what Violet wanted. But I couldn't just ignore what he'd said. I was too curious. "What do you mean?"

"She has lots of bad dreams. She screams a lot in her sleep. It always wakes me up and sometimes she comes and snuggles with me to stop crying. But she didn't do that last night."

"Oh." His words were troubling. Was she having constant nightmares? Or maybe she was reliving something bad that happened to her. Horrible memories. "Well, maybe she was just more relaxed last night. Has she ever told you what makes her upset when she's sleeping?"

"No." He kicked his heels some more. "But I think someone was probably mean to her. Or else she did something really bad. I usually only cry when the other kids pick on me or I'm bad and I know it."

My fingers tightened on the steering wheel. I had witnessed the catty women around town. People were awful to Violet. And I had my suspicions that her home life growing up wasn't exactly a great atmosphere. But I wanted to know if Zeke knew anything else about it. "Have you ever seen her do anything bad?"

He shrugged. "She's bad a lot. She counts things. And forgets things because she can't stop counting."

"That's not bad. She can't help the counting."

"Yes she can. Whenever I tell her she's doing it she stops. Always."

"But she needs you to remind her."

He nodded. "That's why I think maybe she did something else bad before I was here to remind her to stop."

I pulled into the drop-off lane at his school. The line of cars inched forward as Zeke's words echoed around in my head. I was going to have a conversation with Violet later about all of this. I didn't have to question her kid about it too. But it didn't mean I didn't want to. I glanced at him out of the corner or my eye. "What do you think she did?" I couldn't help it. The words just poured out.

"Promise not to put her in jail? She's the bestest mommy in the whole world. And she's my only friend."

"We're friends, Zeke." It was the only thing I could think of to say in response. His words broke my heart.

"You have to promise." He put his fist out in front of him, his pinky extended. "Pinky promise."

When we had first started driving he had asked me whether or not I'd arrest someone I loved. And he wanted to know if I loved his mom. The kid knew something. "Pinky promise." I wrapped my pinky around his.

A car behind us beeped. We had reached the front of the drop-off lane.

He dropped my hand and unbuckled his seatbelt. "She doesn't like to leave the house."

"Okay…" Was that the big reveal? I'd put a little too much hope in this conversation.

"I think it's because of the truck she drives, not the mean peoples. She cleans it a lot more than anything else. The back of it the most. And she's always hardest to get to stop counting when she's cleaning it."

I already knew she liked to do everything in multiples of three. Cleaning a whole truck bed three times would take a while. "That's not bad, Zeke. It's good to take care of things."

He grabbed his backpack and lunchbox and opened up the door. "No, it's different. Like she's stuck cleaning up something on repeat. Over and over and over again." He looked down at his lunchbox and then in a rush he spit it all out: "I think she murdered my daddy and hid his body in the back of it. And I'm only telling you because I don't want her to kill you too."

What the fuck? I thought about her old truck. With all the money she had, it didn't make sense for her not to turn it in for a new one. But a lot of things she did were inconsistent with the inheritance she'd mentioned. Like the fact that they lived in that old house in the middle of the woods. The fact that she was unpredictable was part of the reason why I found her so alluring. Zeke was just confused. He was being manipulated by the rumors too. He didn't give me a chance to correct him, though. He jumped out of the car, slammed the door closed, and ran up to the school.

CHAPTER 25

Violet

I thought back to yesterday in Tucker's car. He said anyone who murdered someone was a monster. No ifs-ands-or-buts about it. No exceptions. Nothing. He was a detective for Christ's sake. Of course he thought that.

And Tucker didn't believe that people could change either. He'd finally altered his answer after I kept pushing it. But that didn't mean he believed what he said. He was just trying to appease me. There was no chance at redemption in his eyes.

Ow. I looked down at my wrist. I had been scratching it so much that my nails had broken through the first layer of skin. There was blood dripping down my palm and embedded underneath my fingernails. *Shit.*

I went to the bathroom and turned on the faucet. The water stung my skin as I washed away the blood. I stared at the pink stained water hitting the sink. What was I doing? I couldn't tell Tucker. I couldn't. I started counting down from three repeatedly, trying to calm myself.

Water splashing onto my thigh pulled me out of my trance. "God." I turned off the faucet before the sink could overflow anymore.

I felt nauseous. I tried to swallow down the bile in my throat as I bandaged my wrist. It was easy to tell myself to calm down. It was another thing entirely to actually do it. I ignored my hands shaking as I finished up with the bandage.

It was hard to talk myself out of something after I decided to do it. I was going to tell Tucker this afternoon. But I needed a backup plan in case things went south. I needed a way out.

I was going to be sick. I grabbed the edge of the counter. No one knew the truth. Sometimes I doubted it myself. The rumors were ingrained in me. Manipulating my mind.

Air. I needed fresh air. I changed out of my robe and ran down the stairs, my stomach churning.

I grabbed my new coat, a hat, and gloves, and shoved my feet into my boots. I pushed the door open and inhaled. The cold air was a slap in the face, but it didn't calm me.

The lake always made me feel better when I was younger. I forced myself to not look at my truck as I walked past the driveway. I just needed one minute of peace. I needed my mind to stop. For just one second. *Please.*

"Big lies have big consequences." My mother's voice seemed to be echoing around the woods.

Stop.

"Consequences, Violet. There are consequences to big lies."

Stop.

I took a huge breath. Three, two, one. Three, two, one. Three, two, one.

Coming out here was a mistake. The lake was a reprieve when I was young. Now? It was the key to my demise. But I couldn't stop walking.

My pleas were answered when I finally reached the lake. It was frozen solid. My secrets were trapped beneath the icy surface.

"I'm sorry," I said into the silence. "I didn't mean to do it."

CHAPTER 26

Tucker

I wanted to be relieved that Zeke didn't know I was hooking up with his mother. But how could I be relieved after what he said? The rumors were getting to him. The poor kid actually believed his mother killed his father. That was a heavy weight to carry around for a five-year-old.

And I hadn't gotten a chance to explain to him that he was wrong. I'd seen the photos of Joel with my own eyes. His father was alive. An asshole, but alive. It was probably best that I didn't get a chance to explain that. It wasn't my place to talk about his dad.

Violet needed to know what was going on with Zeke. But I wasn't sure that was my place either. We hadn't even talked about what we were yet. I didn't know how to handle situations like this.

I walked into the precinct and kept my head down low. I wasn't in the mood to talk to anyone. For just a minute I needed to sort through my own thoughts.

"It's a pretty shitty day to be late," Damien said as I pulled off my jacket. "The captain wants to talk to us."

So much for not talking. "Now?" I asked.

Damien was perched on the side of his desk with his arms folded across his chest, like he was scolding me. "No, actually. Five minutes ago. She's going to be pissed."

I glanced at the clock on the wall. "Sorry. The drop-off line was a little backed up."

Damien's eyebrows rose. "You took the kid to school this morning?"

"The idea of doing it was making Violet anxious. I was just trying to help out."

"So…you were there this morning?"

I shrugged.

"You slept with her," he said way too loudly.

"Would you keep your voice down?" As usual, he was being horribly annoying.

"Well…did you see any scars?"

I hadn't even thought about it until he asked. Her skin was perfect. Flawless like the rest of her. "No. I don't think she had any at all."

"Probably not abused then."

"That's not necessarily true." I lowered my voice, hoping he'd do the same.

"Oh you mean like verbally instead of physically? Poor chick has been verbally abused for years. The question is whether or not she deserves it."

"You know she didn't do what people say. You spent time with her yesterday. I don't think she could hurt anyone, Damien."

"She was pretty good at taking care of me." The smirk on his face made me want to punch him.

I stopped outside the captain's office. "I'm being serious. I think we could help repair her reputation. She doesn't deserve any of this."

"You don't know that for sure. Just because she's nice to us doesn't mean she's not an ax-wielding murderer."

"Violet's innocent. And you know it."

"Are you talking about Violet Clark?" asked our captain. I hadn't seen her come into the hall.

Damien suddenly decided to close his big mouth.

"Yes, ma'am," I said.

"I know you two have already met. She was your lead suspect in the Adeline Bell case, right?" She turned on her heel and walked back into her office without waiting for an answer. She didn't need one, she already knew it.

Damien and I followed her in.

"Close the door," she said as she sat down behind her desk.

Damien shut it and then we both took a seat across from her.

"Violet Clark." The captain opened up a file on her desk. "You are correct, she's been ruled out by the FBI. However, her property has not." She opened up another folder, pulled out a picture, and put it down in front of us. "The FBI uncovered a tooth in the woods behind Adeline's house. They're expanding their search throughout the entire woods, including Violet's property. They're still doing forensics on the tooth, but the original opinion on the scene was that it had been there for several years. Adeline only lived in that house for a few years. I'm pretty sure it's not related."

"What are you saying?" I knew what she was hinting at. But I didn't want to believe the pit in my stomach. Was I the only person on the force that didn't believe in rumors? I thought she was going to call me out for sleeping with a suspect. This was worse. This was so much fucking worse.

"The FBI is waiting it out, thinking the timeline on the tooth will change. So I think we should let the FBI have their unsolvable case. In the meantime, we have a real opportunity to close a cold case. The FBI will think they're unearthing evidence for themselves, when really it will only benefit us. They're going to do all the leg work and we'll be able to take all the credit. Serves them right." She looked so pleased with herself. "Violet Clark isn't Adeline Bell. But that doesn't mean she's innocent.

"I know you've kept on the case without my permission, Reed. You ignored direct orders. But...in this one instance...you were right. So I'm going to let you take the lead on this cold case. You've earned it, she was your suspect first." She handed me the file. "Don't mess this up."

I didn't want anything to do with this case. But I grabbed the file from her. She was trusting me for the first time since I got transferred here. For just a second, I let myself think about the opportunity. But for just a second. The whole thing was ridiculous. Violet was innocent. "It's just a tooth." My words didn't sound convincing, though. "It probably belongs to some kid that was out in the woods playing."

"It's an adult molar, Reed."

I don't know why I was forming a rebuttal on the tooth theory. It didn't even matter. I had hard evidence. "She didn't do it." I pulled out my phone and typed J.J. Walker into Google. I slid her my phone. "Her ex-boyfriend is alive. He just changed his name when he moved to Hollywood."

She looked disappointed. "Have you talked to him?"

I shook my head.

"Get him on the phone so he can confirm his identity. There's still the issue of her stepfather and mother so make sure to question him about that too. I'll let you know when I get the results for the tooth."

I just stared at her. All I wanted to do was tell her to go fuck herself. Instead, I swallowed down the words. Being at the top of this case meant I'd at least have control over it. There had to be a way to clear Violet's name. Getting my badge taken away from me right now would just make that harder.

She cleared her throat. "You can go."

The folder felt heavy in my hand as I followed Damien out of the room.

"Do you want me to call the ex?" Damien asked. "I can't believe you managed to track him down."

"Violet tracked him down, not me. She showed me those articles this morning."

"Trying to prove she's innocent? That seems guilty as hell."

I grabbed his arm and pushed him into the bathroom.

"What the hell?" He pushed my hand away from him.

I ignored him and bent down to see if all the stalls were empty. "She's not guilty. This is a fucking witch hunt. I need to fix this. You have to help me fix this."

"Take a deep breath, man." He smoothed his shirt back into place. "You know I've just been messing with you. If you're 100 percent sure she's innocent, then I believe you. Just tell me what you need me to do. I've got your back."

It was nice to know he had at least one serious bone in his body. The only problem was that I wasn't 100 percent sure.

There was no such thing as being 100 percent sure of anything. And I knew that I was too far gone to take a step back and try to see the case from a new point of view. Asking him to do anything could put his career at risk too. I just needed to ask Violet a few questions before I figured out what the best plan of action was. "I need to go talk to her. Can you cover for me?"

"You heard the captain. We're supposed to be calling her ex to try to get some answers. Running to her and telling her about the tooth isn't going to help anything. The best way to get her out of this mess is by solving the case. Prove her innocence."

I didn't want to prove anything. I wanted to pack her and Zeke up and get the hell out of town before it was too late. She was being targeted because of some stupid housewives' gossip. A tooth found in the woods? Were they freaking kidding me? Anyone could walk around back there. I had just done it the other day.

"Right," I said. "Starting with her ex." I didn't feel comfortable talking to Joel. He was a piece of shit. He'd abandoned his child to chase fame. He'd left Violet to the vultures. As much as I trusted Damien, I didn't want anyone else to hear what Joel had to say. Because if it was bad, I needed to be the only one that ever heard it. I'd already buried one secret for Violet. I was willing to do it again if I had to. "I'll call him as I head over."

"What do you want me to do?"

"Go over the file." I tossed it at him. "Try to see if there's anything to help get her out of this."

"You want me to stay here?" He didn't look down at the file. "I think I should come with you."

"I need you here to tell me if they get that report back about the tooth."

He shook his head. "She'll notify us even if we're both out. I'm coming."

I didn't have time to argue with him. Even though I knew Violet was innocent, there was this fear in the back of my head that no matter who that tooth belonged to, she'd be tied up in it. I wasn't going to let that happen. I was running out of time. "Okay, let's go."

Damien was able to find Joel's number before we reached the car. He hit the speaker button as I pulled the car out of the lot.

This morning Violet had seemed off. She had been talking about regret. She had been asking whether or not I believed people could change. I just thought she was nervous about taking Zeke to school, but now everything felt wrong.

Damien was following our captain's orders to call Joel. At least this way I'd overhear what Joel had to say. I'd be able to see Damien's reactions. I'd know if I could trust him. I pressed down hard on the gas.

I thought the call was about to go to voicemail when someone finally picked up.

"Hello, Joel Walker? This is Detective Damien Torres. I have a few questions for you pertaining to Violet Clark."

There was a long pause. "Is…is she okay?"

I was surprised by his response. He was worried about her now? What about when she needed him?

"She's fine. We were hoping you'd be able to answer a few questions."

"I don't think I can help you, detective. I haven't heard from Violet in six years."

"Fortunately for both of us, my questions have to do with six years ago."

"Am I in some kind of trouble here?"

There was the Joel I imagined. Worried about Violet for two seconds and then putting himself first. It reminded me of what Violet had said, about people showing their true colors when it mattered.

"No, not at all, Joel," Damien said. "But we are aware that you two dated. We were wondering if you have any idea what happened to her mother and stepfather?"

"Um. No?"

"You don't seem so sure about that."

Joel cleared his throat. "I mean, yeah, I heard about their passing. But I don't know the specifics."

"Violet didn't tell you what happened to them?"

"No, we weren't on speaking terms. When I say I heard about it, I meant I read about it. I thought about reaching out but…" his voice trailed off. "I was finding my footing out here. I was trying to keep the past in the past."

Ass face. She needed you.

"Do you think it's at all possible that Violet may have played a role in their deaths?"

"What? No. Absolutely not."

"So you don't think that Violet's OCD ever trended toward violence?" Damien asked.

"OCD? Violet doesn't have OCD."

"Maybe that's the wrong term. I'm referring to the compulsions she has. The obsessive counting."

"I think you have the wrong Violet Clark. Vi didn't have compulsions."

I gripped the wheel a little tighter at the mention of her nickname.

Damien spouted off Violet's birth date and a brief description of her and of Zeke.

"I mean…I guess that sounds like her, yeah. But she didn't have OCD. Not when I knew her."

Damien glanced over at me. I didn't know what to think of the information either. She must have developed it after he left. Sometimes trauma brought things like that to the surface.

"It was a boy?" Joel asked. "She had a boy?"

I grabbed the phone away from Damien. "You'd know that if you stayed around, you piece of shit."

"Stop it," Damien hissed and pulled the phone away from me. "Sorry about that, my partner isn't having the best morning. What he meant was why didn't you stay? To help with the baby? What made you decide to leave?"

"There was no reason for me to stay. There was nothing left for me there."

I wanted to throttle him through the cell phone.

Damien put his hand out like he was afraid I'd steal the phone again. "Being part of your son's life didn't seem important to you?"

"*My* son? That kid isn't mine. We never…" his voice trailed off. "It would be impossible for him to be mine. Did she tell people I knocked her up and left?"

Damien glanced at me and then back at the phone. "I think there's a lot of rumors about why you left. But I'm not calling to discuss rumors. Violet's in trouble. I need to know if there's anything you can tell us that would prove Violet didn't kill her parents."

He sighed. "I thought the Violet I knew would never hurt anyone. But she gutted me. So what do I know?" He cleared his throat. "Is there anything else I can help you with? I'm in the middle of work."

"No, that's all. Thanks for answering…"

Joel hung up the phone before Damien finished talking.

Damien looked over at me as we turned onto the road that led to Violet's house. "I think we should take a minute to go over what he just said before you do whatever it is you're planning to do."

"I'm not planning anything. I just need to talk to her." I was planning something and I didn't have time to think about what Joel had to say. I didn't believe anything that spewed out of his mouth.

"She lied to you, man. Didn't she say that Joel was Zeke's father?"

"She implied it." I put the car into park and started to unbuckle my seatbelt.

"Tucker, she cheated on Joel. Zeke isn't his kid. He doesn't even look like him." He showed me a picture of Joel.

I already knew they didn't look the same. But that didn't mean anything. He just took after his mom. "You believe him over her?"

"Honestly, yeah. She's lived out here alone for years. She's…"

"Don't say crazy." Violet wasn't crazy. She wasn't. "And she hasn't been alone. She has Zeke." She had me too. I believed in her. She wasn't what everyone said she was. She couldn't be. I stepped out of the car. I had parked right next to her truck, so my mind flipped back to what Zeke said about Violet putting his father's dead body in it. He was wrong. Clearly he was wrong. Zeke was right that the truck was insanely clean. But there was nothing at all suspicious about it.

"And Zeke isn't exactly normal," Damien said as he climbed out of the car too.

I was barely listening to him. When I had looked up from the truck, I had seen Violet in the distance. She was standing at the edge of the lake, staring at it. She had to have heard my car coming up the lane, but she hadn't turned to start walking back. She was just staring. Transfixed.

"The kid has dreads and wears boots with cargo shorts when it's sunny out. He's an odd duck. Which he gets from his mother."

Zeke wasn't odd, he was adorable. But things did run in families. Violet had mentioned that she was worried about her mother committing suicide when she was little. She'd been terrified of being left alone with her stepfather. And the way she was staring at the lake…I suddenly knew how she felt. *Jesus.* "Stay here."

"Tucker…"

"I just need a few minutes to talk to her alone." He opened his mouth but I cut him off. "Just five minutes. Please."

Damien leaned against her truck. "Okay."

I starting running down the hill and into the woods. "Violet!" I yelled through the leafless trees. But she didn't turn. Instead, she took a step forward into the lake. "Violet!"

CHAPTER 27

Violet

I thought I saw a flash of red under the frozen surface. My mother had been wearing red the last time I saw her. I took another step onto the ice.

What if I had imagined the whole thing? What if she was still alive? I took another step. I wanted out of this nightmare. I wanted to be able to breathe again.

There was a noise behind me, but I ignored it. I had seen her. Another step. She was trying to get out. I could still save her.

"Violet!"

Hearing my name made me freeze. What was I doing? I looked down at the ice under my feet. Why was I out here?

"Violet."

My mother hadn't even been wearing red the last time I'd seen her. Her shirt had been white. Perfectly pristine. Until it wasn't. My heart started racing. It was easier when I blocked it out.

"Violet I'm here for that talk. Please get off the ice. I want to talk to you."

I turned around to see Tucker standing at the edge of the lake. He was looking at me like I was crazy. Was I crazy?

"How long have you been out here?" he asked. "Let's go inside. It's freezing."

I looked down at the coat, hat, and gloves that were still in my hands. I'd never put them on. How long had I been out here? I needed to get everything off my chest. I couldn't breathe. "I need you to promise me you'll believe me. I need you to promise."

"Just come over here first," he said.

His words made me see red again. "I don't like being told what to do."

"Okay." He held up his hands. "Okay. I promise I'll believe you. But it's barely below freezing, Vi. The ice is thin. It's dangerous. Please come talk to me over here."

I shook my head. This is where I belonged. Tucker had come too soon for me to figure out a backup plan. This was the only choice I had. I'd know what it felt to be them. I'd always known this would be my final resting place too. "I lied to you." God, it felt so good to say. *I lied!* I wanted to scream it.

"That's okay." He took a step forward like he was about to get on the ice too, but he stopped.

"It's not okay."

"It is. Look, I lied to you too. We're even. Please just get off the ice."

"We're not even."

"We are, Vi. I lied too. I went to your childhood home. I saw the way the floor was scuffed up in front of your bedroom door. You used to look out your window at the woods right? You dreamed of escaping? Being out here feels safe?"

I shook my head. I didn't know what he was talking about. No one was safe out here. I certainly had never been.

"The only escape is death?" Tucker was staring at me like his words should have meant something.

I shook my head again. "I don't know what you're talking about."

"I saw the floorboard where you were counting down the days. You etched into the wood that the only escape was death. But that's not the answer. Coming out here isn't the answer. Just talk to me. I can help you."

I was trying to make sense of what he was saying. "My bedroom was in the front of the house. It overlooked the street."

He lowered his eyebrows slightly.

"The guest bedroom overlooked the backyard. My mom would stay in that room when she was bad."

"Bad?"

I felt nauseous. This was my chance. I could come clean about everything. I had his undivided attention. But I still didn't know if I could trust him. Luckily a backup plan was finally forming in my head. "There's exceptions to every rule, right? Like just because you believe something doesn't mean there aren't situations in which you'd change your mind?" I needed to be able to change his mind. I had to. I'd already lost so much. I didn't want to lose him too.

"It depends on the circumstances, but yes. There's exceptions to every rule. Of course there's exceptions."

He sounded genuine. But I knew I was scaring him. He was worried I was going to fall. But the ice was solid here. Farther in, maybe not. I was banking on the fact that it wasn't. "I'm a monster."

"You are not a monster, Violet."

"You lied about one thing. I lied about everything."

"That's okay."

Why did he keep saying that? It wasn't okay. "I need you to take care of Zeke for me. Make sure he knows that I love him more than anything in this world. No matter what happens, I need him to know that."

Tucker stepped out onto the ice. It cracked under his feet and he quickly retreated back to the dirt. "Violet please. I need you to get off the ice before it breaks."

Rip the Band-Aid off. "When my stepfather and mother found out I was pregnant they wanted me to get an abortion. They insisted it was the only way." I touched my stomach. "I couldn't do it. I refused. So they said they were going to take me away from here. Henry bought a home down in Florida and everything. He said he thought it would be better for my mom. Sunnier. I was only18. I was still hung up on Joel. I thought he'd come back. I was young and dumb and I thought he'd come back for me. I didn't want to go with them." *Stop lying. Stop lying. Stop lying.* It was so ingrained in me that it was hard to stop. But the words weren't lies. They were just a piece of a story. The innocent piece. "When I say they wanted to move I use that term lightly. Henry wanted to move. My mom…she wasn't there. She was on new medicine. She was just checked out. I know she was sick, but God I needed her. I needed her to stand up for me for once."

I wasn't sure Tucker was paying attention. His eyes were focused on the ice beneath my feet.

"My mother met Henry on one of her good days. She didn't have many of those days near the end. Barely any really. I'm pretty sure he thought she tricked him. Tricked him into falling for her. She didn't mean to be the way she was. She was just...sick." Like me. "And honestly even on her lucid days she was cruel. She used to drag me out here when I misbehaved and would hold my head under the water. Henry used to laugh." My own laugh sounded strangled. "She was awful. I never told anyone how awful she was."

"Violet, if your mother abused you, you had every right to fight back."

"That's not..." I shook my head. "I knew how to handle her. It was Henry that I couldn't fight off." *God. Do it!* "I looked like my mom. He..." *Damn it!* "I think he thought it was only right that he got me instead." I was going to be sick. "Zeke isn't Joel's baby. I never even slept with him. I couldn't." It felt like I was holding my breath. "Henry would...he never asked. He just took everything from me. For years. I told my mother and she said I was lying. She didn't believe me. Why would I ever think that someone else would if my own mother didn't? She'd lock herself in that damn room and just let it happen. She let him ruin me."

"Violet."

There were tears in his eyes. I hadn't even told him the worst of it.

"How was I supposed to tell the boy I was falling in love with that I lost my innocence when I was 12 years old? I was ashamed that I didn't know how to stop it. I was ashamed that my mother thought I was lying. I didn't know what to do. I didn't know how to stop it." I stifled my sob. It was just part of the story. I had to tell him the rest. He needed to know. "When Joel found out I was pregnant, I tried to tell him but he was so mad. He had been so patient with me. I told him I needed time before I was ready to sleep with him. I was just trying to find the strength to tell him what was going on in my house. But he left before I could explain. He wrote me off so fast. Even if I was able to get the words out, I think he would have left anyway." *I needed him and he left.*

"His foster father, John, overheard our conversation. A few weeks after Joel left, I was at the lake waiting for him like an idiot. John said he'd been trying to get me alone for weeks to talk about what happened. That he'd had foster kids before with the same issues as me...he said he understood. He knew what I was going through and he believed me. I never meant...I shouldn't have asked for his help." *Stop lying. Stop lying. Stop lying.* I shook my head. "He went to go talk to my mother and stepfather right away. He said he'd get me out. I thought he could save me. For once in my life I thought I was lucky."

I wiped away the tears from my cheeks.

"The conversation didn't go well. John kept saying he was going to call child protective services if Henry didn't let me leave with him. When John pulled out his phone, Henry took a swing. It escalated quickly. Henry had his hands around John's throat. I still remember his eyes bulging." I swallowed hard. "I didn't know what to do. I kept yelling for my mom to help. But she just stood there watching like it didn't matter. She had that blank stare in her eyes that I hated so much. I did the first thing I could think of and grabbed a shovel from the garage and swung it around. I was just trying to break it up. I...it didn't work." I could still picture John's body falling to the floor with a thud. I didn't know someone could feel so much horror and relief at the same time. Because when Henry turned around there was a pocket knife sticking out of his chest. "John had stabbed him." I touched the center of my chest. I had never been so relieved in my life. "Henry died." I said it like it happened instantly. But it was slower than that. He gurgled and spat for a few minutes as I tried to resuscitate John. "They both died." I didn't give a shit about Henry. But John? I could barely live with myself. It was my fault that he was dead, just as much as it was my fault that Henry was dead.

"I kept yelling for my mom to call 9-1-1. I told her to get help. When I finally stopped trying to resuscitate John to call an ambulance myself she was standing there with a gun. Pointed at me." I shook my head. "I've told you once, I've told you a thousand times, Violet. Big lies have big consequences," I repeated her words. I couldn't look at Tucker. I stared down at my boots. *Stop lying. Stop lying. Stop lying.* "She used to say that before she'd shove my face in the water. I thought after all the years of abuse she might actually believe what Henry had done to me. But like I told you before, my mother never loved me." I wiped away my remaining tears. I didn't have any left to shed. "She turned the gun and shot herself in the face." I could still see the blood seeping into her shirt. The blood was everywhere.

"I didn't think my mother would ever actually do it. I'd feared it, but only in a far-off sense, like how a kid worries about her parents getting divorced." I wished my life had been that simple. "If I'd ever seen that floorboard, maybe I would have known. I wish I had known. Maybe I could have at least stopped one death. But I didn't know. And I'm what everyone says I am. I'm a monster. It's my fault they're all dead."

"It wasn't your fault."

"Yes it is. I killed them." God it felt good to say it out loud. "That happened because of me. I could have just left. I could have figured it out. But I ran to someone else for help and look what happened? Three people are dead. Three. Because of me." *Three. Three. Three.* I was haunted by that night. It was so easy to get pulled back into the moment. Whenever I was upset or agitated or nervous, I'd see all three bodies. I couldn't escape the memory.

Tucker stepped onto the ice and it started to crack under his foot. "Shit." He pulled his foot back. "Violet, please get off the ice. None of that was your fault."

"All the rumors are true."

"No they're not. You are not what people say you are. You are good and kind and sweet. You've listened to the assholes in this town for far too long. We're going to get all this cleared up. Please, just get off the ice, Vi."

I looked down at the ice. There was a crack trailing toward me. It was too late.

"We can fix this together. That gun I found under your floorboards. Was that the gun?"

I nodded.

"Great. You said you got rid of it, can we get it back? We're going to need that for evidence. Who'd you sell it to?"

"No one will ever believe me. Everyone's already made up their mind. I just wanted one person to believe me. I needed you to believe me, Tucker."

"I do believe you. And the gun will help prove your innocence. There are so many ways to get you out of this. We can clear your name. Where is the gun, Violet?"

"That gun isn't going to fix it. I've cleaned it so many times." So much fucking blood. "I know I should have called the police right away, but I didn't have a choice, Tucker. Everyone had already made up their mind about me after Joel left. They were calling me a slut to my face. No one would talk to me. I lost all my so-called friends. I didn't have anyone to ask for help. And it looked bad. There were three dead bodies in my house.

"I knew no one would side with me. My peers had already made that clear. I was worried everyone else would believe the rumors going around about me. I sat there for a long time, trying to figure out what to do. When it got dark, I thought maybe I'd drive the bodies out of state. I put one of them in my truck, but I freaked out. There's too many tolls. Too many places where they could be seen. So I…I wheelbarrowed their bodies through the woods, lined their pockets with rocks, and dumped them in the lake. It made the most sense at the time. My mother always liked the lake." The crack in the ice had almost reached me.

"When any neighbors would ask, I just said they were on vacation. When they never came back…more rumors spread about me." I could see it on his face. He didn't understand. "I hated Henry. But Zeke? I knew I was going to love him so much. He was already a part of me. And he was going to be so good. He was going to be everything his father wasn't. I needed to protect him. If I got locked up, who was going to protect my son? I didn't want him to become the monster that his father was. He needed me."

"I understand why you did it, Vi. I understand." His eyes were focused on my feet instead of me. "We're going to get you off. Everything's going to be fine. Just…just get off the ice and tell me where that gun is."

I looked down as the thin crack reached my feet. "It's with all the bodies. Underneath me."

CHAPTER 28

Tucker

The cracking noise reverberated through the woods. I was already running onto the ice as she fell through.

"Violet!" I ignored it cracking beneath my feet, shoved off my jacket, and dove into the part of the lake that wasn't frozen over. She wasn't allowed to die. She wasn't allowed to drop that on me and then leave. For six years she'd let everyone in this town convince her she was a monster. She wasn't. She was just a kid when it'd happen. She was scared. And alone. She wasn't alone anymore.

My eyes stung as I opened them under the water. I didn't see her anywhere. I swam underneath the ice, trying to find her. Farther. I was running out of air.

I couldn't actually promise her that I'd be able to clear her name. If there were really bodies in this lake…if she really took the time to secretly put them here? That was fucking bad. That made her look guilty. But I didn't care about clearing her name. That was what backup plans were for.

I turned around in circles searching. The last air bubbles escaped my lips. *Where are you?*

I swam back out to the middle of the lake and barely made it to the surface in time before I inhaled water instead of air. I took a huge gulp of air and was about to dive back under when

I saw her. Her head was bobbing above the water a few feet away from me. Her lips were blue, but she was fucking alive.

"You scared me half to death," I said as I swam over to her.

"I'm sorry, I…"

I silenced her apology with a kiss. I didn't care. I didn't care about any of it. She could have killed them and I didn't think I'd care.

She clung to me like I was her lifeline. And maybe I was. Maybe all she needed was one good person in her life to take away all the bad.

"I threw the gun into the lake." Her breath was hot against my neck.

That gun wasn't going to get her off. I was just trying to tell her whatever she needed to hear to get her off the ice. And now I needed to get us both out of this water before we froze to death. "We'll get it later, okay? The water's too cold to search right now." She didn't resist when I pulled her back over to the ice and hoisted her up, hoping it wouldn't crack again. We both made it back to dry land and I draped my dry coat around her shoulders.

"I lost another freaking coat," she said. It sounded like she was trying to make a joke, but I didn't have time to react like a normal guy with a crush on a girl. We were running out of time.

"We need to get going." I grabbed her hand and pulled us through the woods.

"Going where? I thought you said you believed me." She was shivering. "That the gun was enough evidence…"

"Yeah, well we both confessed that we're liars, Violet. I was just trying to get you off the ice."

"You think they'll put me away?" Her walking had turned into a jog to keep up with me.

"I think justice isn't as black and white as people think it is. And that you shouldn't go down for something just because there's rumors that you're guilty. We're going to skip town."

"We're? I could never ask you to do that."

"You're not asking me. It's my choice."

"But I just confessed. I'm tired of hiding. If it wasn't for Zeke, I would have turned myself in a long time ago. You're a detective and I'm guilty of…"

"You saw three homicides occur. You're not guilty of anything and I'm not going to let you go to prison for the rest of your life for something you didn't do."

"I'm so sick of living in fear every day. You asked me why I never moved. I've been terrified that if I left, someone would come along and go snooping where they shouldn't. I thought someone would find the bodies. I had to stay and make sure my secret didn't come out. Now that it's out…"

"I'm the only one that knows. Your secrets will stay buried for as long as it takes to skip town." *I hope.* "We'll go get Zeke and then we'll just drive. As far away as we can get from here." We finally reached the top of the hill.

"Stop," Damien said as we stepped out of the woods and onto her driveway. He was holding his gun up, aiming it at Violet. "Drop his hand, Violet."

I wrapped my fingers more securely around Violet's to prevent her hand from slipping. "Drop the fucking gun, Damien." I pulled Violet toward my car, knowing full well he wasn't about to shoot either one of us.

"They found a match for that tooth. It belonged to a John Fredrick. Joel's foster father. He went missing six years ago too. Just like her parents. That's too much of a coincidence."

"I'm sorry," Violet said.

She was not making this easy on me. Apologizing made her sound guilty. "It's a misunderstanding," I said. I shielded Violet's body from him as I helped her into the passengers' seat and then slammed the door closed.

Damien was pointing his gun at me now. "A misunderstanding? She just apologized for us finding the dude's tooth in the middle of the woods. She clearly killed all three of them. You're too infatuated with her to see it."

"She didn't. She told me the whole story. She saw them die, but she didn't do it." Even the gashes in the doorframe and flooring in her childhood home lined up with her story. They were the right size to be from the sharp end of a shovel. I could picture the scene so vividly in my head. I glanced at her truck. All the inconsistencies around Violet weren't as inconsistent as they seemed. She kept the truck because she was worried about evidence. She stayed in these woods because she was worried about her secrets being unearthed. She'd done everything in her power to protect her son. She wasn't the monster everyone made her out to be. And I wouldn't let her be labeled as one because of a few rumors.

I walked back over to my side of the car. "I'm getting her and Zeke out of here so they can't lock her up for something she didn't do. The bodies are in the lake. I'm leaving this one to you. Clear her name for me."

"The lake? What?! You can't help her escape! Are you freaking insane? You can't just believe anything that comes out of a beautiful psycho's mouth."

"She's lied about a lot of things to cover it up. But she's not lying about what happened."

"You don't know that."

"She was young and scared and didn't have anyone to help her out of it. She has me now. Would you lower your fucking gun? We both know you're not going to shoot me."

Damien slowly lowered his pistol. "She's killed at least three people, Tucker."

At least? Were they going to pin every death in this town on her? "She hasn't killed anyone." And I wouldn't blame her if she had. Her stepfather had deserved a fate far worse than he got. A quick death after years of abusing her? I would have made it slow and painful.

"What if you're wrong? What if she did it?"

"I'm not wrong." I'd seen the way her face crumpled when she told the story. How guilty she felt for her actions. How much it had haunted her all of these years. She wasn't a monster at all. She had a sensitive soul. She developed a nervous tick, reminding her every day of the secrets she kept. If she had murdered three people she'd be completely lost.

"But what if you are?"

"I'm not."

"Are you leaving me here?!" he yelled at me as I opened the car door. "These woods are fucking cursed!"

I tore away from the house as fast as I could. If Damien thought I was going to bring him with me he was the crazy one. This was career suicide. There was no reason for him to make it too. Especially if he still thought she was guilty.

Violet's lips were more purple than blue now. I didn't know if that was a good or bad sign. I turned up the heat, knowing it wasn't enough to dry our clothes. Stopping for dry ones was the first on my list after getting Zeke. Violet's teeth were starting to chatter.

"I'm sorry about what happened with your stepfather. I'm sorry about all of it." I didn't know what to say to her to make it better. She'd been raped for years with no one to turn to for help. She'd witnessed the unthinkable. Her life had been a living hell for the past six years. Yet she was still beautiful. She was still standing. She was still breathing. She was still strong.

"You can't change the past. I know that better than anyone." She looked up at me. "I appreciate you doing this for me...but you shouldn't be. The last person that tried to help me ended up dead."

I shook my head. That wasn't going to happen to here. What better person to run from law enforcement than law enforcement? I knew how to think like a criminal. And I knew that I had just become one five minutes ago. There was no going back now.

"Why are you? Doing this?"

She had just confessed everything to me. Why sugarcoat things now? I took my eyes off the road for a second. "I think I'm in love with you." No, there was definitely no going back.

"You think you're in love with me?"

I turned my attention back to the road. "Because I know it's crazy to say it. I haven't known you for very long."

"Hmm. Well from one crazy person to another then...I think I'm in love with you too, Tucker."

This wasn't how this conversation was supposed to go down. There should have been roses and chocolates and a fancy dinner. Instead we were speeding through town in a getaway car. I couldn't even kiss her. I couldn't even really look in her eyes when I said it.

I pulled to a stop in front of Zeke's school. "I'll go grab him real quick."

She put her hand on my arm to stop me. "Thank you for believing in me. That's all I wanted." She leaned forward and pressed her lips against mine.

I didn't want to move. I wanted to get lost in one moment with her without any complications. But my life had just become a pile of complications. And Damien had his phone. He knew where I was going. The cops would be here any second. I pulled away from her kiss. "I'll be right back, okay?"

She nodded and put her hands up in front of the heater to warm them.

Getting Zeke out of school wasn't easy until I flashed my badge. After that the principal did exactly as I said.

"I never get out of school early," Zeke said as we walked down the hall together. "Except for that one time when Asher called me a loser and punched me. I got to leave early and stay home from school for two days."

Violet hadn't told me that any of the kids had gotten violent with Zeke. She should have told me. Maybe I could have acted on all this sooner. Maybe we'd already be long gone. I took a deep breath. All that mattered was that I was getting him and his mom out of this shithole. No one would mess with them again. We'd get a fresh start. I'd figure it out day by day, but I wouldn't let them live like this anymore.

"Where are we going?" Zeke asked.

"A road trip with your mom."

"A trip on the road? Cool!" He pushed open the front door of the school. "Do we get to sleep in the car? Or are we only on the road when we're awake?"

"I don't know yet."

"Well, I'm glad I brought my lizards to school with me today." He patted his pockets with a smile on his face.

That kid was really bad at following his mother's rules. I laughed. And then my feet stopped.

"Aren't you coming?" Zeke asked as he turned around to look up at me. "It's going to be so fun!"

"Yeah. I…" I stared at the spot where I had parked the car. It was empty. I had been dumped before. I had milked wounds for months. But in that second? I felt gutted. I was willing to risk everything for her. I was willing to give up my whole life. I didn't know what true heartache was until that second. My chest physically ached.

"Come on," Zeke said and tugged on my hand. He was pulling me away from the front of the school and toward the parking lot.

And that's when I saw her. She was sitting in a beat-up Chevy truck that only looked a few years older than the one she owned. She was hot-wiring the freaking thing. I ran over with Zeke. My heart started to beat normally again. The ache subsided as quickly as it had come.

"Your car is too flashy," she said as she played around with the wiring. "Besides, the cops will be looking for a Dodge

Charger." The car revved to life. "Do you want to drive or do you want me to?"

"You can drive." I probably should have thought it was suspicious that she knew how to hot-wire a car. I was betting my whole life on the fact that she wasn't a criminal. But I just found it incredibly sexy. After all, I wasn't on the same side of the law anymore. I'd made my choice. I hoisted Zeke up into the truck and climbed up after him.

Violet leaned down and kissed Zeke on the top of his head. "Are you ready?" she asked and smiled over at me.

"Road trip!" Zeke yelled.

I smiled back at her. "I'm ready."

"You're sure?"

I had told Damien that I was sure Violet hadn't committed the murders. But there was no such thing as 100 percent certainty. "I'm sure." What could one last lie hurt?

CHAPTER 29

Violet

He loved me. I had forgotten what it felt like to be loved by someone who didn't call me Mommy. I turned onto the freeway and breathed more easily than I had in years.

I'd almost drowned countless times in my youth because of my mother. I'd gotten really good at holding my breath. As much as it hurt my heart, I think I had set Tucker up to die today. I knew he'd believe my lies and try to save me when I fell through the ice. But sometimes life happened unexpectedly. He was a surprisingly good swimmer, and I was glad he was alive. I was glad he was helping me escape. I was glad he was able to love someone like me.

I'd tried to tell him the truth. I really had. But only parts of it had managed to fall from my lips. Because I had killed three people, even though I never meant for it to happen.

I had come back from school late that day. I'd missed my bus and had to walk for over an hour because I didn't have anyone to ask for a ride. Henry was waiting for me when I typed in the code to the garage. I didn't even see him in the darkness, but I could smell the alcohol on his breath. He was always worse when he'd been drinking. I could hear the sound of him unzipping his pants. And I couldn't take it for another second. I wouldn't let him force me to have an abortion. And I wouldn't let him drag me to Florida so he could continue to ruin me. I had a baby to protect.

I'd grabbed a shovel off the wall and ran inside screaming for my mom to help. Begging her to believe me. I just needed her to help me get away from the hell I was living. I just wanted out. Henry tried to shut me up. But I was done being silenced. I was only trying to knock him out. I needed enough time to flee. But I'd be lying if I didn't say I felt relieved when the metal edge of the shovel sliced clean across his neck.

I had hoped my mother would finally believe me. His pants were at his ankles while the blood seeped out of his neck. Not that she needed any more proof; she'd heard him raping me countless times. Shoving a dresser in front of her door may have blocked out demons, but it didn't block out his disgusting grunts. I never had the same freedom my mother did. I didn't have pills to numb my pain. And shoving a dresser in front of my own door wouldn't have helped. It would have just delayed the inevitable.

I had hoped my mother wouldn't wave a gun in my face and yell at me about my lies. Lies? I had never lied. How could she believe a monster over me? Her never believing in me had already ruined my life. I wasn't going to let her end it too. She was weak from the medicine but it still wasn't easy to overpower her. I was just trying to get the gun away from her. I never meant for her to get shot.

That should have been the end of it. I wish it had been. But John Fredrick had overheard me arguing with Joel a few days before. And he'd suspected that my stepfather was abusing me. And he showed up at the wrong place at the wrong time. He arrived right when I was shoving my mother's dead body in my pickup truck. He threatened to call the police. I explained what happened. I told him that both of them attacked me first, but he didn't care. I begged him not to call. It was naïve to think he was ever going to save me. No one ever believed me. I lunged at his phone, knocking him backward. His head hit the tailgate of my truck and made an awful crunching noise. I tried to revive him even though I knew it was too late. He'd snapped his neck. *I'd* snapped his neck.

Everything was too late. I'd accidentally killed three people. Most of what I had said to Tucker out on the lake was true. I was haunted by that night. And technically I had confessed. I told him I killed them, even if everything I said before that was a lie.

Sometimes I wondered what I would have done if John hadn't slipped. I liked to think I wouldn't have killed him. But I wasn't sure if that was true. I was worried I'd become what everyone said I was. A monster. After all, you could only hear something so many times before it became a part of you.

Maybe they were right all along. Maybe I had meant to slit Henry's throat. Maybe I meant to tilt the gun just enough so the bullet would penetrate my mother's skull. Maybe I was fully aware of the tailgate laying ominously open behind John. *Maybe. Maybe. Maybe.*

The rumors swirled around my mind. For six years I let my neighbors define me. But I was finally free from their whispers. I wasn't what they said I was. I was done doubting myself. And now I could finally have the future I'd always wanted.

I looked down at one of the lizards on Zeke's lap. It changed colors to blend in with his shorts. I wanted to believe that people could change that easily. I wanted to believe that I could change. Because I wasn't the crazy lady on the hill. It was easier to believe in myself when someone else believed in me too. I smiled over at Tucker.

He smiled back.

I really did love him.

I thought it would be easy to shove the rumors out of my mind the farther away from town I drove. To stomp out the doubt. To erase the whispers that I was a monster. *I'm not the person they say I am. I'm not the person they say I am. I'm not the person they say I am.* But no matter how many times I said it, there was still a voice in the back of my head that wondered if I'd end up accidentally killing Tucker one day. And if I did, I doubted he'd be my only victim. Sometimes I really hated doing things in threes.

WHAT'S NEXT?

Violet isn't the only crazy housewife in the neighborhood! There's one more, and she might be the craziest one yet! Meet Ensley in Book 3 of the Secrets of Suburbia Series, *Crazy in Love*!

It's beginning to look a lot like Christmas. Mistletoe and holly and lights all aglow. It's my favorite time of year. Until my husband had to go and ruin it.

Christmas is officially canceled at my house now that I've kidnapped my husband and locked him in the basement. And not even Santa can get me out of this mess.

I know what you're thinking. That I'm crazy. But I swear I'm not. I'm going to let him free eventually. Or maybe with a little Christmas magic he'll fall in love with me again.

A NOTE FROM IVY

My husband has told me that I'm evil on several occasions. He says it jokingly after I steal the last bite of bread pudding. Or when I talk about wanting to be respected by everyone in the world. You know...the little things. But sometimes I wonder if it's true. Because I do have a pretty twisted mind.

I mean, when I wrote *The Truth in My Lies* I dedicated it to my husband. It was the first book I wrote after we got married and I wanted to dedicate it to him, which is sweet. But the choice was a bit psycho too - I won't spoil that book here in case you haven't read it (which you should) but it was a pretty strange choice of dedication given the circumstances. Which made this book so easy to write...because I think I might be sweet like a psycho.

Either way, I become what my characters want me to be for the few months I'm in their minds. So while I'm writing this note, I'm definitely twisted. Apprehensive. A little psycho. It was fun for me to write Violet's character and especially Zeke's. I hope this book made you laugh, smile, hurt, and feel a little uncomfortable because it made me feel unsettled too. That's the best part about writing in this genre. That eerie feeling in your bones.

And I'm not going to stop. I think this genre is my happy place (yeah, yeah, cause I'm crazy or whatever). That means another book is coming in the Secrets of Suburbia series!

Ivy Smoak

Ivy Smoak
Wilmington, DE
www.ivysmoak.com

ABOUT THE AUTHOR

Ivy Smoak is the international bestselling author of *The Hunted Series*. Her books have sold over 1 million copies worldwide, and her latest release, *Empire High Betrayal*, hit #4 in the entire Kindle store.

When she's not writing, you can find Ivy binge watching too many TV shows, taking long walks, playing outside, and generally refusing to act like an adult. She lives with her husband in Delaware.

Facebook: IvySmoakAuthor
Instagram: @IvySmoakAuthor
Goodreads: IvySmoak

Recommend *Sweet Like a Psycho* for your next book club!

Book club questions available at:
www.ivysmoak.com/bookclub

www.ingramcontent.com/pod-product-compliance
Lightning Source LLC
Chambersburg PA
CBHW030546310726
48979CB00010B/2052/J

* 9 7 8 1 9 4 2 3 8 1 1 8 1 *